Evan released her and jumped back as though expecting a blow.

"I suppose that was a demonstration of strength against weakness," Judith said hotly.

"No, for women are the strongest of all. Father may think he is in charge, but he must report in to Helen each night."

"She does what he says."

"She may perhaps give an inch here or there, but eventually she will win the war and he will do what she wants even if it means getting rid of me. You could be such a woman. I am yours already."

"I don't want you."

"That's not true," he said, taking a step closer. "Those lips don't lie well."

"I must not want you!"

"You, perhaps, should not want me, but that doesn't change the fact that you do…!"

Dear Reader,

Fans of Laurel Ames and the Regency period rejoice, for this month Ms. Ames is back with her new novel, *Tempted.* This RITA Award finalist is known for her unique characters, and her current hero, military engineer Evan "Mad" Mountjoy, is no exception. Add a heroine with an indiscretion in her past, and a little intrigue, and you have the perfect mix for what *Affaire de Coeur* calls an "exciting, unusual, and delightfully quirky Regency." Don't miss it.

Ana Seymour's sixth book for Harlequin Historicals, *Gabriel's Lady,* is a heart-warming Western set in a gold-mining town in the Dakota Territory. It's the story of an eastern do-gooder who heads west to rescue her brother, only to fall in love with his disreputable partner.

For those of you whose tastes run to medieval novels, look for *Knight's Ransom,* the next title in Suzanne Barclay's dramatic ongoing series, The Sommerville Brothers. And Emily French rounds out the month with her emotional tale, *The Wedding Bargain,* about a Puritan woman who defies her community to marry a bondsman with a tortured past.

We hope you'll keep a lookout for all four titles wherever Harlequin Historicals are sold.

Sincerely,

Tracy Farrell
Senior Editor

Please address questions and book requests to:
Harlequin Reader Service
U.S.: 3010 Walden Ave., P.O. Box 1325, Buffalo, NY 14269
Canadian: P.O. Box 609, Fort Erie, Ont. L2A 5X3

Laurel Ames

Tempted

Harlequin Books

TORONTO • NEW YORK • LONDON
AMSTERDAM • PARIS • SYDNEY • HAMBURG
STOCKHOLM • ATHENS • TOKYO • MILAN
MADRID • WARSAW • BUDAPEST • AUCKLAND

ISBN 0-373-28938-3

TEMPTED

Copyright © 1996 by Barbara J. Miller

This edition published by arrangement with Harlequin Books S.A.

Printed in U.S.A.

Books by Laurel Ames

LAUREL AMES

Although Laurel Ames likes to write stories set in the early nineteenth century, she writes from personal experience. She and her husband live on a farm, complete with five horses, a long spring house, carriage house and a smokehouse made of bricks kilned on the farm. Of her characters, Laurel says, "With the exception of the horses, my characters, both male and female, good and evil, all are me and no one else."

This book is dedicated to my computer expert husband,
Don, who makes all the books possible.

Chapter One

Devonshire County, England
April 1814

Two riders moved up the road through a light rain. It was not wet enough to force them to seek shelter, especially considering that the red Royal Engineers' uniform of the slighter man had already faded much from the weather, and the worn batman's uniform of the larger man covered a frame so substantial it would have taken much to melt him. The young captain rode stiffly, as though it hurt him to move, his servant with a relaxed slouch, partly owing to having to lead two horses loaded with baggage.

They came not to a ruined Spanish village nor to some godforsaken Portuguese valley, but to an ordinary English country house. "It looks different than I remember it, Bose," Captain Mountjoy observed.

"We haven't seen it for ten years, Evan lad. Recollect you were little more than a boy when we left."

"I was fifteen. I think I would have remembered something of Meremont."

"As I said. Let's see if this grandmother of yours is still alive." The older man urged his hard-muscled horse to a shamble and rode not to the main house, but to a smaller house set off to one side. He dismounted, and his mount gave a sigh of relief, waiting patiently as its rider rapped at the door, then tried to peer in a dusty window.

"It's shut up," Evan said sadly. "Gram must be dead. I surmised that when her letters stopped. We may as well go."

"Go? You mean leave again without even inquiring? Are you forgetting I might want to find out if Joan has been true to me after all these years?"

"Sorry, Bose. I am a selfish lout. I was forgetting you have a reason to come back here."

"You have, too. You are the eldest son. There is something owing to you."

Evan winced. "No. I don't mean to go up to the house. You go round to the kitchen and ask after Joan."

"While you wait here in the rain? We'll ride down to the stables, at least pull the horses in out of this weather for a bit. If you've turned chickenhearted on me you can cower there."

An unexpected smile stole over Evan's tired face as he turned his mare and trotted it toward the stable block. They dismounted, and Evan took the bridles as Bose sprinted for the house. The stable boys gaped at Evan, then turned out to attend to a carriage and pair that arrived unfashionably at the back door. The lady who descended from this equipage cast a dark look at him and, rather than entering the house, strode across the courtyard, muddying her hem on the cobbles.

"Who might you be?" she demanded.

"Captain Mountjoy, ma'am."

"And I am Lady Mountjoy, now," she claimed, with a challenging tilt to her chin. "I married your widowed father in good faith and with certain expectations. I tell you plainly, sir, you are not wanted here."

"I know that," Evan said with a certain glint in his brown eyes. "I only came to inquire if Gram—my grandmother—is still living."

"She died in January. She left you something, I believe. You may consult with her lawyers in Bristol."

"No, don't unsaddle them," Evan said gently to the wide-eyed stable boy, passing the lad a coin.

Lady Mountjoy did not like being ignored. "There is nothing for you here," she insisted.

"I know. I'm only waiting for Bose to come back from the house. Is everyone else . . . well?"

"We go on perfectly fine without you. There is no entail, you know. Nothing need be left to you. Nothing *has* been left to you."

Evan's heart thudded to a stop. "Father—he's dead then?" His voice was high, like a boy's. He staggered a little, but the mare propped him up.

Evan took the woman's silence for assent. Why would this come as such a shock, since his father had never once written? And why would it hurt so much? He scarcely even remembered him.

"She's here!" Bose crowed, "and as happy to see me as the day I—pardon, ma'am."

"Who's here?" Lady Mountjoy demanded.

"An acquaintance of mine—Joan."

"And she is also, as I recall, a servant of mine. Keep your distance from her," the woman warned, her blue eyes flashing.

"Bose, this is the new Lady Mountjoy."

"And the new mistress of Meremont. Now be off with you, both of you."

Bose opened his mouth to protest, but Evan said, "It's all right, Bose. I had not meant to stay." The young captain remounted wearily, and his mare stared round at him, realizing the oats and hay she had been contemplating were not to be hers. He rode out, leaving Bose to follow, but stopped and turned at the road to take a last look at his home as he waited for his batman to catch up with him.

"I think I used to call it Merry Mount when I was little. I cannot remember why. I was never merry here."

"You can't just leave. You have certain rights!"

"Apparently not. I knew he had remarried from Gram's letter. She said the new Lady Mountjoy was very protective of 'her' children's rights. I can scarcely blame her. We'll put up in the village till you see your Joan again and settle if she is to come with us or no."

"To where?"

"Most likely America, after my leave is up. Though with the war, they may not let her... Bose! How thoughtless of me. You can leave the army, marry Joan and raise fat children here."

"Not bloody likely. I'd not have a moment's peace, not knowing what scrape you had got into. We will put up in the village, though. Can't push these horses much farther, anyway."

Bose had seen a rider approaching at a trot and gaped in such a way that Evan stared at him.

"So, you're home!" boomed the old man in the saddle.

Evan twisted involuntarily and gave a grunt as he strained his cracked ribs. "Father!"

"Did you mean to just ride by without even stopping?"

"No—yes," Evan gasped, as the constriction in his chest relaxed and relief flooded through him like a strong draught of brandy. "I thought you were dead." He shook his head to clear it of the giddiness. So his father was not dead, after all. Now why had Lady Mountjoy bothered to lie to him?

"All the more reason for you to stop, eh?"

"No! I—"

"Well, you are stopping now. We have things to settle. Your grandmother has left you her entire fortune. She always did favor you over the others."

"Only because no one else cared about me."

"Nonsense. I have always treated you fairly. Too fair to deserve being ignored for ten years."

"But you never..." Evan faltered, for his father had ridden on toward the stable, and Bose had followed with the horses that carried all his dry clothes. He really had no choice but to stop. Oddly, he did want to stay, to speak to his father again. As he rode back to the stable he vaguely wondered if he had been forgiven after all this time. No, that was too much to hope for.

* * *

Evan rode in and dismounted with a grunt. Molly, his mare, snorted her approval of his coming to his senses and went gratefully with the groom.

"Well, come along," his father demanded. Evan followed the older man to the back door through what was by now a downpour, then down the hall to the library.

Evan looked about him uncomfortably. "You've changed the room about."

"No, we haven't," stated his father, looking up from the decanter and glasses. "It's always been this way."

"This isn't how I remember it."

"You were no more than a boy when you left. It's only natural things would look different to you."

Evan ignored his father's invitation to sit, but stood turning himself by the fire, until the worst of the rain had dried off his clothes. The uniform did not actually dry, of course. Rather, the water seeped through to his skin, making him feel clammy. But this was such a familiar sensation by now that Evan did not regard it. Accepting a brandy from his father reminded him of his recent shock and subsequent relief. He should have known the old man would be too stubborn to die. This last thought brought a puzzled frown to his face. Why had Lady Mountjoy lied to him? Had the desolation he must have shown pleased her? He didn't care. He could not say that he loved his father, but it was disquieting to think of him dead.

"As I said, your grandmother has left you pretty well off. Rather cut up poor Terry's expectations."

"Terry?"

"Your brother, remember?"

"Yes, of course. I wasn't thinking."

"You are not famous for your thinking."

Evan smiled. Nothing in all these years had changed. If his father had welcomed him with open arms he would have felt strange indeed. To be cut at, though, was such a familiar feeling he quite liked the man for it. His first impression was that his father looked unfamiliar. The hair, though full and magnificent, was white, the face lined, the body thickening perhaps a bit around the middle. Still and all, he was a fine figure of a man, but not one Evan remembered well except by his voice.

"What happened to your face?" his father asked.

"What?"

"You've a bloody great scar under your lip and, now that I look closer, one on your forehead."

"I scarcely remember. They do not signify."

Lord Mountjoy tugged at a bell, as he had already done several times.

"Bose must be turning the servants' hall on its ear," Evan offered.

"No doubt you are right. Stay here. There is someone I want you to meet."

Evan had an uneasy feeling he knew whom, so he poured himself another brandy and took up a position by the fireplace so that he could gauge his effect on his new mama to the full.

She entered the room, toying nervously with a lock of her brown hair. Her cheeks flushed when she saw him, and she sent him a forbidding stare. She almost taunted Evan to say aught against her.

"May I present Lady Mountjoy? My son, Evan."

"So pleased to meet you at last, dear ma'am."

"Likewise." She plopped down in a chair and continued to stare at him with a puzzled look. He had not snitched, and she could not fathom why.

"May I get you something, my dear?" Lord Mountjoy asked. "Oh, where are the girls?"

"They took the pony trap to Wendover. I expect they will stay there until the rain lets up."

"You'll meet Judith and Angel at dinner, I'm sure."

Evan recalled Gram mentioning that the "new Lady Mountjoy" had some younger sisters.

The door was pushed open by a boy of six or so in ruffles and short coats. He ran to Lord and Lady Mountjoy expectantly, and Evan felt an impulse to warn him not to foist the pup he was strangling onto his father. But the boy laid the whining animal on Lord Mountjoy's knee with impunity. Smiles softened both their faces, and Evan knew a pang of remorse. His parents had never smiled on him in such a way, not that he could remember. And this was the same man who'd had nothing but gruff admonishments for him, to stand up straight, or take the food to your mouth, not your mouth to the food.

Lord Mountjoy glanced up, and the genuine smile was replaced by a forced one as he introduced Evan to his new brother, Thomas. Thomas shook Evan's hand in quite an adult manner. Evan knelt and smiled his own genuine smile, hoping the child would fare better in this house than he had.

There was a firm knock at the door, followed by the entrance of a prim woman in cap, apron and gray gown, whose worried face split into an indulgent smile when she saw the child. "I might have known...." she said, then started when Evan got up from his kneeling position. Her face grew wary, angry almost, and she glanced sharply at Lady Mountjoy to see if this stranger was permitted to touch her darling. Evan had thought that the wispy hair escaping her cap was gray, but he now saw it was blond, and that she was, in fact, not old.

"This is my oldest son, Evan," Lord Mountjoy said. "This is Nurse Miranda."

Evan had a frosty nod bestowed on him.

"Run along now, Thomas," Lord Mountjoy said. "You can keep the pup in the stable, not in the house."

"Yes. Nasty, dirty thing," Nurse agreed. "You must not bring it into the nursery again."

"I must go, too," Lady Mountjoy said, getting up and leading Thomas to his nurse. "I suppose we should kill the fatted calf if there is time."

"I'm sure you shall contrive something equally fitting, my dear."

Evan watched them depart and wondered what the nurse would say to the boy about him, perhaps that he, too, was a nasty, dirty thing that should be kept in the stable. He felt a moment of dizziness overtake him as he put down his glass, and he rested his hand on the table until it had passed. It was caused not only by the brandy, but by riding so many miles in an unfit condition, plus two more or less sleepless nights and a weariness he could no longer shake.

"I hear Bose in the hall. You may have your old room. Terry has Gregory's and I see no point in displacing him."

Evan flinched a little at his dead brother's name and left the library without a word. He climbed the stairs on knees that ached for days at a time now. Twenty-five years old and he was falling apart. He stopped uncertainly on the landing. Then he seemed to hear Gram's voice reciting, "Your room is at the top of the stairs on the left."

"Will I ever live there again?" an uncertain voice—his own, he supposed—asked.

"I don't know, child."

He went toward that door, not so much because of the voices in his head but because of the thump of baggage coming from within. He entered and sat on the bed, to marvel numbly at Bose's eternal energy. It was a small room with a fireplace across one corner. The furniture consisted of no more than a bed, a small desk and a hard, wooden chair. Evan's baggage was piled under the window. It was not as he had remembered it and yet he could not say what was wrong.

"You look all in, lad. Give me those wet clothes and roll up for a nap until dinnertime."

"Perhaps you should be the captain," Evan joked as he rose to strip off his wet uniform. He crawled between the covers, naked except for bandages, and let the sheets dry and warm him.

Evan awoke with a certain stiffness hanging about his limbs. He stretched and relaxed, then took a deep breath and grunted at the stab of pain. It was such a familiar pain by now that he ventured to think the ribs felt a shade better. The knees still ached. "Bose?" he asked experimentally.

"He's asleep, but I can wake him if you really need him," the woman said as she set her sewing aside and got up from the small chair by the window.

The voice was firm, but gentle, and Evan regarded her in puzzlement. It was not that it was odd for him to wake with a woman in his room, but he usually remembered who she was. And of this beauty he had no memory at all. That fine tawny hair, those kind blue eyes and that kissable mouth—those he would have remembered.

"May I get you anything?" she asked, coming to stand over him.

"Just your name. I seem to have mislaid it."

"Judith. I'm your aunt, now that I think of it," she said with a chuckle.

"Uh, I don't have an aunt." *And if I did,* he thought, *she wouldn't stir me like this.*

"You do now. Two of them, though I dare say we are both younger than you. Angel and I are Helen's sisters. But I should not be teasing you when you are not even awake."

"Nor should you be here," Evan said, remembering his naked state.

"I caught Bose preparing to curl up for a sleep outside your door, so I sent him to his own room." She had trouble keeping her eyes from straying to Evan's chest and shoulders.

"We have been away from civilization too long."

"Is he always like that—a faithful hound?"

"More like a bossy nanny most of the time. Now that I come to think of it, I'm surprised he let you send him off."

Judith shrugged and smiled. "Do you need him?"

"No, let him sleep. Believe it or not, he was the one who wanted to get here in such a hurry."

"Ah, yes, our Joan. She has spoken of nothing else since you arrived. She said you rode a hundred and fifty miles in less than three days, and in this weather."

"It's what we're used to."

"Yes, I know," she said sadly.

"You—you have been following the war, then?"

"I have read the accounts in the *Times*," she said warily, unwilling to let him know she had read his letters to his grandmother.

"I should have liked to read those papers myself, to see if the reports bear any resemblance to what really went on."

"Gram saved them. I will find them for you—later. Perhaps you should not come down to dinner tonight. You have a bit of a fever." She almost touched his forehead, as she had while he slept, but stopped herself in time.

"Oh, I shall do," he said cheerfully, sitting up and revealing the bandages around his chest.

"Yes, I'm sure you will," she said, whisking out of the room and closing the door behind her before he could see her blushing.

Judith closeted herself in the room she shared with Angel, and leaned against the door until her heart settled down to a more normal rhythm. She had helped nurse Terry when he was wounded, but had never felt like this. Perhaps it was because Evan was exactly as she expected—handsome, fine and hard muscled, with that understated masculinity. His straight brown hair fell across his brow most charmingly, and the scar under his lip crinkled when he smiled. His eyes were brown and brooding, as though he was always thinking of something else.

She must get a grip on herself. Between the two of them there could never be anything. He was Lord Mountjoy's heir and must marry someone of his own station. And that was the least of the reasons.

Why had she so fastened on his character to the point where she fantasized about him? She realized it was because she envied him. He might have been spurned by his father, but he had not whimpered and cowered in some corner. Instead, he had done something with himself. She wished she could have led such a life, hard though it might have been. She had got from his letters a sense of his belonging where he was, of making a place for himself, just as she tried to do.

She had heard all about him from Gram, but without his letters, she would have known only what he'd been like as a boy. Reducing war news to mere asides, his missives were filled with rollicking tales of camp life, foreign foods and customs. One would have thought he was a young man on a grand tour, with safe conduct through all those foreign parts, rather than a soldier in the thick of battle.

Without knowing it, Evan had made her laugh. Unconscious of her existence, he had made her care about him. And he had been a comfort to his dying grandmother without knowing she was dying. Judith had wondered if any man could ever read as well in person as Evan had on paper. Now she knew.

Owing to his falling asleep again, and Bose's not coming to his room until close on five o'clock, Evan was the last to enter the library, where the family gathered before dinner. It was evident to him, as he scanned their faces, that he had been the subject of their conversation. Lady Mountjoy had high color again, his father was stern, Judith sympathetic. The younger girl—Angel, as she was introduced—looked on him with particular interest. He caught his breath, for she seemed too young, too beautiful to be real. But then she blushed and dropped her eyes and became all too human. Had she faced him down he might have liked her better. A figure moved toward him, one who reminded him vaguely of himself. "Terry?" he asked uncertainly.

"Hallo, Evan. We thought you was dead." Terry shook his hand and left a mist of brandy fumes in the air.

Evan was still struggling for a reply when Lord Mountjoy helped his wife to her feet. Evan would have been inclined to fall in beside Judith, but Angel pushed past her and appropriated his arm. Judith rolled her eyes heavenward in such an automatic response that Evan grinned in spite of himself.

"You don't look that old," Angel confided, staring at the lines around his eyes. "I was thinking twenty-five was very old, but you don't look much older than Terry."

Evan smiled and nodded, wondering how he was going to make it through the evening. He sat up straight at dinner. He hadn't much choice, the way Bose had strapped up his cracked ribs. And he remembered to take his soup to his mouth and not crouch over his food like a hungry animal, as Terry was doing at this moment. Evan could remember many occasions recently when he had hunched ravenously over a crust of bread or a piece of half-cooked meat. But there was a time and place for everything. In his father's house he could not help but sit at attention as he ate.

Evan glanced at Lord Mountjoy, who was staring at Terry. But his father merely shuddered and looked away. Was it possible the old tartar had mellowed? Evan did not care to find out. He remembered his dizziness from before and took only enough wine to dull the ache in his knees. Riding did not bother him in the ordinary way, not even riding for long stretches at a time, but he had been badly trampled at Bordeaux the previous month, and now a dull ache would creep down to his right knee in particular, nagging at him for days on end. In spite of Angel's opinion, he felt worn-out, used-up and numb to anything else that might happen to him.

"I think the courtesy of an answer is due your brother," Lord Mountjoy demanded.

"Sorry, I was not attending."

"I only asked if you had seen many battles," Terry repeated.

"Yes."

"There's your answer, Terry—yes, he has seen many battles," Lord Mountjoy quipped.

Evan smiled. "Such conversation is not particularly good table fare, not for children, anyway."

Angel raised a belligerent chin, as did Terry.

"In that case we shall leave you to your port and your talk of war," Lady Mountjoy declared as she rose with dignity. Judith left them with a sad smile, Angel with a definite flounce.

Evan realized the meal was over, though he had scarcely touched the food on his plate.

"You always were able to clear a room," his father said with satisfaction.

"I don't remember that," Evan answered.

"You also have a very convenient memory."

"I am not a child," Terry interjected, a little the worse for wine.

"I never said you were," his brother answered.

"Who were you referring to then?"

"Judith and Angel."

"But Judith has got to be all of twenty-four."

"Really? Why isn't she married then?" Evan asked, wondering how such a treasure could have been passed over.

"No fortune," Terry said.

"I shall provide for the girl," Lord Mountjoy stated. "A very proper young lady she is, and the greatest help to me."

Evan stared at his father, for now that he thought of it, one of their long-ago mealtime arguments had been over his father's philandering. He couldn't recall the memory so much as he could recite the conversation—his own condemnation and his father's gruff and unconvincing defense.

"How is she a help to you?" Evan asked pointedly.

"Keeps my library in order, helps me write—damn you, boy, you have a nasty mind," his father said as he caught Evan's meaning. "How did you think she helped me?"

"I didn't know. That's why I asked."

"I feel as though she is my daughter. She is too good, almost, for this household."

"That I can belie— Pardon me," Evan said, breaking off abruptly. "I was determined to be polite to you, since you invited me in. I'm sorry."

"Don't strain yourself. I am not used to any consideration from you."

Evan fell silent again. Terry, who had been glancing from one to the other, took his turn at conversation. "So you were in a great many battles?"

"It has all blurred together for me, I'm afraid. I was always knee-deep in mud, working on siege parallels, or up to my waist in freezing water trying to shore up a bridge."

"Didn't you see any real action?"

"Enough to suit me."

"Terry, he doesn't want to talk about it," their father said.

"Oh, you only had to say so." Terry drained his glass.

"You are going to have a head tomorrow," Evan observed.

"Sorry, it isn't everyday one is displaced. I think I shall go straight to bed." Terry rose valiantly, but wove his way out of the room.

"Whatever did he mean, and does he make a habit of that?"

"He is not such an aesthete as you promised to be, but no, he does not in general drink his meals."

"I was wanting to ask about Gram. How did she die, I mean?"

"Who is to say what gives out? The heart, I expect, is what—"

"I know she was old. You don't have to remind me of that. Was she...alone—lonely?"

"God's death! Do you think I have no proper feelings, even for a mother-in-law? Of course she wasn't alone. I was there, and Judith. If you want to know what she said, speak to Judith. She stayed with her more than anyone."

"Thank you. I didn't mean to accuse you of neglecting—"

"You have no right to accuse me of anything!"

A slight flush rose to Evan's face, but he looked his father squarely in the eye—and read resentment and anger there. No surprise; it was what he expected. Evan saw disappointment, too. That also was no surprise. He had always disappointed his father, he thought. He simply could not remember all the details.

Lord Mountjoy got to his feet and walked steadily toward the door, leaving Evan brooding at the table. "Are you coming or not?"

Evan twitched at the summons and stood stiffly, to follow his father back to the library, where candles had been set out on the broad table to light the ladies' embroidery and hemming. Their pale dresses and colorful shawls looked oddly out of place against the dark leather furniture. Evan could remember when the library had been a man's haven and wondered that his father permitted this invasion of his sanctuary. He sat where he could watch Judith, and she gave him a sympathetic smile. He desperately wanted to ask after Gram, but only in private. He would wait.

The conversation was desultory, perhaps owing to Angel's having taken a pout. She *tsked* over her embroidery. Judith, hemming seam after seam, appeared to be making a shirt. And Lady Mountjoy was doing delicate work on a garment so small it could only have been intended for... Evan's eyes flew to her waist. Of course. She was in the early months of pregnancy. That accounted for his father's solicitude, perhaps also for her irrational behavior toward him. He would have found out soon enough that Lord Mountjoy lived. Evan vowed not to make her uneasy during his stay. All he needed was to be accused of causing her to miscarry.

Judith was watching him, and now blushed a little, as though she could read his thoughts. Evan supposed her situation might be hard. It would be easy enough for them to turn such an amiable girl into a drudge. If she had been nursing Gram, perhaps they already had. Something must be done about that.

On the other hand he must remember that he had no say in anything. There was his grandmother's bequest, though. Perhaps he could—

"I asked if those horses of yours are Andalusians," Lord Mountjoy shouted. "Are you deaf?"

Evan twitched. "A little, from the shelling. Two of them are from Andalusia. The gelding I bought in Portugal. Bose is riding the horse he took with him from England. Odd that he should have survived when . . ."

"What?"

"Nothing."

"I only got a quick look at them," Judith said. "What are they like?"

"Lovely when they are better fed. You can ride my mare when they are rested."

"I don't ride."

"Would you like to?"

"No, I don't care to," Judith said softly.

Evan did not know how he knew it, but this was a lie. And there did not seem to be a good reason for it. She was blushing and looked tearful. He felt so bad about causing her any kind of pain that he excused himself and went to bed.

Bose had been waiting for him.

"So when's the wedding?" Evan asked.

"Well, that rather depends on you," Bose said, helping him off with his dress uniform.

"Me?"

"If we mean to stay, she'll marry me on the spot. But if we are to be off junketing again, she isn't sure."

"Bose, this is impossible. You can't link your future to mine. I have no idea what I'm going to do."

"I was thinking we would give it a few days, see what the old gent means to do by you. He was always fair with me."

"He was?"

"He paid my wages the whole time I waited on you at Cambridge, and sent us money in Spain."

"I didn't know that. So that's why I always had something to eat even when no one had been paid for months."

"It strikes me you don't know your father very well. He seems such an amiable man."

"With everyone but me. Yes, I agree, he can be quite charming."

"Perhaps if you didn't argue with him so much . . ."

"But I didn't, at least not that I remember. But there's a great deal I don't remember from before the accident."

"You were groggy for weeks.... Sending you off to school like that was not well-done of him, but perhaps he regrets that now."

"That's past mending. All in all, I'm not sorry. In spite of having you to lean on, I think I amounted to more than if I had stayed home."

"I agree. And an engineer might be much in demand in civilian life, unlike most of these soldiers."

"You think I should muster out?"

"You're not getting any younger."

"Thank you very much. Whereas you, five years my senior, seem to get younger before my eyes."

"That is because you are looking at a man in love."

"Truly, Bose, you are sick of army life, aren't you?"

"It's time to move on to something new, time for both of us to move on. I only hope . . ."

"What?"

"That you won't let your pride stand in the way of your future the way it did before."

"Bose. I have been facedown in mud and blood so many times I don't remember what pride is. I know we won a lot of battles, and that is some consolation, but for myself, I feel beaten by the war."

"Then listen to your father when he talks. Don't take everything he says amiss."

"I shall be polite to him for your sake and Joan's."

"Polite isn't enough. Be kind to him, for your own sake. If we ride away from here now, you might never see him alive again."

Evan recalled how empty he had felt when Lady Mountjoy let him believe his father was dead, and knew Bose was right. If he left Meremont again, he would not return. It hurt too much, and he wasn't entirely sure why this was so.

Chapter Two

Evan rose at dawn and dressed himself. He realized it must be hours until breakfast, so he took a walk to the stable to check on their horses. He then wandered down the lane toward the fields. If the house mystified him, the grounds disoriented him. He expected things would have changed, but there were huge trees growing where he did not even remember small trees. The only familiar parts were those Gram had described. He could call up her voice telling him about the lane with the bridge over the stream and the cottages beyond. And there was the small beech wood where one could walk quite unobserved from the lane.

Evan found a path that he must have taken as a boy. It had been kept open by some inveterate walker, and he felt a friendly sympathy for the unknown boy.

He sat down on a rock to rest and try to puzzle out the past, but the crucial memories eluded him. It seemed such a profitless task. He was what he was now. Why unearth memories that were likely to be painful?

He started at a movement among the new foliage, and almost dropped to a crouch before he remembered where he was. A lithe figure picked its way along the path. Not a boy though, but a girl, wearing a shawl and bonnet that looked old-fashioned even to a man who had been absent from England for years.

"Good morning, Judith," he said quietly, so as not to startle her.

"I didn't even see you there, you were so still."

She sat down beside him, which spurred him to ask, "Do you often stop to rest here?"

"Not rest, just listen and think. The way through the wood is too short otherwise. I was just taking some bread to Mrs. Gorn. She's quite alone now."

"Isn't that a job for Lady Mountjoy?"

She looked at him accusingly. "She would do it, if she could."

"Sorry, that was a stupid thing for me to say."

"Especially now that you know she is increasing. I saw your face when you guessed. You looked—well, satisfied, as though you had caught her out at something."

"Did I?" Evan thought back over the previous agonizing evening. If his face was that easily read, they must all think him a cold, brooding fellow. "It had only solved a puzzle for me, about why she doesn't want me to stay. Her irrational dislike for me makes sense in light of her pregnancy. Women do often act out-of-character when pregnant . . . don't they?"

Judith hesitated, and Evan thought she was on the point of denying that her sister disliked him, but instead she asked, "Had you ever thought that perhaps that is the one time they are more truly themselves, when all that matters is the baby and providing for it?"

"I had not thought about it, but then I have not had much time to observe women, let alone wonder about them. You, for instance, are a complete mystery. I would have guessed you to be the type of person who likes horses, not hates them."

"But I love them!" she said passionately, then looked away.

"But not to ride?"

"I drive tolerably well," she said, clasping her hands in her lap.

He looked at the strong, competent hands laid against the faded material of her gown and inspiration hit him. "A riding habit. You need a new one, don't you?"

"No, I don't want one. What are you that you read my mind like that? It's not fair."

"That had to be it. You would love to ride, but you must have a riding habit to do it in. We will go into Exeter and buy you one."

"We will not. What would people think of me? Men do not buy women clothes."

"Not even their aunts?"

"I am not related to you by blood at all. It would be highly improper."

"Improper for me to bring gifts to my family—all my family? You could help me pick out exactly what Helen and Angel would like. We'll go before breakfast, if you can drive me."

"I can't. I have work to do."

"What sort of work?"

"That's none of your business."

"You don't strike me as the sort of person who would put your own interests before your family, even if it meant putting off your work."

"No, of course not. I mean—"

"You were just using that as an excuse not to help me. Very well. I shall go myself. But I fully intend to buy you a riding habit, whether you want one or not. Of course, left to my own devices, I shall probably choose red, or make some other crucial blunder, but there you have it. I am a soldier and prone to blunder." He got up decisively.

"No, you must not," she said, jumping up.

"Not red?"

"No, you must not buy it at all." She stamped her foot in frustration. "They will think I coerced you."

"No one coerces me. Hasn't Father told you how stubborn I am?"

"Time and again."

"What else did he say about me?"

"Only that you were very unforgiving."

"Me unforgiving? That's a good one. Well, do you mean to come with me or no? For I am off now."

"I will help you choose gifts for your father and the others, but you must not buy me anything."

"Oh, well, half a loaf... Come then." He held out his hand to her so commandingly that she took it, and he very nearly dragged her the rest of the way through the wood. She fetched it back when they came at last to the stable.

Before Judith fairly knew what had happened, they were on the road to Exeter, with not so much as her reticule about her, and Evan thrusting the reins upon her. She did not like being poor and resented being made to feel poor by someone she held in awe. She would rather have had her reticule, even if it was empty. But that was what she was like—a sham.

"We shall be late to breakfast," Judith warned as Evan helped her carry the pile of packages from the stable to the house.

"I'm sure there'll be something left for us. Then we will go riding and see if that habit looks as good with you on horseback as it did in the shop."

Judith thanked him hastily and ran up the stairs with her plunder, leaving Evan to find the breakfast parlor on his own. The main hall ran from front to back; cross halls ran the length of the house. Evan opened several doors on the north end of the house before concluding that the shrouded ballroom, salons and drawing room were not much used. If they had been in use when he was a boy, he could only think that he had been barred from them, for nothing looked familiar. The south end of the house contained the library and dining room, what looked like a morning room full of sewing baskets and, finally, the breakfast parlor.

"Where the devil have you been?" Lord Mountjoy demanded of Evan as he sat down.

"Exeter, shopping. We have bought you some tobacco."

"What nonsense! Haring off first thing in the morning to go shopping. I said I had things to discuss with you."

"Oh, did you mean this morning?"

"Of course I meant this morning."

"Could you please pass the ham?" Evan asked of Judith, who had just slipped in and seated herself.

"I want you in the library directly after we've eaten."

"Sorry, I have an appointment," Evan replied.

"A what? A what?" his father sputtered.

"Evan, it can wait—" Judith started to say.

"Judith has promised to show me the countryside."

Lady Mountjoy frowned at her sister, and Angel increased her pout. Evan could not help noticing that Angel was dressed in a new muslin of the latest cut, and thought perhaps she was expecting a compliment.

"I should be available in an hour or two if that is convenient."

"No, it is not! You be in the library in ten minutes—ten minutes!"

"No, I don't think I can manage that. I suppose tomorrow will do as well."

"No, it will not." Lord Mountjoy threw down his fork and left the table. Evan merely cocked an eyebrow at his fuming exit.

"Now see what you have done." Lady Mountjoy rose from the table and with a penetrating stare commanded her sisters to come with her. Angel went in a pet, but Judith sat gazing at her plate.

"We do make a spectacle, don't we?" Evan asked of Judith.

"Evan, please have this meeting with him. We can go riding afterward. Besides, it will take me an hour to change."

"I see," he said suspiciously. She rose then, forcing him to do so, and he walked with her into the hall. She ran up the stairs, but turned to look back at him with an admonishing expression.

"I'm going. I'm going," he promised with a laugh and went to knock at the library door.

"Come!"

Evan entered the room as he would that of a commanding officer who had sent for him without telling him why.

"So you have finally found it convenient to talk to me?"

"I'm sorry. I did try to be civil, but I am so unused to it, it is a bit of a strain."

"For me as well. Look that over and tell me what you think." His father tossed a document across the desk.

Evan sat down and read for a moment only before he said, "This isn't Gram's will. It's yours. Why do you want me to read this?"

"Just read! You did learn that at your expensive school, didn't you?"

Evan sighed and read slowly through the document, not believing any of it.

"Have you finished?"

Evan jerked as he had always done at the sound of his father's voice, bursting on the silence like a shot. It was a habit he resented. If the French cannonading had not made him blink, why did this old man set his nerves on edge? "Yes, I've finished, but I don't understand it."

"I had thought you intelligent enough to comprehend a simple testament—"

"I mean, why me? Do you really mean to leave everything to me, when we have not spoken for ten years? Surely Terry has a better claim on you. If not Terry, then Thomas."

"Thomas is as yet unformed and too young to worry over. Terence is ... not like you."

"Which is to say he does not drive you to the verge of apoplexy."

Lord Mountjoy gave a grudging smile. "No, he does not. In fact, he agrees with every judgment I pronounce, even if I am dead wrong."

"Are you?"

"What?"

"Ever wrong?"

Lord Mountjoy leaned back in his chair and braced his elbows on the arms, his fingers propped together in a steeple as he regarded Evan. "More than once I have erred quite fantastically, especially where you were concerned. I feared I would never have a chance to set that right."

"If you mean to buy my loyalty after all those years of neglect, you cannot." Evan resisted the impulse to fling the document in his father's face, but merely laid it on the edge of the desk.

"I had no such thought. I am merely doing what is best for Meremont and everyone concerned. I have already spoken to Terry about it."

"Let me guess—he agreed with you."

"He is the most exasperating boy in that respect. Yes, he did."

Suddenly Evan chuckled. "This is absurd. We should never get along."

"I do not expect us to. In fact, I don't want you under the same roof with me. Even I cannot take being rubbed raw at every meal. You may refurbish the dower house for your own until my death, then I'm sure you will give it over to Lady Mountjoy for her use."

"A rather bleak future for a young mother. I wish you a long and prosperous life, Father."

"She is not the most biddable of women, but she does give in to me."

"Not too soon, I hope. Otherwise, you might hold her in the same regard as Terry."

"No, we have had some rare battles, especially over you."

"Indeed. I still don't see what you want with me."

"I don't want someone who only agrees with me. I want someone who knows about things. The buildings need repairs. We need a new bridge over the stream to get our crops to market. I want to build a canal—"

"A what?"

"A canal to the Exe. I have bought up almost all the land I need."

"Oh, no, Father. Not a canal. Have you any idea of the expense?"

"Some idea, but I'm sure you can work that out exactly... Don't argue for just one moment, until I finish my thought. I also want someone who will disagree with me when the need arises."

"And not out of mere playfulness?"

"Do you imagine we could ever be on such a footing?" His father looked at him intently.

Evan took a moment over his answer, sighing heavily at the wasted years behind him. Then he thought of Judith and smiled. "I can imagine it, with the right woman to keep us from each other's throats, but I do not think we will come to such a state painlessly."

"Then let us come to it by whatever road we must. It is the only way I can see for this family to survive. Do you agree?"

"I agree to try," Evan said, rising. He looked at his father's extended hand and shook it.

"Good. We'll discuss the canal later."

Evan opened his mouth, then closed it and went up to his room, shaking his head.

"You just had to do it, didn't you?" Bose demanded. "You had to argue with him." He tossed a pair of Evan's boots to the floor with enough force to draw a complaint from him.

"Mind what you are about."

"Disappearing for half the morning, then arguing the entire way through breakfast. What could you have been thinking of?"

"My head was turned, and I did apologize."

"There should have been no need. I thought you were past such raw-recruit antics. I shall most likely never win Joan now. Don't expect much dinner, is all I can say, for she is in tears in the kitchen, expecting us to be thrown out at any moment."

"Bose, you are an admirable traveling companion, and sometimes even a passable batman, but your intelligence gathering leaves much to be desired," Evan said, as he straightened his stock and searched out his riding crop.

"Don't even speak to me. I shall hope to be taken on as a groom here. I wash my hands of you. What do you mean, intelligence?"

"Any moderately well run establishment would allocate at least one footman to stand outside a door where a crucial conference is being held, and keep the maids from crying into the shelled peas by reporting that everything is going to be fine."

"It is? But you just had a rousing fight with him."

"Yes, that's what he likes about me. At least that's what he says."

"That makes no sense. Are you sure you have it right?" Bose asked, as Evan was about to leave.

"Seems odd to me, too, but he wants us to stay. He means to leave the place to me to run. Of course, I shall be instantly saddled with a family who doesn't like me, with one exception. But that's no worse than breaking in a new troop, don't you think?"

"I'm sure there is a difference, but I don't know what all it might be," said Bose in awe.

"No sense borrowing trouble from tomorrow in any case. Of course, there's no saying what might happen at dinner."

Lady Mountjoy had watched Evan and Judith ride out and had waited by the morning-room window so that she could speak to her sister directly once they returned. When they came up the back steps of the house, Judith saw Helen staring at them and wiped the smile from her glowing face.

"Angel, leave us a moment," Helen Mountjoy commanded a few minutes later, planting herself in her sisters' bedroom.

Angel grimaced at Judith on her way out, drawing a smile from her. Judith was sitting on the bed in her shift and reached for her tired blue evening frock. Helen helped her pull it over her head.

"Where did this riding habit come from?" Helen asked as she turned to shake out the creases from the long green skirt hanging by the mirror.

"Evan bought it for me," Judith said calmly, thinking of their first ride and how Evan had praised her natural riding ability.

"That's not proper. It's also very dangerous."

"So I told him, but somehow he managed to talk me into it. I keep going over it in my mind, and I can't quite make out how I agreed to it. It must have been when he threatened to buy me a red one."

Helen sat on the bed beside her sister. "I know you are very sensible in the ordinary way, Judith, but he's a man."

"I know," Judith said, combing her hair.

"And a soldier."

"Yes, I know," she said emphatically.

"I fear he may persuade you to some indiscretion."

Judith went pink in the face, but not from anger. "After being tricked once, I could never be taken in again. Besides, Evan is different from Banstock. Evan is a war hero. While Banstock's troop never left England."

"And Evan is stronger. He could take what he wanted, and you could never stop him."

"But he would not do such a thing under his father's own roof. Besides, I feel I know him already from his letters, and from Gram talking about him. I think he will be a very good friend to me."

"Friend? Does he know the sort of relationship you have in mind?"

"Do not worry. I shall keep him at arm's length. He will be the big brother I never had."

"Do you mean to stick by your decision never to marry?"

"We did agree that it is best this way. At least I will never have to deceive anyone."

Helen hesitated as she ran her fingers in circles on the coverlet. "You don't mean to tell Evan the truth, then?"

"And give him a disgust of me? No, I could not bear it."

"I don't like him, Judith. I tell you, I don't like him."

"Merely because he is a soldier and strong?"

"He is also dangerous," Helen said ominously.

"Nonsense, Helen," Judith said, as she rose to arrange her hair. "I can handle him."

"I don't mean physically dangerous. When he arrived, I tried to send him packing."

"You didn't!" Judith whirled. "I know you don't like him, but this is his home."

Helen pushed herself to her feet with much less grace than her sister. "Well, it didn't work. Then, when Hiram introduced us, Evan acted as though we had just met."

"But that was very kind of him."

"It was very clever of him. I warn you, Judith, behind those sad, hurt eyes lurks a formidable intellect."

"You make it sound as though he is plotting against us."

"He is a soldier and not one to miss the main chance. What better way to entrench himself here than to marry you?"

"But that's silly! We've only just met. Besides, I will never marry."

"Captain Mountjoy does not know that."

"Then I have only to tell him so."

"There is no reasoning with you when you have taken one of your romantic starts."

"If we are speaking of romantic starts, what about a new widow who suddenly marries a man nearly twice her age?"

"That was different," Helen said, holding her head up proudly. "I had advertised as a housekeeper, not a wife. I think in the beginning Hiram simply felt sorry for me, caught with young Ralph and almost no pension."

"Not to mention two sisters, one of whom was a fallen woman."

"But that wasn't your fault. I advised you to go with Banstock. I believed him when he said he preferred to be married in Bath rather than Bristol."

"I believed him, too. So do not worry about me being taken in by another man. I mean to be very careful."

"Very well." Helen kissed her lightly on the cheek. "We must go down now. I so hate to be the last to go in to dinner."

"Helen?"

"Yes, dear?"

"You do love Lord Mountjoy now, don't you?"

"Very much. You see, I thought he was only trying to save us. I never expected he actually wanted me, or that I would be having a child to him." She stroked her round stomach affectionately. "He is the best of men."

"Yes, I know."

After Helen left, Judith stroked the green dress that became her so well. Evan had picked the color. If Helen perceived that he was no gudgeon, then Judith herself should be wary of him. Still, Gram had had a high regard for her grandson. Judith supposed that she should not let one devastating experience color her judgment of all men. But what did it matter, really? She was going to be a spinster aunt and remain at Meremont forever. So why should she not enjoy Evan's gallantry? She was completely safe from him.

Evan determined to show Bose that his fears were ungrounded. By dint of speaking only when he was spoken to, Evan made it through the evening meal without a single hitch, though he was called to attention half a dozen times for not answering. He could not help noticing that Judith wore the same gown she had the previous evening, and that when the candles were set out in the library, she picked up a basket of mending. He occupied himself with ruses for providing his future wife with a more extensive wardrobe immediately. She could sew; that was something. So all he had to do was put the materials into her hands. That was surely not the same as buying her clothes. It came to him that he was taking a lot for granted in expecting her to accept his proposal. She was too good for him. But he had better ask her. Then, of course, he could say she was working on her trousseau. Yes, that was the best plan of action. He nodded to himself as though he had just finished the work plan for the next day and was surprised that the table did not contain innumerable maps and drawings to roll up and put away.

His father was staring at him, and Evan smiled blankly. Lord Mountjoy scowled. "I asked if you were going to ride about the place tomorrow with me. But I suppose you are too deaf to hear me."

"Sorry, I was not attending. May Judith come as well?"

"If she wishes."

"I want to go, too," Angel said.

"Not on one of my horses," his father declared.

Angel looked appealingly at Evan.

"Afraid I can't afford to have one of mine lamed, either," he said warily, assuming the worst.

"It's not fair."

"Best stay home, child," Lord Mountjoy said more kindly. "You would only hold us up. You are forever dropping things."

"Terry, may I ride one of your horses?" Angel asked sweetly.

"No, absolutely not. You don't even like to ride."

"How shall I ever grow to like it if I am not given the chance?"

"Liking it isn't enough. You have to be good at it," Evan said, but he was looking at Judith, who blushed becomingly.

"Is Judith good at it?"

"Very."

"I believe the ladies will go up now," Helen interrupted ruthlessly. Evan soon followed them, since he had no desire either to drink or argue, and Terry's less-than-coherent grumbling would lead him to one or the other. He was interrupted in the process of undressing himself by a knock and threw his shirt back on before opening the door to Lady Mountjoy.

"I mean to talk to you."

"Sit down, please."

"I shall require only a moment. I may have to put up with you, but I will not have my sister preyed upon by you. If you lay one finger on her I will—I will shoot you."

Evan blinked at her and then smiled. "I admire your fortitude, and I should have spoken to you before, so as not to worry you. My intentions—"

"I know what a soldier's intentions may be. I cannot live in a house without being aware of what is going forward below stairs."

"Oh, Bose. But he and Joan have known each other for decades. It's only to be expected that his affair progresses more rapidly than—"

"His affair, as you name it, disgusts me."

"But his goal is marriage, as is mine, I assure you."

"A man may promise anything...."

"If you have been disappointed by some man at some time, that does not mean we are all cut from the same cloth."

"I flatter myself I know what cloth you are cut from. I'll send her away if I have to. You will not have Judith."

"But I want to marry her. She will be Lady Mountjoy someday...or is that it? A sister you have taken for granted for years, almost turned into a drudge, might someday have precedence over you?"

"I'll see you in your grave before I'll see her married to you."

She turned on her heel and exited, with Evan thoughtfully closing the door behind her. He realized he might have to revise his plans. But what could not be taken by direct assault could be had by patient siege, and he knew how to be patient.

The ride about the estate was not the casual affair that Evan had anticipated, but a tour of the lands acquired in anticipation of his father's canal project. They were all under cultivation, as it happened, but the acquiring of them might well have beggared him. Evan could see some point to it, if they had a manufacture to ship goods from or even a woolery, but with the current price of corn and cloth, it would never pay for itself. He did not, however, ruin the ride by saying so. Judith was in her glory, garnering compliments on her new skill from both Lord Mountjoy and Terry. Evan liked to see her smiling shyly at them, since most of the things he said to her drew a suspicious look.

They returned to the house with hours to spare before dinner, so Evan invited Judith for a walk. He led her toward the dower house and found them a seat in its neglected garden. Even in its overgrown state it seemed very familiar to him. It should. He had spent many days here recovering from the accident that had claimed his brother.

"I miss her," Judith said, picking a flower and twirling it sadly between her fingers as she sat sideways on the stone bench.

"So do I. I would have come if I could."

"She did not expect you to. She would not even let me write that she was ill until she knew she could not—"

"It was your hand that wrote those last letters for her then?" He took her hand and turned it over, to regard the ink stains lovingly.

Judith swallowed but did not pull back. She liked the touch of him too well. What harm would it do, after all? "I suppose you did not get them all, if you didn't know she was dead."

"I must have been on my way home by the time those would have reached me."

"It was little enough to do for her. We used to sit out here and she would talk."

"Of what?"

"The war."

"She did not know about our victories then."

"She had every confidence you would triumph in the end. She—she let me read your letters." Judith stared down at the flower and their joined hands, and wondered if she had said too much.

"Then I fancy you know me a great deal better than I know you."

"I know that there was a great deal you left out so as to spare her. She used to rant at your lack of detail."

"That sounds like her." Evan smiled. "If I could not be here with her, I'm so glad you were. There isn't anyone else I would rather have had with her."

"Lord Mountjoy was not inattentive. He—he read your letters, too. Or rather, I read them to the both of them. He has them now. It was the only thing he wanted."

"Father? I'm surprised."

"I do not know what is between you two," she said finally, drawing her hand back, "except that it is in the past. I only know that I like you both and would rather not see you at odds with one another."

"He must have mellowed indeed."

"He has always treated me gently, as though we are old friends."

"Why is that?" Evan asked suspiciously.

Judith studied her hands for a moment. If ever there was a time to tell Evan the trials that his father had shared with her it was now, but her courage failed her. "I think because of the time we spent here together," she lied, her voice milky with tears.

"I would not have thought it of him."

"People can change. They can see what they've done wrong and try to make up for it," she pleaded.

"Are we talking about him or me?"

"I had meant . . ." She stopped when she realized she had been speaking about herself. *Tell him,* she thought, but any way she arranged the admission, it sounded sordid.

"Yes, if the shoe fits . . . Is there the slightest chance that an educated and proper girl such as yourself would ever consider marriage to a worn-out soldier?"

"No, never!" She jumped up in shock.

"Oh," he said, slowly rising, knowing he had moved too fast and not wanting to panic Judith further.

"I mean I shall never marry." She turned her face away.

"But why not?"

"I have found a . . . higher pursuit—my studies."

"Do they consume all your time?"

"Nearly all."

"When you are not sewing."

"Yes." She looked from side to side, as though searching for a means of escape.

"How is it that you sew a great deal and have nothing to show for it?" He could see a tear sparkling on her eyelashes. "Don't mind me. I'm just a clumsy soldier. Think of me as your brother if it will help."

"I have to think of you as a brother or I will not be able to think of you at all," she said desperately.

Evan studied her intense face and knew she was not indifferent to him. "And as a brother I should be able to buy you some bolts of fabric to sew with. Once again you had better help me pick them out."

"Why are you doing this?" She looked into his eyes.

"There is so little I can do. Humor me?"

"It is not right. People will talk."

"Who are these unnamed people who talk so much?" he asked with a forced laugh. "I think they should mind their own business."

She nervously brushed away a tear and said, "I don't know. It's what Helen always says when she does not want us doing something."

"People will talk no matter what you do. It's a waste of energy to pay any attention to them."

"I should like to ignore them, all of them," she said wistfully.

"Good, we will go shopping again tomorrow."

As they found their way back to the house, Judith thought again that she should tell Evan why she would not marry. But she could not bear to think of him disgusted with her, angry even. In spite of reading all his letters over and over, she did not know him well enough to guess how he would react. If he pressed her, of course, she would have to confess, but she rather thought that she had nipped his suit in the bud, that he would become much like Terry. Now she had only to worry about controlling herself around him. His slightest touch, whether to help her off her horse or up from a seat, made her heart pound with desire.

gate moved back slowly into the engine, but Terry was not where he'd headed. There was, instead, reclining in one corner, Diane, a very young lad of five, more than three years, was barely recognisable to single. In one of her poses.

"I won't go to Leo. Run to church. You made it through asked. If he has a home-make with it of you—

"Not Tuce have—her—not pull the way—

"Sure," the knight. I'm unrecognisable. Bell."

"Sure," she said. "I'm—on—to go—a saw of the book to that I had—

"And I did not know of germs, but today." Robin said laughing.

Chapter Three

Evan's inspiration to include Angel on this next shopping expedition was a wise one, since she chivied Judith into more extravagant fixings for finery than would have occurred to Evan. He drove the gig home himself. Such intense discussions of hemlines and laces would have distracted even such a staunch mind as Judith's from her driving.

They heard Lord Mountjoy shouting in the library from the courtyard and ceased their merry laughter. Evan shooed the girls upstairs with their packages and wondered whether he should intervene on Terry's behalf. Having listened to many such lectures, Evan was not cowed, except to shrug in sympathy at the monologue that issued from the library. His father might have been speaking to him, for some of the lines were the same. And yet the words were all he remembered, his father's disembodied voice nagging at him. He looked around the hall. Unless it had changed vastly, he did not remember it any more than he did the library or dining room, or even his bedroom. But he knew he could walk into the dower house and go through it blindfolded. What freakish tricks the mind played.

The library door burst open. "I thought I heard you come in."

Evan jumped at his father's intrusion.

"Get in here. I need you."

Evan moved reluctantly into the room, but Terry was no-where in evidence. There was instead, lounging in one of the chairs, a surly young lad of no more than fifteen years, who bore a resemblance to Angel in one of her pouts.

"I want you to take him in charge. You made it through school. If he has a prayer in the world, it is you."

"Me? Take him in charge? But who is he?"

"Helen's son, Ralph. He is incorrigible. Well?"

"Sorry to be struck stupid, but I did not know of his ex-istence until this moment."

"And I did not know of yours until today," Ralph said resentfully.

"So we are even then?"

"Not by a long shot. I suppose I won't even get the bar-rens now," Ralph countered.

"The barrens?" Evan asked.

"Don't you remember anything?" his father demanded. "The moorlands. Not good for much except pasturing sheep, but they would yield a living if properly managed."

Ralph looked up, a spark of malice in his eyes. "Is that where Terry is to be exiled now?"

"That is none of your affair, you young cur."

"Do you like farming?" Evan asked blankly.

"No, I should sell it and go back to London."

"Back to London?"

"He was sent down from school a month ago, but he copped the letter out of the post and has been philandering in London."

"Pretty exciting this time of year, all littered with the ton?" Evan asked.

"And expensive."

"He ran out of money and into debt," Lord Mountjoy said, as though Ralph could not hear him.

"How many subjects did you fail?" Evan asked casu-ally.

"All of them," Ralph said proudly.

"A great temptation, the life at Oxford or Cambridge, as I recall. Better than half my class got sent down, for one reason or another, by the middle of each term. Their fathers got them back in, of course, for as long as it seemed worthwhile."

"It's a total waste," Ralph said.

"Not to the fathers, who have got rid of a troublesome lad for months at a time."

Evan had not been aware of his father leaving the room, but when he bothered to look around, he noticed his absence.

"Were you sent there to get rid of you?" Ralph asked.

"Oh, yes."

"Toying with the maids, or was it the bottle?"

"I killed my elder brother."

Ralph gasped. "You never!"

"Ask anyone. Tell me, of all these subjects you failed, does any of them have an appeal for you?"

"No."

"You're telling me you are interested in absolutely nothing?"

"I like poetry."

"Poetry? That's a tough one. Never could quite get it myself."

"I only like it because it's quick to read."

"Quick to read, long to understand. Suppose we make a deal. You teach me poetry and I'll tell you what I know about geometry."

"What use is that to me?"

"Can't fire a gun, even a little one, without geometry."

"I'm a fair shot."

"But could you fire a twelve pounder and have the vaguest notion where the ball would fall, what elevation to use to hit your target?"

"With practice."

"Not good enough. You can't be all day finding the enemy's range or you would be blown to bits while you are about it. Take it from me, geometry can be useful for a variety of things. Of course, we shall have to tackle algebra first. You will need to know how to solve a formula. Tell you what. You pick out a book of poetry for me to study and I will hunt up my textbooks. They must be at Gram's house. We'll start after lunch tomorrow.''

"I didn't agree."

"Well, I think if you understand poetry, the least you can do is help me out. It isn't easy courting your sister when I am only an ignorant soldier."

"You and Angel?"

"No, Judith, but keep that quiet if you would. I'm not entirely sure she will have me."

"She'd be a fool not to."

"What, a murderer? It's only by the greatest exertion that I will ever prove myself worthy of her."

Evan left young Ralph staring at his back. The boy was not much different than the regular run of recruits. One had only to find a common ground, appeal to that and establish a rapport. About lying to the boy and manipulating him, Evan had no qualms. One did what one had to in time of war.

But this was not war... or was it? Perhaps he had not exaggerated his fears of gaining Judith's hand, if Lady Mountjoy had any say. What better way to win that good lady over than by helping her recalcitrant son?

Was there another reason? Perhaps he did see a bit of himself in Ralph. His own rebellion had not been as blatant and he'd had more cause.... Of course, he did not know what Ralph's upbringing had been like. Perhaps it had been worse than his own. He did know his father had a talent for mishandling striplings.

There was also Judith. Perhaps she was attached to this brooding nephew of hers. Any way he looked at it, helping Ralph had to be a winning proposition, but only if he succeeded. He went to get the key to search for his old textbooks in the attic of the dower house.

He was right about remembering the place. Except for the covers over Gram's furniture, it looked the same, and it was heavy with memories of her. She had been like a mother to him. Why this was, he could not quite remember. He thought his own mother must have been rather sickly. He found his trunk of books in his bedroom. It was a room he remembered well. "Why didn't I come back in time?" he asked the empty air, then went back to the main house.

"Well?"

Evan jumped, despite his prone position on the bed. That one word shouted at a man comfortably ensconced in the *Times* made him cringe. "Am I the only one you shout at?"

"You don't attend me half the time," his father said from the doorway. "How else am I to get your attention? Are you going to take the boy in charge?"

"On one condition."

"What is that?"

"That you do not interfere or question what I am doing."

"Interfere?"

"I had a commander who always trusted me. I might not do things the way he expected, but I always got results. That was enough for him. I should think you could trust me that far."

"I have no choice. Nothing I say makes the slightest impression on Ralph."

"Well, as long as he regards you as our common nemesis, I may be able to gain his confidence. So have a care you shout at us both in equal measure. I would not want him to think I am conspiring with the enemy."

"Nemesis indeed! Do you think I don't have the boy's best interests at heart?"

"No, I believe you do." Evan's eyes had strayed back to the paper when a sudden thought struck him. "Only tell me truthfully, was I ever that callow?"

"You were worse, and sanctimonious into the bargain."

Evan shuddered a little. "I am justly punished then. How could you stand me?"

"I couldn't."

"Oh, yes, I was forgetting."

"And don't think you can steal the paper away to your room every day when others might wish to read it."

"Sorry, Father."

Lord Mountjoy harrumphed and left. On the way down the stairs he tried to count the number of times Evan or Terry had said that to him, not paying the slightest attention to what they had done, so that he had to issue the same command again the next day. He would never understand these young bloods—never.

Evan rode with Judith again in the morning, and she showed him her favorite paths. Some of these were not entirely suitable for riding, in that they had to duck limbs and brambles and even get off and walk in places. They fetched up in the garden of the dower house to cool the horses. "Father says I can take up living here," Evan remarked, glancing up at the dusty windows.

"Oh, I am glad. I do not like to see it shut up like this."

"I was thinking of that, too. It's a big house. It will take some work to set it to rights."

"Let me help. I would love to do it."

"It strikes me you already do enough for others, perhaps more than you should."

"I owe them something, Helen and Lord Mountjoy. They needn't have brought me here."

"But to be ordered about by your sister when you might very well be managing a house of your own . . ."

"I am content. I do not know what would have become of us if not for Lord Mountjoy."

"How did they meet, anyway?"

"Sister advertised herself as a housekeeper, but she insisted Angel and I would have to come with her."

"Surely she did not offer you as servants?"

"No, and I believe that is what intrigued Lord Mountjoy. Her very helplessness in the face of financial disaster had a certain appeal to him."

"How can you speak about it so objectively? It was your future, too, your disaster."

"I had an offer of marriage." Judith blushed and studied her gloved hands. "At least I thought it was an offer of marriage." She was feeling more courageous today, perhaps because of the horse.

"A good offer?"

"Don't look at me so. You have no idea what it is like. I did it to help my family, and when he...when it didn't work out, it seemed wiser to cling together if Lord Mountjoy would allow it." She finished with a blush, embarrassed once again that she had not confided in him.

Evan had a notion there was more to the story than this, but only the present concerned him now. "Well, he always was a managing fellow."

"I feel almost sorry for him, having all of us thrust upon him. Especially me, which was uncalled for, and Ralph. What was the row about yesterday?"

"Ah, I am to whip Ralph into shape for school. He, in turn, will teach me poetry."

"What?" she asked, halting Molly and turning to stare at him suspiciously.

"You were probably unaware I have such aspirations."

She laughed in his face. "You have not, and you know it."

"Ah, but Ralph does not know it, so take no notice if we wander about discussing odd bits of verse. Who knows but what I may gain a little polish, after all—at least do not laugh in this disarming way. It is infectious."

He put his free arm around her back and silenced her with a kiss. She countered with a blow that fairly made Evan's head ring. It also startled Taurus into a rear, which nearly dragged Evan off his feet.

"I'm sorry," she gasped, one hand thrown up over her mouth, the other still clutching Molly's reins.

"So am I," Evan said, giving his head a shake and calming his horse.

"I didn't mean to hit you so hard, but you caught me off guard."

"I should hate to think what you are capable of when prepared for a kiss," he said, feeling his cheek.

"You must not! You must never do that again."

"And you must think me a beast. But war has a way of giving one a certain impatience with life."

"Things done impatiently are usually done unwisely," she said almost to herself.

"That has the ring of your sister about it."

"I'm sure she has had reason to say it often enough."

"I must agree with it, even knowing it comes from her. Can you forgive me?"

"If you promise never to do that again."

"I promise I will never force myself on you again. But you do see what I mean about needing polish?" he asked with a grin.

"Why are you helping Ralph?" she demanded. "And do not continue with this nonsensical story about wanting to learn poetry."

"Perhaps I am doing it to get in your sister's good graces."

"Even if that would work, why would you care what she thinks of you?"

"I should like her to be more at ease, for the babe's sake if for no other reason."

"What would you care about her baby, another half brother?" she taunted callously.

"The way you say that, so coldly...it gives me a chill. Do you imagine I went about putting infants to the sword? When you have been engaged in such a ghastly business as war, any baby, no matter whose, is a ray of hope, a promise that something will continue."

She stopped ahead of him, saying nothing. He dropped the reins and walked around in front of her to discover tears on her cheeks. "What is it? I know, my rude talk. I am hopeless."

"No, it's not that," she said, thinking how sweet it would be to have a baby and be allowed to keep it. "I have tried to imagine what it was like for you." Her voice was rich with the wetness of the tears. "I would rather have been there...."

"In Spain?"

"Anywhere but here."

"But it is fairly pleasant here."

"I am talking foolishly. Please don't regard it." She brushed the tears away with her gloved hands. "Are the horses cool?"

"Yes."

Judith let Evan lead the horses to the stable and retreated to her room to change. She had missed another chance to tell him, but it wasn't the sort of thing one blurted out to a near stranger. The quandary was that the more she knew him, the better she liked him and the more difficult it was to tell him she had been ruined. Except for the rides she must not be alone with Evan again; it was as simple as that. If they became no closer, there would never be a need to reveal her guilty secret.

As promised, directly after lunch, Evan and Ralph tackled algebra for two hours. They were consigned to the breakfast parlor for this exercise, since Helen and Angel went to sew in the morning room, and Judith and Lord Mountjoy conducted business in the library during this part of the day. The post had been fetched by then, and there were always letters to be answered, after which Lord Mountjoy would retire to peruse the *Times* and perhaps catch a nap. Evan was well aware of the schedule and, intentionally or not, was always plotting how he could get to the newspaper before his father. No chance of it today. The post, which was deposited on the hall table, had been taken up by Judith on their return, and she had gone directly to the library to sort it in preparation for the afternoon work. Evan had not as yet discovered where she secreted the paper, but he would.

By dint of presenting each lesson as a useful means of solving a practical problem, Evan managed to hold Ralph's interest. But nothing could alleviate for Evan the dullness of

Chaucer. He had not thought Ralph would take him seriously enough to present British poetry from a historical perspective.

Within a day Ralph proved to be a welcome addition to the household in several ways. Not only did he now share the bite of Lord Mountjoy's tongue, he brought a wealth of gossip from London to enthrall Angel and delight Judith in spite of her pursed lips. He also made a fourth for whist, which was the only game Lord Mountjoy countenanced of an evening. That is not to say the play was peaceful. Terry was hounded for his dullness, though Evan guessed this was from a surfeit of drink. Evan himself was constantly chastised for not attending, and Ralph for being cocky when he won.

Evan sensed there was trouble brewing with Terry but could not conceive how to stop it. It came to a head the next morning when Evan caught his brother returning from a night's carousing, mounted on Evan's Andalusian colt.

"He's come to no harm," Terry claimed.

"He might well have. You had no right to take him without asking. Surely you knew I meant to ride him myself this morning."

"Why ask you, then? You would have refused. You never gave me anything. Now you have taken everything." Terry's broad gesture swept full circle to indicate Meremont.

"I never meant you any harm. I scarcely know you."

"Is that my fault, cooped up here with Father while you were off in Spain, covering yourself with glory?"

"It was mud."

"What?"

"Mud was the only thing I was ever covered with in Spain!" Evan shouted.

"You..." Terry lunged, but failed to connect with a blow, flailing away, rather, as his brother tried to hold him up. Finally Evan pushed him, and Terry, enraged at falling in the muck, grabbed a pitchfork and ran full tilt at him. Evan sidestepped and tripped him up.

"Give me that before you hurt someone," he commanded as he wrested the pitchfork away from him.

By this time one of the stable boys had run to the house for help.

"I hate you!" Terry shouted. "You were supposed to be dead. You were supposed to die in Spain. Why did you come back? You ruined everything."

Evan got him in a headlock, but Terry struggled desperately against his grip with the violence of the berserk as his air was slowly cut off. "Do you mean to kill me, too?" he gasped.

Evan let go his hold and took a step back. "I didn't mean to kill Gregory. I felt very much toward him as you feel toward me now. He had everything, even Father's love. And I had nothing. I did not mean to ruin everything for you."

Terry's resentful look was mixed with puzzlement and defeat. "It doesn't matter. Father is probably right. I would only waste it all anyway." He stared at a steaming pile of muck.

"What the devil is going on here?" demanded Lord Mountjoy as he burst through the doorway and pulled up short at sight of his filthy sons.

"Nothing, Father," Evan said in that automatic singsong of his.

"Nothing! But what—? You don't intend to tell me, do you?" He looked pointedly from one son to the other. "I thought not. Everything has to be a conspiracy against me. Well, I should be used to it by now. I don't know why I worry...." Lord Mountjoy stomped out of the stable and toward the house, talking to himself.

Evan chuckled first. "Does he often do that?"

Terry snickered. "More and more of late." He wiped his eyes on his sleeve. Evan went to him and put his arm about his shoulder, causing Terry to wince a little. "I hurt you, didn't I? I'm sorry. Just tell me when you want to borrow the colt. You're more important to me than him."

"Do you mean it?"

"Of course I do. You're my brother."

"No, I meant the part about borrowing your horse."

"Yes, I mean it. Let's get you cleaned up and to bed. You will look rank at breakfast if you don't get an hour or two of sleep."

"I am a mess."

"You should have seen me at your age."

Judith encountered the unlikely pair on the stairs and gave them a wide berth. "I shall be a bit late," Evan warned.

"Take your time," she said with amusement, wrinkling her nose at the stench they were carrying in with them.

"A madhouse!" Lord Mountjoy shouted, coming out of the library. "I live in a madhouse! Oh, Judith, where is yesterday's paper? I've searched the entire library."

"I put it under the blotter on your desk so no one else could get at it."

"Bless you, my dear. You're the only one, the only one who cares about me at all." The force of this was somewhat lost on Judith, since it was bellowed up the stairway for the benefit of his sons.

"What the devil is all the racket?" Ralph complained, coming out of his room with his robe askew.

"Racket, is it? Back to bed with you, you ungrateful whelp," Lord Mountjoy shouted.

Ralph's face disappeared, and Angel only peeked over the banister before disappearing again. Judith thought perhaps she should go check on Helen, but sat on the stairs instead, listening to both the ranting of Lord Mountjoy in the library and the rumblings from Terry's room. Evan finally tramped down the stairs and lifted her to her feet.

"What's the matter, Judith?"

"Our lives were sadly dull before you came to Meremont."

"God grant we may enjoy some dullness when I am safely ensconced in Gram's house."

Lady Mountjoy, far from being asleep upstairs, whirled out of the breakfast parlor. "You! I thought I told you no more riding alone with this—this soldier. It is highly improper for you to go unescorted in his company."

"But—"

"She is right, Judith," Evan agreed.

"What?" demanded Judith and Helen in unison.

"I have been giving it some thought, and as we are not related by blood, I think we do need a chaperon to protect your reputation, especially since I am a soldier. So nip upstairs and get Angel into her riding habit. Run along. Taurus will be rested enough to ride by then."

"But—but will she come?" Judith asked uncertainly as she groped her way up the stairs, not at all sure of Evan's sincerity in wanting Angel to join them.

"She has been wanting to learn to ride. Of course she will come."

"You think you have got around me with this trick, but I won't countenance your attentions to either of my sisters," Helen said.

"Even a soldier could hardly seduce both of them at once."

"Watch your mouth, young man, or I will do as I said."

Lady Mountjoy exited just as her husband came into the hall. "What is going on out here? I cannot even read in peace."

"Nothing, Father," Evan said innocently.

"Nothing, is it again? If I hear that from you one more time I'll strangle you with your own stock. What are you doing standing in the hall?"

"Just waiting to take the girls riding."

"The girls? Both of them?"

"That's right."

"I won't have that Angel on one of my horses, do you hear me?" Lord Mountjoy pointed an accusing finger.

"She may ride my gelding."

"We haven't had a moment's peace since you returned. It's a madhouse, a madhouse!" He slammed the library door after himself.

Bose peeked around the door frame.

"The coast is clear for the moment," Evan said with a vague smile.

"Have you any idea what that sounds like from below?"

"No, are we vastly entertaining?"

"Don't give me that innocent look. What have you been up to?"

"Other than a brawl with my brother and a shouting match with Father and Helen, nothing. Make us something fortifying for breakfast, will you? I shall need it after Angel's riding lesson."

Bose went grumbling down the back stairs to the kitchen, Judith reappeared with an excited Angel and Evan stared only momentarily at the concoction on the child's head.

True to form, Angel lost her hat at the slightest hint of a canter and clutched the saddle so desperately she made no pretense of reining her horse. That was a mercy, since she could not then jab the animal in the mouth. He and Judith had a tolerable time laughing at Angel.

Breakfast was strangely quiet after the commotion of the morning, each of them avoiding the prospect of another argument. Lord Mountjoy stared hard from one to the other of his strange family, almost daring them to break the peace. He did not do so himself except to adjure Ralph to mend his dress with some shirt points he could see over. To this end the algebra lesson was cut short and the poetry skipped altogether in favor of Ralph going shopping.

Evan found Judith in the garden beside the house, fitting Thomas with a new jacket. Thomas was talking quite volubly to her about his puppy, which he was leading by a piece of rope thick enough to tether a bull. Evan laughed at this arrangement and wrestled with the pup with one hand, as Thomas looked on proudly.

"Aunt Judith, are you sure you have taken all the pins out this time?" Thomas asked cautiously in his high, light voice.

"I thought I had. Why? Is one sticking you?"

"No, I just hoped you had made sure."

"It's a wonder you trust me at all, Thomas, as many times as you have been stuck," she said, and smoothed the fabric along his arm with a loving touch.

"It doesn't hurt. It's only a bit of a surprise."

"Like falling off a horse, then?" Evan asked. "You usually don't get hurt, you're just taken aback to be suddenly on the ground."

"I have seen your horses," Thomas said, round eyed. "They are tall but not as fat as Father's."

"They will be if they keep eating their heads off in his stable."

"I shall have a pony next year, but I would rather have a horse."

"A pony is more of a challenge," Judith said bracingly. "I have more trouble getting Betty to do what I want than I have with a horse."

"She's right," confirmed Evan. "Ponies are much smarter than horses. If you can manage a pony and get it to like taking you about, you will be able to ride anything in future."

"Truly?" Thomas questioned, then flinched as he caught sight of his nurse approaching from the house. Judith saw her, too, and there came into her face such a look of resentment that Evan was shocked. Judith quickly removed the garment and helped Thomas back into his old coat, buttoning it up as she would if she were sending him someplace cold. She hugged him for a moment, as though she were not going to see him again for a long time. "All finished, Miranda," she said in that tearful voice Evan was coming to know.

"You spoil him more than his mama," Miranda said, taking the boy's hand possessively and giving Judith an admonishing look. Evan supposed this frown was for letting him talk to the boy. The pup trailed after them, valiantly trying to hold his head up on the end of his heavy tether.

Judith's face was a swirl of emotion—regret, longing, jealousy. "You could have a little boy like that," Evan said.

She flashed him a look of horror.

"I mean when you are married and have a home of your own."

"No!" she said, shaking her head slowly. "I can never have a son like Thomas."

He would have pressed her, but he was afraid to make her cry. What did she mean? That she thought herself to be barren? If a doctor had told her this for certain perhaps that's why she spurned his advances.

"Why does Miranda always drag him away when I am about? Does she think I will eat him?"

"I don't know," Judith said, carefully folding the coat as though the warmth of the child were still in it.

"I expect the other servants have filled her head with stories about me killing Gregory."

"But you did not. Overturning the curricle was an accident."

"Why then?"

"It must be because Thomas was so sickly when he was little." The way Judith forced the explanation out, Evan knew she was lying to him. "If not for Miranda, we might have lost him. He is almost as much her baby as ours." Evan nodded vaguely as she gathered up her sewing rather distractedly and fled toward the house.

Evan was nonplussed. Judith seemed such a sturdy, good-humored soul most of the time. It was only the mention of anything relating to marriage or children that disturbed her. It wasn't going to be easy courting her then. He would have to go slower. Perhaps he could learn to pace himself to civilian life. He would certainly try for Judith's sake. To this end he decided to go fishing.

Judith lay facedown in her pillow. It had been a long time since she had cried like that. It had a cleansing effect. The world was no brighter when she finished, but she felt emptier, which was somehow better than feeling as though she was going to burst.

"What is it, Judith?" Helen asked. "Is Evan bothering you again?"

"No," she said, sitting up on the bed. "I didn't hear you come in."

"That's because I didn't knock. I saw you run from him. I knew I would find you crying. He's bringing it all back, isn't he?"

"It isn't Evan. It's—it's everything. Do we still need Nurse Miranda? Thomas is nearly six now."

"We will need her when the baby comes. She may as well stay."

"But she scarcely ever lets Thomas play."

"She plays with him. I have seen her. She loves him very much."

"I just think, as badly as we need money, we could do without her. I could take care of Thomas."

"Now we all agreed that was not wise, didn't we?"

"That was a mistake. I should never have given him up. Never!"

"But what were we to do?" Helen asked. "I was the one who was getting married. Are you jealous of me?"

"No, I'm not jealous. I just want my son back."

"But you have him. We all live in the same house."

"I don't have him. He is your son now, but you don't love him—not like I do."

"Of course I love him. You tell me this is not Evan doing this to you, but I don't believe you. You never regretted your decision before. It was the only way."

"I know. It's not fair."

"Life is not fair. If the world made any sense, men would ride sidesaddle and women would run the government."

Judith gave a reluctant laugh.

"When my baby comes," Helen said, patting her stomach, "Nurse will be so busy with it, you will have Thomas all to yourself. Mark my words."

"Yes, I'm sure you are right. You almost always are."

Evan borrowed the gear he needed from Terry and worked his way down the stream from where it ran past the stable to near the bridge. It was a shallow stretch of water now, but from the breadth of its bed and the height of the banks, in flood time, he guessed, it could not be forded. It had quite a few inviting pools that he did not so much remember as instinctively find. He knew he used to fish here, for his grandmother had told him so, but there was nothing familiar about it.

He pondered this as he tried one pool after another. He supposed a stream would change a good deal in ten years, but why had everything else changed so much? Indeed, some of his memories were truly faulty. Perhaps it was him. Perhaps he had remembered wrong or the memories had become distorted with time. He also remembered things that were not there, trees and pieces of furniture. He supposed he could have invented these, but why would he, since he tried never to think of home? He had, he realized, spent a lot of effort wiping out all thoughts of the place.

He had only just baited his hook atop a big rock by one of these pools when a shot whistled past his head. He rolled off the rock backward, landing in the shallows and staring through his wet hair at a figure in white. Much as he wanted to right himself, his every instinct was to lie still on his back and hold his breath. After regarding him for a moment, the woman moved off into the woods, a dark object showing up against the white of her dress—a pistol.

Evan breathed and rolled over, watching as a drop of blood splashed onto the wet stones and washed away. He felt his head and located the cut near his hairline. He was about to bind that up when he discovered, to his dismay, that the fishhook had gotten lodged in the skin between his thumb and forefinger. He really felt like weeping, but instead he laughed. It was the sort of thing that had got him his half-mad reputation in Spain. He could laugh in the face of the worst disaster because he could not do anything else.

He collected his gear and stumbled toward the house. Ralph gave him a start when he appeared out of the small woods in his shirtsleeves. He waved a dark object at Evan, who almost crouched to duck until he realized it was only a book. He waved back, paused and racked his brain to try to remember if the figure in white could have been a man with his shirttail hanging out because of the heat. No, he could not be sure. With the blood and water in his eyes he could not even say for sure if the figure had been wearing white. It might as easily have been cream, buff or light gray.

"What happened to you?" Judith asked, making him flinch again and driving his heart against his ribs. "You're soaked, and why do you look at me so oddly?"

Evan had by now ascertained that the dark object Judith held by her faded muslin dress was also a book and not a pistol. Why had such a thought even come into his head, and did everyone have to be walking about with books like this? His nerves had not been so badly knocked about when he had been in Spain.

"Fishing," he gasped with relief.

"It looks like the fish won. You've got a hook in your palm."

"I know."

She took his hand and turned it over to examine the position of the hook. "It would probably be less painful to push it the rest of the way through and nip it apart rather than trying to extract it."

"Can you do it?" he asked, fascinated by having her handle him rather than the other way round.

"I do have a brother. I can manage it if you don't wince too much. Come to the stable. There are sure to be some cutters there."

"What did happen to you?" she asked, to distract him as she deftly twisted the hook and exposed the barb on the other side of his hand. He did not flinch at all, just watched dispassionately.

"I fell off that big rock at the end of the path."

"Hence the cut on your head. But why?"

"If you must know, someone took a shot at me," he said with a reckless smile.

She looked suitably horrified. "I thought I heard shooting." She bound up his hand, which was not bleeding at all, with her worn, lace handkerchief. It was a quite unnecessary operation, but Evan would never have said so. He did not mean to return the handkerchief, either.

"What are you two doing, or shouldn't I ask?" Terry propped his shotgun against the wall.

"Someone fired at Evan near the stream," Judith told him.

To Evan's surprise, it was Terry who glanced at the shotgun, not Judith.

"It was a pistol shot," Evan supplied. "I saw who did it, but only at a distance."

"I heard the shot and went to investigate, but I didn't see anyone by the time I got there. What did the person look like?"

"I was upside down in the creek with blood and water in my eyes. I have only the vaguest impression of someone in white."

"And yet you made out that the shot came from a pistol?" Judith questioned.

"I could tell that from the sound as it whizzed by."

"They don't sound anything alike, Judith," Terry advised. "Someone in white?"

"Is that significant?"

"No, why should it be?" Terry asked with a laugh.

Evan did not like the way Terry and Judith glanced at each other. They knew who it was and they were not going to tell him. He had never felt like one of the family, but had never felt such an outsider as at that moment.

Evan had been under fire for years, sometimes for days at a time, yet none of it had unnerved him as much as that one bullet, perhaps because it had been fired by a woman. And neither Judith nor Terry had said "he," though the natural assumption would be that it was a man.

It had to be Lady Mountjoy. She must be unhinged to think she could get rid of him this way. He had already decided that she was unsettled by her pregnancy. And she had given him fair warning. He would just have to be careful...but for the rest of his life? He thought of carrying the tale to his father for only a moment before discarding that idea. How could he tell such a man that his wife was mad or close to it? He certainly could not tell Judith he suspected her sister, even if she suspected her as well.

By the time Evan delivered his battered body into the hands of the stunned Bose, he was in the mood to pick up and leave, and said as much.

"I knew it! I knew it couldn't last! You've argued with him again, haven't you?"

"No, as it happens. But someone shot at me near the stream. I might as well stay in the army, if—"

"Are you serious? They shot at you on purpose?"

"Yes. It wasn't you, was it?" Evan asked playfully.

"Don't tempt me. Did you get a look at him?"

"No."

"Then how do you know it was on purpose?"

"You're right. It was probably an accident," he said to appease Bose. Being sniped at was such an ordinary thing to an engineer that, after the initial surprise, he was inclined to shrug it off, anyway.

Chapter Four

Ralph's shirt points drew no more than a sniff from Lord Mountjoy at dinner. Evan had gone to the library early so that he could observe Lady Mountjoy when she came into the room, but she did not seem at all surprised to see him alive, merely offended at his stare.

Perhaps she did not even remember shooting at him, Evan decided. It was possible that once the child was born the madness would leave her—or get worse. He glanced anxiously at her and drew such a look of sheer hatred that he had no stomach for dinner.

Perhaps Judith's reluctance to accept his attentions came from her sister's poisonous comments about him. And why not? They were probably true, whatever she said. He was a soldier, flighty, unreliable, violent. He must have done far worse things than even Lady Mountjoy could imagine.

"Stop it!" his father said in the middle of the second course.

Evan froze, convinced his abstracted crumbling of his bread had drawn this censure. But when he looked up, it was Lady Mountjoy his father was staring at.

"Helen, I won't have you looking daggers at the boy all through the meal."

"Father, don't," Evan pleaded.

"Then I will eat in my room, sir, until you find your wife's company more to your taste than your son's." She rose and left with the stateliness of a queen.

"You don't help matters by saying nothing." Lord Mountjoy turned on Evan this time. "Have you no conversation?"

Evan sighed. "It's not working, Father."

"Ralph!" Lord Mountjoy shouted, redirecting his attack. "Tell me what you have learned so far from this wastrel."

To Evan's surprise, Ralph threw himself valiantly into the breech and discoursed on algebra for a good three minutes with more enthusiasm than accuracy. Judith then filled the ensuing silence by leading her nephew on to speak about his poetry.

"I didn't know you wrote it yourself," Evan finally said in amazement, comforted by the assurance that Ralph, at least, was not his would-be assassin.

"Mere schoolboy stuff," Ralph declared.

"It is not," Judith vowed. "He sends me a poem in nearly every letter, and they are good."

"Why does he never send me poems?" Angel demanded.

"You wouldn't understand," Ralph said. "It's no good if you have to explain them."

"It's always the same. I'm too stupid or I wouldn't understand. Nobody thinks I know anything."

"Would you be willing to read some for us tonight?" Evan suggested. "I'm sure I won't understand them, either, but I would like to."

"Stuff and nonsense," Lord Mountjoy grumbled under his breath.

"Oh, but it's not," Evan said spontaneously. "Everything we do—the wars we fight, the work, the struggle to farm the land—everything is done to make such things as poetry and art possible."

"Well, I know that," Lord Mountjoy said. "I stay here and work like a laborer to keep that young lounger in school so he can write poetry."

"I'm sure Lord Mountjoy would not want to hear my poetry," Ralph mumbled.

"Of course I do. Haven't I just said I do? You will read for us tonight. I should get something for my money."

Ralph had taken the request quite seriously and scurried to his room after dinner, to meet them all in the library with a sheaf of papers. Lady Mountjoy was there and so pointedly ignored Evan that he wasn't sure if it was better than being hated. As soon as the women had settled to their work, Lord Mountjoy looked expectantly at his stepson, and Ralph stood, with more relish for the task than Evan would have expressed under similar circumstances.

"'The Torn Soul,'" he read.

> "Another bitter morning.
> The full moon sees me to my classes
> With a smudge of blue across his face
> As though he has been tending my fire.
>
> I go where they send me to learn
> Prudent lines of language,
> The science of machines and
> The vagaries of politics and wars,
>
> When all I really want to think about is the moon.
> But there is always the night."

"Is that it, then?" Angel broke the silence to ask.

"Yes. What do you think?"

"Well, it's bit short, isn't it?"

"The length has nothing to do with it," Ralph said defensively. "It's the meaning—"

"It doesn't rhyme," Lord Mountjoy rumbled.

"I know it doesn't rhyme. I do know how to make a rhyme. But there is a difference between rhymes and poetry."

"I like it," Evan vowed. "I'm not quite sure why I like it. Maybe because it does not rhyme. Too much of the singsong is distracting from the meaning for me. Now that I think of it, I'm quite sure that's why poetry usually makes me nod off."

"You mean, like when you say, 'Nothing, Father'?" Lord Mountjoy asked.

Evan glanced at his father in amused surprise.

"The moon is always a woman," Terry said a little blearily, but with great conviction.

"It needn't be," Ralph maintained.

"In every poem I have ever read, the moon is feminine."

"He's got you there, Ralph," Lord Mountjoy said with satisfaction.

"Let me see," said Judith, taking the sheet and reading it over. "You know, Ralph, I like it already, but perhaps it works even better with the moon as a woman."

Ralph thought through the poem in his mind and finally took the paper and made a note with a stub of pencil he pulled from his pocket. "I think you're right. It does read better."

"Aha, so we are right," Lord Mountjoy said.

"An intelligent man is always open to good ideas, no matter who they may come from," Ralph said. Terry smiled crookedly, and Lord Mountjoy looked at Ralph a little suspiciously.

"Why a woman?" Angel asked. "Why would the moon always be a woman?"

"Tradition," said Ralph. "It was the smudge of dirt that threw me. One does not think of a woman with a smudge of dirt on her face, but I suppose she might have if she were tending a fire."

"That's no answer," Angel complained.

"It has to do with the changeableness of woman," stated Lady Mountjoy. "They are well-known for their inconstancy, whereas men are so reliable," she added without looking up from her work.

Evan chuckled in spite of himself. "Poetry and satire in the same evening," he said. "My cup runneth over."

Lady Mountjoy's mouth softened, not into anything approaching a smile, but at least she did not glare at him.

"I don't understand," Angel protested.

"I knew you wouldn't," Ralph declared.

"You know so much just because you have been to school. Why does it cut off like that? What do you mean by 'There is always the night'?"

"I mean I may be at someone else's beck and call to study and learn what they please in the daytime, but at night I can dream or write whatever I please, that they can't kill the romance in me."

"You see," said Judith helpfully, "the moon is a metaphor, for dreams, romance, whatever you will."

"A what?"

Ralph turned back to Angel. "It means it stands in place of just saying those things—"

"It would be much simpler all around if you did just say those things without all the bother. I don't like your poem at all," Angel said defiantly.

"Well, I do," said Lord Mountjoy. "It tells me more about Ralph than I have found out all the times I have talked to him. Now if we could just get it to rhyme," he mused.

"Thank you ever so much for the help. If you don't mind, I shall go upstairs and work on it some more." Ralph bolted from the room before he was likely to be subjected to Lord Mountjoy trying to impose a rhyming scheme on him, and Evan caught Judith grinning at the same thought.

"You were going to tell me about your canal, sir," Evan said, to distract his father.

"My what? Oh, yes, yes, the canal. Terry, bring one of those candles over to the desk. I have my plans right here."

As the clock chimed ten, the ladies rose and put away their work. It struck Evan that they led a very dull life here. He could not remember exactly what life had been like at Meremont before, but his Gram had always served tea in the evening, and they had had three meals a day instead of two. He knew that this present situation was not from any paucity of food, but due rather to the scarcity of help. Witness how Bose had been pressed into service in the kitchen in his spare hours. Of course, that might be voluntary, for nothing would put him closer to Joan than helping out at the house rather than lounging about the stable.

Once Evan looked at the map and realized how much land his father had bought up, he could see why they might be beggared. There had to be close to a thousand acres. That brought the size of the contiguous holdings of Meremont to nearly two thousand acres, if one counted the barrens. He stared at his father, trying to divine if the man had become unhinged. Several things suggested this: the will, for one; now this talk of the canal. Lord Mountjoy glanced up at him for approval of the route he had mapped out.

"What's this bit of land here?" Evan asked. "You haven't inked it in yet."

"We haven't got it yet. Fifteen acres of worthless riverbank. It belongs to Lady Sylvia Vane. With any luck we shall get it for free."

"How so?"

"We shall if Terry does not drink himself to death before he has her promise of marriage."

"I suppose I am good for something," Terry said.

"Such a sacrifice for a bit of land," Evan said with a smile. "Is she worth it?"

"She's beautiful," Terry said.

"Do you love her?"

"I don't love anyone else. I may as well marry Sylvia."

"I hope you show her a little more ardor than that," his father said critically, and Terry smiled crookedly.

"I hope you have not got another aging spinster with an odd plot of land you need. I would not be willing to make such a sacrifice."

"All that I require of you is that you build the canal. How many men will it take, do you think?"

"Hundreds, unless you want it to take years."

"We cannot wait years. We need it done in a year."

"Impossible!"

"Then we will merely hire more men."

"Have you any idea what this all will cost?"

"That's the other thing I require of you. You must work out what it will cost."

"I'll start surveying it tomorrow," Evan agreed wearily, hoping that he could discourage his father from the foolish scheme by laying in front of him the figures, before his brother leapt into what was bound to be a disastrous marriage.

Judith rode with Evan as usual in the morning. Angel was not yet up, so Evan made Bose go with them. They went north to scout again the area where the canal was to go, the canal from nowhere. Where on earth was he to start from? There would be water aplenty to feed the thing from all the streams that ran through the district, but the point of origin was only vaguely sketched in on the map. The gap in the hills, he supposed. There was a group of buildings there, and he asked Judith what they were.

"A factory village where they used to fire pottery. There's still plenty of clay left, I hear, but since the owner died the place has been shut up."

"Then how can Father think this canal will be profitable?"

"You think it's a bad idea?"

"I think it's a disastrous idea. I'm just putting off telling him so."

"That will cause an explosion," she said.

Bose looked accusingly at Evan.

"Bose, go scout about that village. You can catch up with us later." Bose clenched his teeth and rode off. Judith followed him with her eyes but made no objection.

"When you first came here you seemed to enjoy setting your father's teeth on edge."

"I really didn't do it on purpose, but he was so prepared to take umbrage it took no effort at all."

"In fact, you fell in to the way of it quite naturally. Was that what you were like when you were young?"

"I can't for the life of me remember if I used to bait him or not. That was all so long ago. If I was in the habit of discomfiting him on purpose, I would have thought I would have outgrown it."

"If you had grown up here, perhaps you might have."

"What do you mean?"

"Even though Helen is a decade older than me and practically raised me, we relate as adults because I have grown into that role. Our relationship has changed because we have always been together. Your attitude toward your father has never changed, since you haven't seen him in all this time."

Evan reined in his horse. "You're telling me that I'm still playing the rebellious youth to his authority figure?"

"Even though he has no authority over you at all."

"In other words, I should grow up," he said with a grin.

"Or at least strive to act as though you have," she countered with a prim smile.

Evan gave a crack of laughter. "You don't pull any punches, do you, my dear?"

"I am not your dear."

"That is what Father calls you," he said, kneeing Taurus into a walk. "I'm merely trying to act grown-up, like him."

"If you want to do so by bantering at me instead of him, I am agreeable. At least it will be fair play."

"Meaning you are more able to defend yourself. Yes, I am well aware of that." He felt his jaw.

"Whether you seek to or not, you do hurt him, and I don't like it. I care about him too much."

"Why do you care about him so much?" Evan asked, reining in his horse again. Judith pulled up beside him.

"Because he is a kind and good man. That should be enough."

Evan stared at her, but the sincere look she returned convinced him to accept her assertion at face value. "Perhaps he has mellowed."

"Evan, he is embarking on the last great enterprise of his life. This canal project is the last thing he will have a chance to do that will make a difference in the world. I will not have you dashing those dreams. Can't you just agree to build it?''

"I suppose I have done more for lesser reasons. Very well, *mon général*,'' he gibed, saluting. "I will do as you say. But I am doing it for you, not for him.''

"Do it for yourself, for your sons.''

"I won't have any sons.''

"Of course you will . . . eventually.''

"But not by you?''

"No,'' she said with a shudder.

He studied her face. Her expression was stubborn, but in defense of his father or in a determination not to cry?

"Then I will do it for Terry's sons.''

"Don't lay that at my door, Evan,'' she snapped. "It's not fair.''

"No, it's not. I'm sorry. But I don't think I want sons, anyway. Not if they have to go through what I've gone through. It's just not worth it.'' He urged Taurus to a canter, and Molly fortunately followed him without command, for Judith was too numb to guide her.

She could not always tell if Evan was joking. He did so often use a joke to turn aside her sympathy or concern. It was as though he could not handle someone caring about him, since he'd never been used to it. Instead of eating up attention, he shrugged it off very much like a little boy who feels he has outgrown the need for mothering. She had watched it happen with Ralph, and she was watching Thomas begin to spurn that sort of coddling. It broke her heart to steal a few moments alone with him, then have him get impatient when she only wanted to love him a little.

She supposed men eventually grew mature enough to accept affection again and return it. But Evan had never known it, except from Gram, and she was gone now.

They rode the rest of the way home in silence and stopped at the dower house out of habit, to walk the horses in the garden.

"I'm sorry if I was cruel to you. I cannot imagine what you went through in Spain. It was very bad of me to rip up at you when you have already suffered so much."

"What gave you the idea I suffered? I had the time of my life."

"Your letters."

"I thought I was careful—"

"Not to put anything worrisome in them? Yes, I grant you were skillful at that, complaining of the food and pay in that jovial way, as though trivialities were uppermost in your mind, and sloughing off the battles as of little interest."

"I can see I shall have to get hold of those letters and read them again. I'm blasted if I can remember what I wrote."

"You're not serious?"

"If I concentrate, I can call to mind a certain battle or day." He kicked some gravel off the walk. "But the days, some of them, went on for eternities. I do not lightly call them up. The whole mess is best left forgotten." He looked up at the vacant windows of the house, as though he might see Gram there.

"Your father was right then. You really don't want to talk about it."

"This house is the only place of which I have any happy memories."

"Your father said you spent far more time here than at the main house. Why was that?"

"I'm not sure, except that Gram did understand me. That is saying something, considering I did not understand myself—still don't. God, I miss her. If only I had got trampled a year earlier, we would have had some time together."

"Don't say that. You might have been killed."

Judith looked at him with that half-worried smile of hers that made her eyebrows so delectable he wanted to kiss each one. Something in his expression made her look down, and her fine, long eyelashes caused him to catch his breath. "I never would have expected I could fall in love, that there was any love in me.'' He had not even realized he spoke his thought.

''Evan!'' she warned.

''No, don't hit me again,'' he said with a chuckle. ''It just came out. I'm sorry, but I can't help it, you know.''

''You turn everything into a joke.''

''Sometimes it's the only way to survive. I meant what I said back there. I have no desire to pass my blood on to another generation. If you cannot have children, then it works out perfectly. Terry will—''

''How dare you?''

''What?''

''How dare you arrange my life as though I have no say— as though I can do nothing for myself?''

''I only thought you regarded that as an impediment to marrying me. There are men who would care—''

''You listen to me, Evan Mountjoy!'' She grabbed his cravat and pulled his face down to her level. ''If I wanted you, children or the lack of them would be no impediment.'' Then she kissed him bruisingly and let go of him, causing him to stagger into the already nervous Taurus. Molly snorted contemptuously as Judith led her off.

''What the devil is that supposed to mean?'' Evan asked the horse, who shook his head and nudged Evan in the direction of the barn. ''Lucky fellow. You know what you want and how to get it. We humans make it so complicated.''

Judith returned her horse to a pair of subdued stable boys, so she assumed they must have overheard her ranting at Evan. She had kissed him! What wild impulse made her think that such an act would convince him to let her alone? And what deceit had prompted her to vow that children didn't matter, when they mattered so much to her? Being let alone was not what she wanted and she knew it. She wanted Evan, but she could not have him without telling him the truth, and that was unthinkable, especially after her recent demonstration. She held her gloved hands against her cheeks to try to cool her face. When she entered the hall, she could hear Lord Mountjoy thundering at someone and could only think that Ralph must have done a horse an injury.

Helen was in the hall wringing her hands, but Ralph came out of the morning room.

"What's happened?" Judith demanded.

"It's Thomas's pup," Helen said, drying her eyes at sight of Evan coming in the door behind Judith. "One of the stable lads found it strangled, hanging by that rope Thomas was dragging it with. It bit him this morning, but I never thought—"

Evan heard his father demanding over and over an explanation from someone whose tiny voice did not even carry through the oak panels of the door. "I'm surprised Nurse Miranda is not here defending him."

"She was," Ralph informed him. "But Lord Mountjoy routed her."

Judith moved with determination toward the library door, but Evan stopped her with a gentle hand. "This is something I can handle better than you."

"I wouldn't go in there if I were you," Ralph advised. "He's already thrown me out."

Judith looked toward Ralph with sympathy.

"You will only make him angrier," Helen warned.

"Yes, but at me. With any luck Thomas will be able to slip away once Father starts thundering at me."

Evan opened the door, to have Lord Mountjoy immediately demand to know what he thought he was doing, interfering.

"Don't you think the boy has had enough?" Evan replied.

"He won't answer me."

"Let me put it another way. Don't you think you have worried your wife enough?"

Lord Mountjoy fairly trembled, swallowed and finally said, "Thomas, this isn't over. You will not get your pony now, nor any other pet until I have an explanation and an apology from you. Now go to your room."

Thomas rose slowly and left in silence, bursting into tears as soon as the door was shut behind him.

"How dare you interfere? How dare you countermand parental authority?"

"I really don't know. I have never done anything so fool-hardy in my life before. Fellow feeling, I suppose."

"At your worst you never brutalized an animal."

"Who witnessed this crime?"

"No one. The pup bit him this morning. An hour later the lads found it hanging in the stable."

"But—but anyone could have done it."

"Anyone didn't. There has never been anything like this at Meremont before. And why wouldn't he answer me?"

"Paralyzed with fear, I should say."

"He acts guilty."

"Or frightened?"

"Don't start this again. You were always covering for Terry when he got into trouble."

"I was? Oh, the chicken peeps. I had forgotten. But he wasn't really trying to drown them, you know. He was only giving them a drink."

"And what was Thomas trying to do to his puppy?"

"I thought we agreed that we don't know what happened."

"He knows something he won't tell me."

"A soldier accused of treason would get a fairer hearing than you gave that child," Evan shot back in a tone his father had never heard before.

Lord Mountjoy glowered at his son, then some fire died out of his eyes and he sat heavily in the great chair behind the desk. "I have tried so hard to do right by the boy." He picked up a paper, and Evan noticed for the first time that his hand was not steady, that it in fact shook with a regularity that was alarming. That was why Judith wrote his letters. He could not do it anymore.

"My interference was inexcusable," Evan said more gently, "and you are probably right in thinking I have done more harm than good, but I could not help myself."

"You always were too soft."

"You always were too hard. When I first saw you with Thomas, I thought what a lucky little fellow he was to get you as a father rather better worn than when I had you."

"Perhaps I have been too well worn. Three sons, now two more. God help me if Helen is carrying another boy. I will never be able to raise him. Why couldn't I have had daughters like Judith?"

"We must all play the hand that has been dealt us."

"I seem to have got more than my share of bad cards."

Evan nodded and left, deciding he would prove his father wrong.

It was Judith who carried the weeping child upstairs, but not to the cold nursery. She took him to her own room and sat holding him in the rocking chair by the window until the racking sobs had resolved themselves into hiccups. Just when she thought he was asleep, he turned his drained face up to her and said, "I did not do it, Aunt Judith. I didn't!"

"I know that, Thomas. You loved your pup."

"And now he's dead and I shall never have another, nor any pony, either." He stared sadly out the window.

"Lord Mountjoy only wants to know who did it. Do you know?"

"He would never believe me if I did tell him. He would believe Evan. He's come home to take his place now. Papa would never believe me over Evan."

"I know Lord Mountjoy is a fair man. You should confide in him."

"Papa used to like me, but now Evan is back. It's all ruined."

"I am quite sure you are wrong about that. Lord Mountjoy loves you still. He's just worried about you."

"Nurse says she is the only one who really loves me."

"Well, you know that is not true. I love you. So does Helen and Angel. Even Ralph was defending you."

"There is no place for me here."

"Of course there is. Nothing has changed."

"You don't know that, Aunt Judith."

"Sometimes things change for the better, Thomas. Now I am going to lay you down on my bed for a nap, and when you wake up I will take you down to the kitchen for tea. Perhaps Cook will have made something good for you."

"You won't leave me?"

"I will be right in this chair when you wake." Thomas sighed and let her cover him with a quilt. "I will never leave you, Thomas, never."

"Would you like to test some of your knowledge first-hand?" Evan asked Ralph when they were about to sit down for their customary lessons. "I could use some help with this survey."

"Really? That would be fascinating." Ralph followed him to the stable and inspected the surveyor's kit Evan was strapping to the spare horse.

"What it will be is a lot of work, and so far I am just running a rough line to estimate how much dirt we would have to move if we were to build this canal."

"I should be glad to have something useful to do."

"Father never gives you any work?"

"Like riding into the village for the paper and the post?"

"No, I mean with the farm. Did you say you were to have the barrens?"

"Yes, and the flocks to manage. It doesn't matter. I don't know a blasted thing about sheep."

"Neither do I. Does Terry?"

"I don't know. We don't talk much. He must have learned something, being raised here. I should be grateful for what I am being given. Why do you suppose your father bothers with me? Why would he even care about me?"

They mounted and rode out the lane as Evan considered his answer. "He's in love with your mother." He nodded to himself, then glanced at the grinning Ralph. "And if you are as disrespectful a lad as I was, I suppose he may like you."

"And he wasn't in love with your mother?" Ralph asked as he urged his horse to catch up with Evan's.

"No, he wasn't," Evan said with a grim smile. Even as he said it, he realized it was a truth he had always known but never acknowledged. "I suspect it was a marriage of convenience. Her family had money. Father had lands and a title. That's what is different about Father now. When I see him with Helen and little Thomas, he looks happy, and I cannot remember seeing him happy before."

"I shall try not to wreck that, and I shall try to be grateful...."

"As to that, no matter how grateful you are, no one can give you an education. They can make an opportunity for you. The education you must work for."

"You are right. So, will you show me how to use the transit?"

"Yes, but first you must learn to use the stick."

"Why does that sound like less fun?"

"Because it involves more walking."

They began the line where three small streams joined and ran toward the river. Evan sighted down the stream valley and showed Ralph how the drop and the amount of earth to be moved would be calculated.

"Will we have locks?" Ralph asked breathlessly as he came back with the elevation stick and measuring rope.

"At least two sets, by the looks of it, besides the ones between the canal and the river. That will give us more control of the water level, anyway. With a few catchment ponds we should have no problem, even during a dry spell."

"What is the drop?"

"Five feet in the first quarter mile."

"How far can you raise boats with locks?"

"It's practical to lock up to a hundred feet or more. Whether it is worth it or not rather depends on what it is for."

"I hope it is worth it. I want to see this thing built."

"You will do more than see it. You will have to help."

They came in late to dinner, very weary, but Ralph was so full of the day's adventures that he did not care. He had been doing real work. Terry stared at him resentfully until

Evan suggested, "I wish you would come with us tomorrow, Terry, or we shall be at this forever. It goes much quicker with three. Are you busy?"

"No, I could come," he said almost eagerly, before glancing at his father for confirmation. Lord Mountjoy nodded his approval.

"Good," said Evan. "What draft of boats is this canal to accommodate, Father? I need to know that if I am to do any serious estimating." He grabbed a roll and tore off a mouthful before he remembered his table manners.

"You are asking what I mean to ship?" Lord Mountjoy returned in annoyance.

"If you mean to have only canal boats for corn, hay and fleeces, we can get by with a three- or four-foot-deep channel, but if you mean to have heavy barges or oceangoing packets, it must be deeper and wider. The least depth of water should be one and a half feet deeper than the greatest draft of boat, the least width of the bottom of the canal twice the greatest breadth of boat," Evan recited as he filled his plate with eagerness and set to eating. Judith stared at him raptly, for he rattled these rules off as though they were some codification of engineering law.

"What do you mean 'least width of bottom'?" Lord Mountjoy asked. "I had assumed it would be the same width top and bottom."

"Only if we were going through rock," Evan said with his mouth full of beef. "Then the sides could be nearly vertical. The more likely the ground is to wash away, the more slope the sides will need. Clay is best, of course, and I am glad to hear there is still a supply of it in the hills, since we may need it for liner over the more porous ground. We will need a quantity of gravel, of course, but not until we are nearly through. That must go at the water-level line to prevent washing out." Evan looked up, suddenly aware that he was the only one talking. "Sorry to be boring you with this."

"It's only that you so seldom say anything," Helen explained. "One thinks you quite stupid in the ordinary way."

Evan laughed with the rest of them.

"Perhaps I am quite stupid in the ordinary way."

"I had no idea it was so complex," Lord Mountjoy said. "You're telling me that you must have specifics in order to estimate the amount of dirt to remove?"

"What did you think a canal was?"

Terry filled the uncomfortable silence. "Well, as you only see them with water in them, we rather assumed they were just very large ditches."

"And it will cave in like a large ditch if you don't have a care how you are building it. There won't be much current, but larger boats give more of a wash. That will affect how we lay the sides, too." Evan looked expectantly at his father.

"Work it out for both canal boats and large barges."

"That's no answer."

"It's the only answer I'm prepared to give you at the moment."

The next morning Lord Mountjoy determined to ride out with the rest of them to see what they were doing. Judith did not have to coax Angel to get her to agree to go as well, once she had awakened her. Judith discharged the duties of a maid for both of them, so Angel was in her riding dress in no time.

"What do you think of him?" she asked as her sister did up her hair.

"Who?" Judith asked obtusely.

"Evan, of course. He does have that scar by his lower lip, but I just think that makes him all the handsomer, don't you?"

"I had not thought about it," Judith lied.

"What a bouncer, when you have eyes only for him. You think about Evan all the time."

"I feel sorry for him," Judith countered. "Here we've been enjoying his home all these years while he was off fighting, and Helen does not even make him welcome."

"His presence does change everything. Poor Terry is very cut up by it. And Ralph will be left with nothing. Poor Thomas will fare no better."

"Did you say that to Thomas?"

"No, of course not. The little fellow is so upset about his puppy. Besides, he would not understand about the future."

"I think he understands more than we expect. And I think Lord Mountjoy will provide an education for both Ralph and Thomas. That is the best they can hope for. He says he means to see you creditably married."

"What about you?"

"I am perfectly happy here, acting as his secretary," Judith stated calmly.

"Don't lie to me, for you are not happy—not all the time, anyway."

"I am as happy as I can be. We are not all meant to bounce around in the sunshine like you," she said, plunking Angel's ridiculous hat on her sister's head and pinning it ruthlessly in place.

"Ouch, you're hurting me."

"Sorry, Angel. Do please watch me and at least try to look like you are riding."

"Everyone criticizes me, even you."

"You have to improve or Evan will lose patience and not let you ride his horse."

"I think Evan was stunned by me at first, don't you?"

"Yes, but I expect he had no idea you are so young."

"You do like him, don't you?"

"Yes, he is very likable. Are you coming now? I see them leading the horses out, and Lord Mountjoy does not like to keep them standing."

"How much?"

"Angel, stop it. I like Evan as a friend—no more."

"The same way you like Terry? Almost like a brother?"

"Yes, like a brother."

"I was just checking, for I mean to have him."

"You what?" Judith stopped as Angel flitted out the door. She poked her head back in.

"I mean to marry him."

"But Angel, he is so much older than you," Judith said, as she followed her sister down the stairs, sorting through her feelings as she did so.

"But now that Terry and I have broken off, I must marry someone, and Evan is the only one around. I see no impediment."

"I think Evan will see many."

"Don't worry. I shall be very good and not argue with him at all. You won't even know me."

Judith was still shaking her head as they reached the stable yard. Angel grasped Evan's arm before he realized what was happening, so he had to assist her to mount, while Lord Mountjoy helped Judith up with a rueful shake of his head. Evan looked at Judith in appeal, but she only laughed at him—a bit uneasily, to be sure. She had best get used to keeping her good humor, just in case Angel's foolish plan came to pass. Judith had told Evan she was not interested in marriage. Terry was keeping his distance from Angel after their flamboyant breakup. There was no reason Evan should not marry Angel. After all, Helen was only thirty-five and Lord Mountjoy was sixty.

Then Judith watched Angel clinging to her mount's back and knew from the look on Evan's face that he could never tolerate a wife who made not the smallest attempt to learn to ride. But was that what she wanted? Evan to stay a bachelor, unfulfilled as she was? What sense did it make for both of them to be unhappy?

Evan's stolid gelding conveyed Angel to the site as though he were carrying a load of baggage, albeit one that bounced and squeaked a lot. The horse turned a weary eye on Evan as he helped Angel dismount. Judith smiled at both of them and slid off herself, getting a nod of approval from Lord Mountjoy.

Stakes and flags seemed to have sprouted in the fields. While Angel amused herself by picking flowers, the men paced and pointed and measured. Judith followed after them, making notes with a lead pencil when Lord Mountjoy addressed any comment to her.

More and more Evan realized that Judith served his father in the stead of a secretary. That meant she probably knew as much or more about the affairs of Meremont as Terry. She certainly seemed to care a good deal more. She would make Evan an admirable wife. Somehow, no matter how long it took, he must convince her. Otherwise, was it even worth staying? Of course, there were Bose and Joan to think of. He must stay if he could at all stomach it.

After breakfast, a peaceable meal for once, Evan was sitting in his room with his feet up on his small desk, deep into the pilfered *Times,* when Terry burst into his room.

"Oh, there you are. Good news. Father had arranged everything. I am to have a commission."

Evan's feet hit the floor as he stared at his brother in consternation. "What can you possibly mean? I thought you were marrying Lady Sylvia."

"I can do that as well. You—you seem upset. I thought you would be happy for me."

Lord Mountjoy entered then, smiling with satisfaction over an open letter he was consulting. "Oh, Evan. I have news."

"I heard," said Evan, rising warily.

"Father, I don't think—I don't think he's pleased," Terry warned.

"Whatever do you mean?" Lord Mountjoy demanded.

"I had no idea Terry wanted to be a soldier."

"Surely you might have guessed that. I had thought you meant to muster out. That leaves Terry free for the army."

"But I don't want him in the army," Evan protested.

"I had assumed you two had discussed this," Terry said resentfully.

"Tell him he can't go, Father," Evan pleaded. This sounded childish to all of them, as Lord Mountjoy's impatient expression indicated.

"Terry, do you think I want to see you shot up, to know you will be out there starving, freezing and getting blown to bits?" Evan was clutching his brother by the shoulder. "I couldn't bear it. I'll leave, instead, if that's what it takes."

"That's quite enough!" Lord Mountjoy said, trembling a little.

Evan stared at him, realizing he had said too much. He let go of Terry with that mad laugh of his and received a demolishing stare from his father. When he could talk again, Evan said, "You have to understand, Terry, that we two are not in the way of discussing things. We merely blunder along, misunderstanding each other. It's our way of doing business."

"Surely you meant to leave the army?" Lord Mountjoy demanded.

The question hung suspended in the air for a moment before Evan could formulate an answer. "No, I had originally meant to visit with Gram, if she were alive, and then be on my way again. I had not meant to stay."

Terry slumped down on the bed, casting his father a beseeching look.

"Surely you came home to stay. What else was I to think?"

"Considering the welcome I got from your wife, sir, what was I to think? That I was not wanted was clear— I shouldn't have said that."

"You have to understand about Helen. She had certain expectations."

"That I would be dead."

"That Terry would have Meremont and that Ralph would have the barrens. She has had to adjust her plans."

"Has she, if you are now meaning to send another son off to war?"

"The war is over now that Toulouse has fallen and Napoleon has abdicated. Terry would never be sent to France. The worst that can happen is that he will be posted to America and have a fine time with his friends."

"I hope it will be more exciting than that," Terry replied.

"Worse yet in America," Evan warned. "I wish you would not romanticize it. There was nothing fine about it."

"Not for you," his father agreed. "You have always been a scholar. I was never more shocked than when your grandmother rushed up here to tell me you meant to enlist in the Royal Engineers."

"But . . . you had always said I would go into the army. I thought . . ."

"I never said that!"

"Yes, you did. I may be foggy on a lot of things, but I remember you telling me I would be a soldier someday."

"When you were five or six, perhaps. But I could see from your marks you were cut out to be a scholar. I assumed you would take up law or go into the church."

Evan ran a hand over his eyes in exasperation as grim details of the previous decade flooded through his mind. But even as they did he realized they had not been wasted years. He had entered the army a boy. He was a man now, perhaps a rather shaken and tired one, but a man nevertheless. Once again he laughed and shook his head.

"You laugh at the oddest moments," his father complained. "People sometimes look at you as though you are not quite sane."

"Well, I'm not. I think it must be a requirement for a soldier to be not quite sane."

"Why did you want the army? Tell me the truth for once," his father demanded, as Terry stared at both of them.

"Well, I was finished with school and I had no idea what to do then. I thought it was what you expected of me. Acting on last orders, don't you see?"

"You mean to tell me you built your whole future on a comment I made when you were six?" Lord Mountjoy shouted.

"It was all I had to go on."

"I expected you to come home and take up your place here."

"I have no place here. I never had!"

"I cannot help that you were jealous of Gregory."

"Jealous?"

"Yes, you were always brooding whenever he had done anything extraordinary. You would have gotten your chance."

"But I thought you didn't like me."

"What absurdity is this?"

"How could you like me when I killed him?" The comment slipped out quickly and fell like a brick between them.

Lord Mountjoy glanced at him, then looked away.

"Yes, we two don't speak of a lot of things," Evan said to Terry, "but above all others, we do not speak of that. I did kill him."

"Nonsense, it was an accident," Lord Mountjoy said uncomfortably, looking out the window. "An accident and a bad business all around. I should have brought you back to the house, not let you stay at the dower house with your grandmother. I should have insisted."

"What do you mean? It was you who gave the order for me to be kept there."

"You remember that?" he asked, the paper he still held shaking to the rhythm of his heartbeat.

"Yes, those were the last words I heard you speak. 'He is never to set foot in Meremont again.'"

"Oh, God! I had not thought you were conscious." Lord Mountjoy passed a hand over his eyes, trying to erase the memory that his son had recalled.

"It doesn't matter," Evan said gently, sorry now that he had hurt his father. "That's all over with. But you have to consider how little I had in those days. No past, no future and no word from you. At least now I have a past, and one of my own making, even if I have no future."

"Don't be absurd. Your future is here."

Evan rubbed his forehead tiredly. "If there is one thing I am not cut out for, it is being a gentleman farmer."

"Farmer? That is not what I need! I mean to make use of your education, the one that put me to such considerable expense. You are an engineer of some note, are you not?" he asked hotly, pulling himself erect.

"You have a fortress you want besieged, perhaps?" Evan asked with a grim smile.

"No, I want my canal, and three bridges across it where it intersects the roads."

"I hate bridges," Evan said petulantly.

"Will you do it?"

"Very well. I'll build them, but then..." Evan caught sight of Bose in the hall, looking as though he were having an attack "...then we'll see."

"Fair enough," Lord Mountjoy said as he left, casting an admonitory glance at the letter before he tore it in half. "And you, Terry, will help him."

Terry nodded and went away in disappointment.

"I can't leave you alone for one minute without you getting into a scrape." Bose came in and hung up the coat he had been brushing.

"They caught me off guard. You heard what he said. He was ready to send my brother into the army. Terry wouldn't last a month."

"There was a time when I wouldn't have thought you would last a month, but the army was the making of you."

"I don't want Terry made into someone like me," Evan said passionately.

"And what did you mean by 'then we'll see'?"

"I meant that for now I mean to stay, since I have been trapped into it. Unless things get very bad, of course."

"That can happen at a moment's notice."

"I know. What would it take to set Gram's house in order?"

"The hiring of half a dozen servants, for one thing."

"Find them. Then will you believe I am committed to staying?"

"May Joan be one of them?"

"Only if you find a suitable replacement for her here. And see what you can do about getting another subscription to the *Times*. That alone should alleviate a lot of squabbles."

Chapter Five

Evan was surprised when Ralph proposed that they take turns reading after dinner. As an alternative to having the lad's poetry hacked apart, of course, Evan could see why the idea recommended itself. But he was startled when Angel took a turn. True, she stumbled over some of the words and looked mulish when Ralph corrected her. She kept doggedly at it, however, bringing a smile to Helen's lips.

Judith took a turn at reading then. Evan could have listened to her forever. She had a voice like his grandmother's, a voice to delight children and comfort a man. How could she vow never to marry when it was what she was meant for? But he could see her point. If she were caught up with raising children, she would have less time for reading and studying, even considering the amount of work she did here.

The girls were each wearing a new dress of figured muslin. Evan had said he did not want to see a new garment on Angel unless Judith made one for herself as well. He must have been staring at her, for he intercepted a sharp, quick look from Lady Mountjoy, no more than a glance, but with its usual menace. He smiled at her, very nearly used to being hated by now. Upon reflection, he had decided that she could not possibly have meant to kill him; she had only wanted to scare him. Perhaps she had been as shocked as he that she had come so close to hitting him. He thought they had achieved a tolerable truce. Besides, life would be boring if everyone liked you. There would be no challenge to it.

"I said our evenings must seem extremely dull to you," his father nearly shouted.

"Oh, no," Evan answered automatically. "Not compared to sitting around a smoking camp fire."

"But there must have been talk of battles and such," Terry prompted, still moping for his lost military career, Evan thought.

"Yes, but that wears thin when you have been living with it and nothing else, day after day."

"You are never going to tell me, are you, about your battles?" Terry finally asked with a sad shake of his head.

"My battles? I scarcely even knew what was going on. I was mostly in the trenches, trying to sap up close enough to get the cannon into place."

"Then how did you get wounded?" Terry demanded.

"Fell into one of my own siege parallels in the dark," Evan said amiably.

His father gave a snort of laughter.

"What's a siege parallel?" Judith asked.

"Trenches laid out parallel to the fortification. After you get the first complete, you cut zigzag trenches up and start another parallel."

"Why zigzag?"

"So that you can get your men within range without taking the brunt of enemy fire."

"I see."

"Also, if you are pursued by the enemy down the trenches, you can ambush him the easier."

Judith nodded, but Helen merely stared at him.

"These trenches are deep enough that you could break a leg?" Terry asked.

"Yes."

"Well, did you?" his father demanded.

"I thought I had," Evan continued. "Bose pulled me out and set me to rights, of course. Another time I—"

"I don't believe a word of it," Terry declared. "I heard you were one of the first into the breach at Badajoz."

"One of the first into the ditch, anyway. Who told you that?" Evan asked angrily.

"Lady Sylvia's cousin, Captain Farlay, and he should know, for he was there. He said you were like a madman."

"They should have surrendered," Evan said, shaking his head in denial.

"What?" Terry asked.

"Those are the rules, the ones we were taught," Evan said desperately. "When the wall is breached you are supposed to surrender."

"What difference does it make?" Lord Mountjoy asked. "You took the city."

"The difference, Father, is in what happens to the civilian population," Evan said bitterly.

"What does happen?" Helen demanded before Judith could lay a restraining hand on her arm.

Judith did not like the hardness in Evan's voice, the horror in his eyes, and the grimness of his mouth. She feared he would break into bits before their eyes.

"The city is sacked. The army commits all manner of rapine and atrocities. There is no stopping them! There really is no stopping them!" Evan realized he was on his feet and that he had been almost shouting. "Sorry, excuse me," he said quietly, and left the room.

"What was that all about?" Terry demanded. "It's not as though it was his fault. He wasn't in command."

Lord Mountjoy frowned at him. Judith was still staring at the door. "But he had a part in it," she explained, her voice thick. "If not for his work, the city might not have fallen. It is rather like Evan to take responsibility for it even if it wasn't his fault."

Helen looked up at this. "How would you know what Evan is like?"

Judith looked at her measuringly. "Why, he is much like Lord Mountjoy in many ways. I merely assumed this was one more trait they shared."

Helen looked down and Lord Mountjoy smiled. "Well, well, Evan like me! I can't credit it. Do you really think so, Judith dear?"

"Yes, very much so."

"Perhaps you are right, my dear."

Terry scowled into his brandy glass.

"I can't stay, Bose." Evan threw himself sideways on the bed, facing the window.

"God help us! What have you done now?"

"They know. They know about Badajoz."

"The world knows about Badajoz. My advice to you is to forget it. That shouldn't be a stretch, as you have conveniently forgotten so much else that would be useful to you."

"Forget it? The women screaming, some of them no more than children, many of them younger than Angel, not even knowing what was going to happen to them."

"You didn't do it."

"I didn't stop it, either."

"You couldn't, not without shooting our own men."

"I could never feel the same toward them after that. It's grim to realize that man is merely an animal who happens to wear clothes."

"All the more reason to give up the army and settle here. If it's peace you want, this is the place for it, so long as you can dodge your father for the better part of the day."

"I don't know." Evan turned and buried his face in his pillow. Bose left him.

After a few minutes Evan got up and paced, but the room was far too small for that, so he went outside and strode about the grounds until he fetched up at the dower house. The door was unlocked, since some rudimentary attempts at cleaning were being made—by Judith, he supposed. He went into the small sitting room and pulled the shroud off the chair he used to occupy. He could hear Gram better in his mind here than anywhere, but she had nothing useful to say to him tonight—just vague assurances that he would do well to learn all he could, that he would have a place someday, that she would see to it. Perhaps she'd meant to leave him her fortune even then. He did not know what all it entailed. His father had been rather vague about it, and Evan did not like to ask, except he would like to buy Judith something extraordinarily expensive.

He lit a candle, found tinder and made a small fire in the grate. The room began to take on its accustomed warmth. He rummaged in the pantry until he found a bottle of Gram's homemade wine. He could not tell by sniffing it what was in the dusty bottle except that it was strong after aging so many years on the dark shelf. Rhubarb, he decided from the bite, but it fit his mood. Life was bittersweet at best.

Here was the perfect woman for him and she wouldn't have him. Perhaps he had moved too fast with that clumsy offer of marriage. She had been hurt by a man—badly hurt. Of that he was sure. Perhaps she had been raped and that was why she could not bear children. He had meant it when he said he did not need sons. As a soldier he had never even expected to marry, let alone have a family.

But he did need Judith. If only he could show her that all men were not monsters, that she did not need to be afraid of love. Somewhere underneath her calm and docile exterior was a volcano of passion, if only it could be unleashed. He called to mind that impetuous, almost punishing kiss that had startled him so. He could almost feel it on his lips, but he wanted more, so much more.

As badly as his outburst had affected Evan, it was even harder on Judith, who turned sleeplessly on her pillow. If ever she had entertained any thoughts of telling him about her past, she dismissed them now. If he was that horrified by what had happened at Badajoz, he would never forgive that she had let herself be duped into a compromising situation. She must keep him at a distance. It was fine to admire him and defend him, but there it must end. She must never love him.

But when she thought of him at all, she could not help herself. How could she be so decisive and sensible in the ordinary way and still be reduced to a state of trembling desire by his mere presence? Her greatest fear was that he would always affect her so.

She slipped out of bed without waking Angel and went to sit by the window. Perhaps Thomas had been right; everything would be changed now that Evan was here. She had been reconciled to her life as she defined it. Now Evan had come to destroy her complacency.

Her wandering gaze found the dower house in the darkness. She had thought she saw a light. Had she left a candle burning when she finished there today? She had better check. She could not be responsible for burning Evan's future home to the ground. She threw her cloak on over her nightdress, slipped on her half boots and made her way downstairs and out into the night.

Evan was half-dizzy from the wine. He had dispensed with the glass by now and was swallowing it out of the bottle, as they had in Spain. It brought back memories, but not welcome ones. He had often turned to the bottle to numb his aching need and forget his unsuccessful attempts to satisfy himself. None of those women had really wanted him, either. They had only submitted for money to buy food. Love could not be bought, and trying to do so left the ache still there. Unfortunately, he could remember them and their foreign words, whispered desperately into his ear as he emptied himself. Evan shook his head, but they would not leave him. And now he would much rather think of Judith.

As though his brooding had called up a spirit, she appeared in the doorway in a long cloak. He started, then blinked, but the woman and her sympathetic look did not disappear. She crossed the room to him.

"I thought the house was on fire," she said as she picked up the glass and tasted its contents. She gave a shudder and sat beside him on the sofa.

"Sorry. I didn't mean to worry you." He saw her night-dress under her cloak, and his groin tightened. He looked at the fire. "The chimney draws well. It always did." He started to take another drink, but filled her glass first.

"If you want to forget about the war, they should let you," she said, taking another sip.

"It's not so much wanting to forget as not wanting Terry to think it was a rousing good time. Did you know Father almost bought him a commission?"

"Yes."

"Why didn't you tell me such a thing was going on? I managed to talk them out of it, but it wasn't all that easy."

"I didn't know how you felt about it. I knew you hid a lot in your letters, but I didn't know you hated it."

"Only the parts I remember."

"How much is that?"

"Not much," he said, thinking again of the Spanish women. He watched the fire leap in the grate. The logs looked like a little city put to the torch. "That reminds me of something. Did you say Gram saved the newspapers?"

"A great many of them. She would reread them and discuss with me our chances, and where you were likely to be."

"What a terrible way to end her life."

"I assure you she was quite proud of you."

"I am not proud of me."

Judith could think of nothing to say and finished the wine in her glass. "I'll look for the papers for you." She swayed a little as she rose, and he lunged to his feet to steady her.

"Where would they be?" he asked. "The attic? I can get them."

"No, last time I saw them they were in the back bedroom."

"You really should not be taking on the cleaning of this place," he said as he followed her up the stairs, ready to catch her if she should slip.

"I don't mind. I enjoy having something different to do." She opened the door and carefully put the candle she had been guarding on the nightstand. Then she threw open a trunk and began to hand Evan bundles. "The oldest will be on the bottom." He restacked them as she handed them out. When she finally stood up, she staggered a little, and he caught her, helping her to the bed.

"I should never have given you that wine. It is rather potent when you are not used to drink."

"Perhaps it will give me the courage to tell you the truth for once."

"The truth?"

"The truth is... I am not indifferent to you."

"Not indifferent?" he said, lounging beside her. "You mean you do love me?"

"Perhaps, since I hardly know you, love might be too strong a word."

Evan saw Judith cross her ankles and press her knees together, and felt an answering pull in his groin to know that she was not physically indifferent to him, either.

"How long you know someone has nothing to do with it," he said, toying with the fine burnished ringlets of her loose hair. "I felt it the moment I saw you." He lifted her chin and kissed her and was surprised that she neither drew back nor tried to strike him. It was the wine, of course. She had lowered her guard at last.

I'm drunk, he thought, but he knew that wasn't true and could not be used as an excuse for what he was contemplating. He told himself that if he made love to Judith he would be no better than the rabble at Badajoz. But those lips of hers, drinking away his sorrow, breathed a life into him he thought had been long extinguished. She wanted him! In his whole life he could never remember anyone really wanting him. Judith wanted him not for his skill, nor for his money, but only for his poor, pathetic self.

"Look at me, Judith," he pleaded. The eyes that opened to him seemed to be a reflection of his own—full of hurt and hunger, of not being wanted. He laid her gently back on the bed and kissed her longingly, feeling the urgent response from her lips.

"You love me," he repeated. "That's all that matters, isn't it?"

"I...I don't know. What was I going to tell you?" she caressed the scar under his lip with her fingertips.

"The truth. You love me."

"Yes, I do love you, especially after tonight, now that I know all you have suffered." Her breath caught on a sob.

"Your love makes up for all. My love for you will do the same. We will heal each other. You do want that, don't you?"

"Yes, more than anything, but..."

Evan stood and frantically stripped off his clothes. She could stop him if she liked, he thought, for she had done it before. But how could he not respond to such a hungry look when the cure was so easy?

Even in the dim light of the candle she could see the other scars. They captured her interest almost to the exclusion of the erect member that confronted her. She licked her lips and tried to rise, but her head swirled giddily. She had seen Banstock, but he had been nothing like this. Evan was hard and lean, and when he positioned himself over her she did not feel threatened.

She eyed his bare chest and arms with wide-eyed fascination, then fixed her attention on the scar on his arm. "Who did that to you?" she asked, tracing a finger along it in a strange, possessive caress.

"A French *Voltigeur*," he said with a shiver as he tugged at the strings of her cloak.

"Is he dead?" she demanded, her lips trembling and with tears in her eyes.

Evan stared at her. "Yes." He knelt over her, deliberately letting her see how aroused he was. Now was the time for her to stop him. Surely she would stop him.

"And this one?" She ran her finger along his thigh, drawing a shudder from his nerve endings.

"A Spanish traitor."

"A man?" she asked, her eyebrows drawn together in concern.

"Yes, a man," he said with a chuckle.

"You make light of everything." She reached for him and drank of his lips until she was breathless. His pulse beat steadily in her ear, like a promise of life continuing. She was vaguely aware that he was undoing the ribbons of her nightdress, but it was too hot in here, anyway. Besides, he only wanted to kiss her throat. She felt a shudder of excitement as his warm lips caressed her breast and drew a groan of need from her. He suckled one soft mound until it was erect, then teased the nipple of the other. She arched her body against him, and he moaned in turn.

"I hurt you," she said in surprise.

"No, and you must believe that I would never do anything to hurt *you.* You need never be afraid of me."

"It's not you I'm afraid of," she said vaguely.

"Who then?"

"Myself, I think. I can't remember."

"Don't be afraid of this. You are a normal, healthy woman. Did you think only men derive pleasure from this?" As though to demonstrate, he slipped her nightdress up and found his way between her thighs with his kisses. It did penetrate to his befogged brain that even if he were not drunk, at least Judith was. How could he live with himself if he took unfair advantage? That he suspected she was not a virgin did not even come into it. That sort of invasion and despoiling lost none of its horror the second time. There was only this—that she could not get with child, no matter how much she wanted to. If he could not give her that, he could at least love her, prove to her that all men were not beasts. Then surely she would marry him.

Judith was running her hands through his hair. She was amazed that she let him kiss and tease her most intimate parts, that she wanted him to do something she could not even define. She knew that she could stop him if she wanted, that he would never force his way in.

He kissed his way up her taut stomach to nurse at her breasts again. His hand slid between her legs, and she shuddered as he begged for entry. "Judith, are you sure?" he asked breathlessly.

"Evan, something is happening to me. I cannot pretend to understand it."

"You've never felt this before?"

"It wasn't like this with him. Nothing like this. I had not thought myself capable of catching fire like this. You seduce me by merely looking at me, without even trying or caring."

"But I do care. I love you more with each passing day. I would never have stayed if not for you."

It was the truth, and she knew it. Elation rose in her like a powerful tide. She held Evan to Meremont when nothing else could. What harm to give him what he needed, what they both needed? And if there was another child? No, that could not happen twice. Life could not be so unfair. Life owed her something, if only a few moments at the heights. She held her breath in the rarified sunlight of the mountaintops as she parted her legs for him. There would be no force this time, no tearing, no pain.

Grasping his hair, she pulled him up to kiss him. Her lips were parted, as were her legs now, and he entered through both doors at once. The shudder that went though her was so profound she almost believed it was Evan, but he was not moving. He was waiting. For what? she wondered impatiently—a blow? an invitation? When she moved, another exquisite spasm wrenched her, arching her upward and causing Evan to moan. He moved inside her tentatively, and she reached behind to grasp his buttocks and get in rhythm with his thrusts.

There was no thought anymore, only unreasonable desire. She gripped him with her internal muscles, delighting in the hard feel of him inside her, but when he gasped, she relaxed again. Another tremor shook her, and this time Evan picked up the pace, his breath rasping as he paused at the height of one stroke to swell inside her. "Now!" he gasped, and she gripped him, taking in his seed in the elemental hunger of a woman in love. A final spasm shook her and left her as breathless as the sweating Evan, who had collapsed on top of her. She tried to keep her head in the vapor and ignore the chasm where things happened, but her exultation slowly ebbed.

He slipped to one side, and she dreamily noted the relief on his face. He pulled the dust sheet over them, thinking she might be cold, wanting to protect her from every chill and care in the world. He was pleased when she let him lie against her warm body. "We can have the banns posted the next three Sundays and be married by the end of the month," he said into the nape of her neck.

"Banns?" she asked vaguely, her intellect beginning to rouse itself and pull free of the animal part of her. "What banns?"

"For our wedding." He raised himself on one elbow to look at her, to stroke the hair away from her face. "Of course, if you prefer, I can go for a special license, but that might take—"

"No."

"No special license? Then we will just have to wait out three weeks."

"No, I cannot marry you," she said firmly.

"But—but we are married in the sight of God. You must marry me now."

"Must? Is that why you did this? To force me into marriage?"

"Force you? No, but I naturally assumed...I mean, what did you think all this meant?"

"I don't know. I wasn't thinking."

"But why won't you marry me?"

"That's what I was trying to tell you after I drank that wretched wine. There was someone before you." She wrenched the sheet away from him and covered only herself with it.

"I understand that, but you didn't love him."

"No, I hated him."

"All the more reason to marry me."

"And live here?"

"Yes, provided I can keep peace with Father."

"But if you left I would have to go with you, and I will not leave Meremont," she said forcefully.

"But I might live here, in this house."

"I cannot even move as far as this house. I belong at Meremont."

"But, Judith, you are being unreasonable."

"Leave me," she commanded, turning her face away.

"But I love you. Tell me what I have done wrong." He sat helplessly on the edge of the bed.

"It's not you, Evan. It's me. If only the wine were not gone I could tell you. Now leave me." Marriage translated to a trap for Judith and triggered in her mind all the ill effects of her short, disastrous engagement to Banstock. Thomas was the only saving grace in the whole affair. Marriage to anyone, including Evan, might mean being expected to abandon her baby. How could she have pushed Thomas aside for a few moments of guilty pleasure?

Evan stared at the weeping girl for a time, then numbly picked up his clothes and went out to dress in the dark hallway. He waited on the stairs, but when Judith hesitated in the doorway, he went back into the sitting room. He thought he heard her calling a name as she fled across the wet lawn toward the house, but he could not make out whose it was. He spent the rest of the night sleepless on the sofa.

It rained the next day, and Evan did not know what to do with himself. He desperately needed to speak to Judith, but he had to get her alone to do so. He paced about the library, disrupting Judith's letter writing and his father's dictation, until Lord Mountjoy asked pointedly if he did not have something to read elsewhere. When Evan had left, the old man turned to Judith.

"What do you think, Judith? Will he do it?"

"Do what?" she asked, caught off guard.

"Build the canal."

She wetted her lips and cleared her throat. "We may have to tell him more of our plans. He is no fool."

"Let's see how far we can get without revealing more. It's not that I don't trust Evan."

"He can't be the one who let out news of the canal. He wasn't even here when Lady Sylvia bought up those acres."

"We aren't sure if she knows about the canal. She does know we are planning something."

"But if she didn't know, why did she buy the land?" Judith asked.

"Terry must have let something slip though he denies it, but why else would he agree to marry her to get the land for us if he was not feeling guilty?"

"I can't believe Terry would be so stupid."

"Not on purpose, perhaps, but you have not seen him when he's crashing drunk."

Judith looked up at him. "I mean, I cannot believe he would call on Lady Sylvia in such a state." She blushed, but Lord Mountjoy took no notice.

"He needn't have said it to her. He had only to mention it at an inn. Word might have got back to her another way."

"What reason did she give for buying them?"

"Said she wants to build a cottage by the river."

"Surely you were not taken in by her!"

"Sometimes she seems so genuine, one cannot help believing her."

"She is a consummate actress."

"Now, Judith, are you sure you are not a trifle—"

"Jealous? Of Wendover, that dowdy little farm? It can't be more than ten acres. It's a toy compared to Meremont, and a toy she is tired of. She is a woman looking to enlarge her scope. We are building something genuine here, something that will last for generations. She's smart enough to know that, and to want in on it."

"We may have no choice but to let her in on it. That is why Evan must be in control by the time I am gone, for Terry is too biddable."

"I know," Judith said wretchedly. "But will Evan be willing to take up this burden and stay here forever?"

"If I had my wish," he said, taking her hand and holding it comfortably between his own, "I would leave you in charge of everything. You are the most capable, the most trustworthy, and after you, Evan. But we do need him. All will be ten times as hard if we cannot bring him back into the fold. I don't suppose you could—"

"Don't ask. I must stand by my decision. If Evan were to leave . . . No, I will work here for the rest of my life in whatever capacity I am needed, but I will not marry."

After breakfast Evan and Ralph stayed in the parlor for a session with Shakespeare's poetry. Except on rainy days, Ralph's lessons were now conducted in the field and resulted in useful work being accomplished. This more than anything else impressed Ralph with his own worth and welded his loyalty to Evan into a solid friendship. Moreover, Evan treated him like a man, not a surly boy. So Ralph found himself acting mature, and he liked it.

As for the poetry, Evan could have wished Ralph's devotion to him did not take that particular form. He was in deep waters with it, for he still found a great deal of it incomprehensible, especially when the problem of Judith's refusal was gnawing at his mind. Evan dare not even call up the memory of their lovemaking. It took his utmost concentration to find an answer when Ralph had finished reading a piece and asked, "What do you think?"

"I like it."

"But why?"

"There I'm at a loss. The rhyme and meter are so subtle you almost don't notice them, and the final rhyme comes as a nice, surprising wrap-up. It gives one a feeling of such completeness." All this sounded rather lame and insincere, for Evan was feeling anything but complete.

"But you must look deeper than mere words."

"Ralph, the words are beginning to blur together on the page. Other than a pleasant picture, there is nothing in this poem I particularly want to pry into. Why should one dissect a pleasant bit of verse? Why not let it remain pleasant?''

''But don't you want to find the hidden meaning?''

''No, I am afraid of what I might find. One does not go turning over rocks without eventually uncovering something rather nasty.''

''Evan, you are hopeless.''

''You are more right than you know, Ralph.''

''Read these three for tomorrow and please try to find something in them.''

Evan rose with the intention of seeking out Judith.

''And Mother wants to see you directly we are done here,'' Ralph added. Evan's mouth dropped open, as though one of his professors had mentioned in passing that the dean was requesting his presence.

''Ralph said you wanted to see me?'' Evan said warily.

Helen looked up from her work as Evan came into the morning room. The sun streamed warmly through the windows. The ladies worked in here only in the daytime and invaded the library at night to share the fire, all other fires in the downstairs rooms having been let go out. He shuddered to think what the house was like in the winter. He didn't mind the cold himself, but he was thinking of Judith, Angel and little Thomas.

''Ralph likes you,'' Helen stated flatly, as though it were an accusation rather than a compliment. She poured him a cup of tea and handed it to him. He took it, guessing that it was an extravagance she did not often indulge in of an afternoon.

''I can't make out why. I force him through those dreaded formulas.'' He sat down in the chair opposite, prepared to be friendly, but very unsure of himself. Had Judith confided their encounter to Helen? Evan felt himself flushing as he stared at her over his teacup.

''The same reason, I think, that Angel is in such awe of you.''

''And what is that?''

"You are dangerous, and the young are attracted to danger. They flirt with it, like moths about a flame." She put down her sewing and stared at him with her hard blue eyes.

"You're saying I am a bad influence?" he probed, but she had only mentioned Ralph and Angel, not Judith.

"I'm saying you are an unwelcome one."

"Do you really think I would hurt any of them? What reason would I have?"

"Being the eldest, none. But then…what reason did you have for killing all those French?"

"It was my job," he said numbly, not having anticipated this attack.

"Does that make it right?"

"I don't know."

"Should you not have made sure before you did it then?"

Evan shook his head, trying to grasp her point. "You're telling me not to interfere, without knowing what the consequences might be?"

"I already know what the consequences will be."

"What am I to do then? It strikes me I tread a narrow path to stay within Father's wishes without trampling on yours."

"Then tread warily. I warned you what I would do if you tried to force yourself on Judith."

Evan stared at her quizzically. But if she knew he had already seduced Judith, she would surely be more angry than this. "I can accept that you hate me. I am used to being hated. But why turn everyone against me?"

"Should I have them adore you rather, the man who destroyed their chances?"

"By coming back?"

"Yes. It would have been so much easier if you had not."

"I am forced to agree with you. If not for me, Terry would have been in my place. I've no doubt you could have managed him."

"And he would have married Angel."

"But he doesn't even like Angel."

"They *were* in love."

"What?"

"Now that is not to be thought of."

"You're telling me a child such as Angel has already been through one love?"

"Women mature younger than men. Now Terry will offer for Lady Sylvia, and Angel has decided to marry you. And I am convinced that will be the best course."

Evan coughed hoarsely on a sip of tea and gasped, "What?"

"Angel will have to marry you."

"Good Lord! What are you saying? She's no more than a baby. And you have just been complaining of my influencing her."

"Nevertheless, since the damage is already done..."

"Surely you haven't discussed this with her." He put down his cup and saucer with a clatter.

"A married woman such as myself must prepare her sister for whatever sacrifice—"

"Sacrifice! You will wait a long time before I make the sacrifice of allying myself with that child. She may amount to something eventually. But for the moment she drives me mad." Evan rose and paced about the room.

"I'm sure your father will make you see reason."

"He never has. Why do you throw Angel at my head when it's Judith I want? I should think you would want her to marry first."

"Judith will never marry!"

"That's what she says, but is that her wish or yours? Do you mean to keep her by you as some convenient drudge to do your bidding all her days?"

The shock on Helen's face made him choke back further expansion on this. "I'm sorry. I vowed I would not upset you again, but I have. Can you at least tell me why?"

"No."

"Why can she not leave Meremont? Is it you who holds her here? She once gave me think she was so engrossed in her studies that she had time for nothing else, but now—"

"Yes, the library. It is a particularly excellent one. She cannot leave it. She has decided to remain unwed to pursue her writings. A husband is out of the question for her."

Evan almost asked about the other man, but was not at all sure Helen was privy to that. "Does it have to do with the church?" he asked lamely. Perhaps Judith felt she should be punished for succumbing to a man—two men now. Evan had only wanted to show her how much he loved her, and he may have made the situation far worse.

"What?"

"Does she have Catholic leanings or—I had not thought to ask—are you Catholic yourself? Does she mean to take holy vows or something, the way she keeps saying she will never marry?"

Helen looked up in surprise at this. "Yes—yes, you have guessed right. My first husband was Catholic. Influenced by him, Judith vowed to devote herself to the church and works of charity. She has spoken of it for years now, of leaving the material world behind."

"Oh, no! I was afraid of that. She is determined in this course?"

"Yes, it would be evil to try to dissuade her."

Evan studied Helen. She looked more open to him, as though she could talk freely now that the secret was out. But why had she not told him before? Did she think him intolerant? Something was not quite right, but he could not make out what, because he could think of no reason for her to be still lying to him.

"Very well, I will not . . . corrupt her, as you fear."

The words were bitter in his mouth, more bitter than the wine. What was he thinking of to seduce a girl with no real experience of the world? He had ruined her already. And he had only wanted to demonstrate how much he loved her. He could not even use the wine as an excuse. He had known exactly what he was doing. Judith had been victimized again.

* * *

Evan left abruptly, and Helen congratulated herself on grasping at that particular straw, until she went to the library to warn Judith about the conversion.

"You told him what?" Judith demanded in shock, leaving a large blot of ink on her paper.

"I told him you had Catholic leanings and were thinking of becoming a nun."

"What could you have been thinking about, Helen, to concoct such a tale?" Judith threw her pen down angrily. "I cannot credit it. And to use the church in a lie! Whatever made you do it?"

"Evan did. He wouldn't have suggested it himself if he hadn't considered the possibility."

"But what is he to think when I don't hie myself to a nunnery? Sister, I wish you had not even talked to him. You have made things ever so much worse. What will he think of me after last night?"

"What happened last night?"

"Nothing."

"At any rate, he may let you alone now. He is the sort who would have respect for the church."

"But you have fixed it so that I have to lie to him now."

"Judith, we are all lying to him all the time."

"I know. I know. He keeps pressing me, and I cannot tell him the truth. I almost did, when he first came, but I liked him so much I couldn't bear the thought of him hating me. I almost did again last night."

"When?"

"Never mind. My courage failed me at the last moment. I would not have made a good soldier."

"It doesn't matter, dear. But he is not going away. Hiram means to keep him here."

"What am I to do?"

"Perhaps you could read some ecclesiastical books," Helen suggested, glancing around the room.

"Helen!" Judith moaned.

* * *

Judith had difficulty facing Evan over dinner that night. He seemed to sense her awkwardness and smiled sympathetically to put her at her ease. That only made her catch her breath, for he looked so sad. She had no right to hide behind such a lie. If she had only a hundredth part of his courage, she would tell him why she would not marry. Why did he look so apologetic? It only made him more appealing, for none of it was his fault.

She had a daydream somewhere between the first and second courses about their recent encounter at the dower house and nearly overturned her wine. She decided she had better do only hemming tonight. Otherwise she would surely sew a right and left sleeve together.

"I thought I would read some cantos of *Childe Harold's Progress*," Ralph announced as they gathered in the library after dinner. This met with general acclaim.

"Do you fancy it?" Ralph asked Evan.

"I never read any of it."

"What?" demanded Angel. "Even I have read *Childe Harold*."

"I'm afraid it hasn't come my way."

"I suppose there aren't many lending libraries in Spain," Terry observed.

"Of course, you have been away," Angel conceded generously. "You've read Wordsworth, haven't you?"

"Well, no," Evan said with a sheepish grin, enjoying Angel's superior attitude even more than she was.

"What have you read besides your textbooks?" she demanded, putting aside her sewing.

Evan thought for a moment. "There was Tousard's *Artillerist's Companion*."

"Something an engineer would carry about in his pocket?" Lord Mountjoy inquired.

"Well, it is a rather useful work, but amusing in its own way."

"How could artillery be amusing?" asked Helen.

"Well, Tousard advises against setting up your guns behind your own infantry and firing over their heads."

"Why?" Ralph asked.

"It makes them uneasy."

"Uneasy!" Terry said with a laugh. "Seems a bit of an understatement."

Judith smiled, but then looked back at her hemming.

"He also advises you never to engage in artillery duels. Your chances of hitting a gun are much less than of hitting men. There are so many more of them, don't you see? The only exception is if your troops are more annoyed by their fire than their troops are by your fire."

Judith laughed in spite of herself.

"Annoyed?" Lord Mountjoy demanded amid Ralph's snickering. "What does he mean, annoyed?"

"Rendered incapable of maneuvers," Evan answered.

"Does that translate to killed?" Terry asked.

Evan shrugged.

"I think I should like to read Monsieur Tousard's book, if you still have it," Judith said meekly.

Evan was rather enjoying pulling Judith out of her mopes. Perhaps he had not done as much damage as he'd thought. Perhaps there was still a chance he could persuade her that he was not so unreliable and would make a good husband. "He also advises against lighting the fuse on a bomb you are planning to fire from a mortar. It could go off prematurely, you see."

"But how..." Terry began.

"Firing it out of the mortar ignites the fuse, anyway."

"Seems extraordinarily dangerous to me either way you do it," Helen said.

"But it's war," Evan explained. "Everything is dangerous."

"Why all this talk of artillery?" Lord Mountjoy asked. "That was no concern of yours."

"I had to get the artillery as close to the fortifications as I safely could. That often involved contriving portable fortifications of our own, gabions and bundles of twigs and such. They weren't much cover, but were better than nothing. Once the artillery was in place, my job was done. I could sit back and watch the show. I was always rather partial to the rockets myself, although the horses hated them.''

"Why was that?" Terry asked.

"Because of the noise, and then they were apt to land anywhere. Even the rocket battery had no notion where the things would end up. They never did much damage unless they landed in an ammunition wagon, theirs or ours, but they were rather fun."

Judith chuckled again.

"Judith," Helen reprimanded. "Do you really think this is funny?"

"Sorry, Helen." Her reply so mimicked one of his own apologies to his father that Evan grinned at her in sympathy, and she smiled back.

"But enough of war," he said, "Let us hear *Childe Harold*."

Chapter Six

"Do you walk out here often at night?" Evan asked. Judith whirled to face him. "Sorry, I didn't mean to startle you. I found the book. The volume of plates is gone, I'm afraid."

She took it from him and hugged it as though it were a precious part of his past. "That banter reminded me of your letters to Gram. You always sounded as though the war was the biggest lark of your life."

"It was. So long as you did not take it seriously, it couldn't really hurt you. It was best to always be thinking about something really important, like your dinner and if you were likely to get it."

"When you look back on it now—"

"I don't!" he declared, taking a step nearer. "I don't look back on it except in idle conversation. I don't look back at all. I've cut off all my yesterdays. It's all a lot of dead weight, anyway. There's only today, tonight and perhaps tomorrow. There's no point in worrying about anything else." He reached for her hesitantly and laid his hands on her arms. When he could feel the gooseflesh there he pulled up her shawl protectively.

"But there is a point in remembering," Judith said breathlessly. "Else how can we learn from our mistakes and keep from repeating them?"

"Mistakes?" Evan questioned warily. Was she talking about last night? "It's been my experience that men never learn from history, not even their own. Otherwise there would not have been more than one war. These papers I have been reading—it could have all happened a hundred years ago for all it means to me, and I have no doubt that we would all march off again tomorrow if another war started up."

"But if it is so horrible, why do they do it?"

Evan relaxed and rubbed her arms. She was not talking about them; she was playing student again. "Sometimes for food or land. It amounts to the same thing. Sometimes for glory. Sometimes even for God."

The last word hung between them like a barrier as he waited for her to say something. She took a step closer, deciding to tell him finally, but that gaze of his set her heart pounding. He pulled her against him powerfully and kissed the pulse in her throat.

"Evan, we must not do this again."

"I promised I would not force myself on you," he mumbled.

She tried to draw back.

"Have you ever watched a pack of dogs or even a herd of cows or horses?" he asked urgently.

"What has that to do with anything?" Judith whispered. "Let me go." But she said it without conviction.

"I'm trying to explain war, not in terms of men, but in terms of animals. Always they will push the weakest one away, even when there is plenty of food. They will all pick on the weakest for no other reason than to feel more powerful. Have you seen this?"

"Yes, but that is among animals. They don't know any better. I expect more of men. Let me go," she whispered.

"You are apt to be disappointed," he said, working his way around to her mouth and feeling a certain easing in her resistance. She gasped and returned his kiss as though she could no longer contain her need.

"This isn't right," she whispered between kisses.

"How could this not be right? I love you."

"You scarcely know me."

"I know all I want to know."

"Evan, stop," she said as he worked his way to her breasts. "Evan!" she warned, grabbing a fistful of his hair. "I said let me go."

He hesitated. He had not a glass of wine to help him hold his enchantment over her. She really did mean it.

"Do you promise not to hit me?"

"Only if you let me go now."

He released her and jumped back, as though expecting a blow.

"I suppose that was a demonstration of strength against weakness," she said hotly.

"No, for women are the strongest of all. Father may think he is in charge, with me, Terry and Ralph taking our orders from him, but he must report in to Helen each night."

"She does what he says."

"She may perhaps give an inch here or there—witness my case—but eventually she will win the war and he will do what she wants even if it means getting rid of me. You could be such a woman. I am yours already."

"I don't want you."

"That's not true," he said, taking a step closer. "Those lips don't lie."

"I must not want you."

"You, perhaps, should not want me, but that doesn't change the fact that you do."

"And that makes me weak."

"No, it makes me weak, but I don't care." He came toward her again, and she brandished the book.

"Don't come any closer."

"That would be an interesting use for Tousard. I'm so glad I was not lending you a pistol. It's only that after you laughed at me this evening I thought you had forgiven me for last night."

"There is nothing to forgive."

"I took advantage of you. I wasn't thinking of how the wine would affect you."

"Do not make excuses for me! I knew exactly what I was doing. But it was a mistake."

"A mistake? You give me the most passionate experience of my life and you call it a mistake?"

"I was feeling sorry for you. I should not have chosen such a way to express it."

"Sorry for me?" He stared at her.

"Must you repeat everything I say? I think we should both forget about last night and attempt to go on as before."

"Forget? Never!"

"Isn't that what you advocated? Cutting oneself off from all yesterdays?"

"But I had assumed that meant today would be better."

"It is better. I have come back to my senses."

"How can you say that, after what happened . . . ?"

"Nothing happened."

"Nothing!"

"Nothing of any moment," she said coldly.

He stared at her as though she had struck him a blow. She had meant to hurt him and she had succeeded.

He walked away, to leave her breathing hard and wanting him with half herself, while the other half warred against passion. If ever there was a war, Judith was fighting it.

She sank to her knees, clutching the book to her as though it were Evan. She had not had the courage to confess, but at least she had sent him away from her, as surely as though he were riding down the road toward the coast.

"You aren't dressed for riding," Angel said, as Judith came into their room next morning.

"I'm not going anymore."

"But you like to ride. I know you do."

"The less I see of Evan the better. You can get a groom to go with you."

"Won't you ever ride with us again? I don't like to see you unhappy."

"Someday, when Evan is safely married and can be no danger to me."

"If he were engaged, that would be as good as married. He would be as unavailable?"

"Oh, yes, I suppose so."

"Then I will get him to propose to me, and you can ride with us again."

"Angel, don't be so foolish. Men like Evan don't just get engaged for no reason. Not quickly, anyway."

"But he has taken an interest in me. He is teaching me to ride—well actually, he is shouting orders at me. That means he is interested. If I make myself agreeable to him, he cannot be so very far from making me an offer."

Judith was speechless for a moment. "You have to remember he is a soldier. The attention he pays you may be more casual than that you receive from another man. It might even be friendship," Judith suggested hopefully.

"You don't want me to marry him?"

"It's not that. I have heard of Helen's scheme and it won't wash. Evan can't be bounced around like a ball. He has feelings."

"Feelings for you. But have you any feelings for him?"

"I feel . . . sorry for him. I did even before I knew him."

"Then if I marry him we can all be comfortable again, except maybe for Terry. Poor Terry. There's nothing I can do about that."

"You're too young for these games."

"Helen does not think so. Besides, what else am I good for?"

"I wish I could promise you that if you waited patiently, the right man would come to claim you, but I know that isn't always true."

"I can be happy with Evan. I don't care if he is grumpy sometimes."

"You'd better go. You are already late. I can hear them talking in the yard."

* * *

Besides riding with the men that morning, Angel coaxed Evan into giving her a riding lesson that afternoon. Even though Angel's attention wandered during it, Evan thought he kept his patience admirably. When they were walking back to the house from the stables, he spoke what was on his mind.

"Angel, why did Judith not come riding with us? Is she avoiding me?"

"Well, since I am going to marry you, she did not want to be in the way."

"What?"

"You can hardly say anything romantic to me with my sister along!"

"Now see here, I am not going to marry you."

"Well, why not? There is no one else here for you to marry."

"That's a stupid reason for marrying someone."

"It is not. Sometimes that is the only reason a woman has. We cannot get about and meet men. We have to take what we can find readily available."

"You make us sound like cattle."

"I don't know why you are raising such a fuss. I think we should get on admirably."

"I don't merely want to 'get on.' I had entertained some notion of falling in love."

"We can do that, too."

"No, we cannot. I am not in love with you, and you are certainly not in love with me. You don't even know what it means to love."

"Yes, I do. I have been in love. It just did not work out. Now I must do what is best for everyone."

"You don't know what you are talking about. You are just a child."

"I am not a child! I'll show you!"

They were at the base of the house steps when Angel lunged at him with the intent of planting a passionate kiss on his mouth, but she overset his balance and landed on top of him on the stone steps. Evan was breathless for a moment, then swore vehemently, for she had split his lip with her teeth. As he wiped the blood away and saw it on his hand, he laughed hysterically.

Angel righted herself, straightened her hat and said, "So there!" before flouncing up the steps and into the house.

A rich ripple of laughter raised Evan's hackles, until he realized it was Judith out picking flowers. "Need any help?" she asked.

"This is a damned dangerous family to have fallen into," he said as he scrambled up and dusted off his coat.

"Poor baby."

"Easy for you to laugh. She hasn't broken your jaw," he said, feeling it anxiously. "You are a violent bunch of females."

"Your jaw is not broken or you would not be able to talk such nonsense." She took out her handkerchief and dabbed at his mouth, thinking how very kissable it was. She could not really blame Angel for wanting him.

He must have recognized some look of desire on her face for he said, "It's not fair," as he seized her arm.

"No, but that's the way it is." She pulled away. "You came too late."

"How can you say that? I'm here. We're both still free."

"But I'm not."

"What does such a vow mean? Hasn't it occurred to you that you might serve God even better as my wife than as Father's secretary? As Lady Mountjoy you could make a difference in the world."

"And as plain Judith Wells, I cannot?"

"I didn't say that. I only meant—"

"I have a life of my own, Evan. I had one before you came. It will continue whether you stay or not."

"Whereas mine won't," he said in defeat.

"What are you talking about?"

"I only stayed because of you."

"Don't say that. That's very dangerous."

"The truth is sometimes dangerous."

"That I know." She teetered on the point of telling him the whole truth. She had borne much in her life, but his scorn she could not endure.

They heard Helen calling Judith from inside the house. Evan picked up her basket. It was heavy, so he did not give it to her, but carried it up the steps and opened the door for her.

"How will you say you cut your lip?" she asked, to change the subject.

"I'll say I rode into a tree limb. Father will believe that. He has always regarded me as a clumsy oaf."

"I don't think so. I always had the impression he was rather proud of you, especially that 'Mad Mountjoy' name you made for yourself."

"Oh, Lord, has that got back to him? I simply have the most awful habit of laughing when everything has gone awry and I don't know what to do. It is never appropriate."

"It did no good with Angel. She means to have you."

"Well, stop her!"

"I can't, and I'm not sure it wouldn't be for the best."

"I think you are the one who is insane. I love *you*, not her. I have told her that more than once. She simply ignores me and goes on."

"I told her to— I mean, I said I have no interest in you."

"I see!" he said hotly. "You have tried me and have no interest in me anymore, so it's all right for her to have a go at me. Is that how it is?" he demanded.

"That is not how it is."

"You make a fellow feel like an old pair of shoes. Once you have done with me, you pass me on to someone else."

"That is not what happened. I told you from the beginning there could be nothing between us. You just weren't listening."

"I was listening to your eyes, not your words. You toyed with the idea of marriage to me, admit it."

"Never. I told you from the beginning I would not marry. I have treated you fairly."

"You encouraged me. Then something happened. Perhaps you found out Gram's money doesn't amount to that much and can't help you keep Meremont—"

He gasped as she delivered a blow to the ribs that all but brought him to his knees.

"How dare you!" Judith said with menace, her eyes flashing. "I would never treat a man the way...the way men treat women."

"The way you were treated, you mean?" Evan asked. "Your offer of marriage—was he the highest bidder?"

"If you must know, he was the only bidder. The price was nothing to be proud of, and he did not even keep his word about that."

"So you sent him on his way."

"Something like that."

"I shall leave then."

"No, you must not. Lord Mountjoy is counting on you. You promised to build the canal."

"I did not promise."

"You let him think you would do it, which is the same thing. You're just like all the others. You only keep your word so long as it is convenient."

"That's not—" Evan broke off when he saw Helen observing them with satisfaction from the end of the hall. Of course she would like them to be at odds with each other. Judith wrested the basket away from him and earned that slight smile of approval from her sister that Evan had come to hate.

He refused to answer Bose when he demanded what had happened. It seemed such a silly incident that Evan did not want to talk of it. He washed up and changed quickly so he could be the first to the library. Judith hesitated in the doorway when she arrived and realized he was there alone.

"I'm sorry I was such an ass," he said to keep her from retreating. "You're right. You did warn me. It's only that when I am hurting I get a bit unreasonable."

"A bit?" she queried, trying to stay angry with him. It was her only defense.

"Very well, when I am hurting, I am not at all rational."

Try as she might, it was not in her to reject his apology. "Then I didn't help matters by hitting you in your cracked ribs."

"No, it's the other side that's injured, and I was glad of that. You pack a powerful punch."

"Perhaps you should remember that, to forestall you from ever becoming unreasonable again," she warned.

"I shall certainly try," he said, rubbing his bruised side.

"And you'll stay?" Judith demanded.

He nodded.

"And finish the canal?" she persisted.

He looked a little mulish, but finally nodded. "Even if it ruins us all."

"Oh, it won't," Judith said blithely.

They were soon joined by the rest of the family and sat down to dinner on schedule. The soup burned Evan's lip, and he dabbed at it to see if it had started to bleed again.

"What the devil happened to you now?" Lord Mountjoy demanded, grasping his jaw and turning it to the light as though Evan were a child. "Fighting with Terry again?"

"No, I rode into a tree limb," Evan said resentfully as he shrugged off his father's hand.

"That's the stupidest excuse I have ever heard."

Terry peered across the table in amusement at his brother. "Someone has clipped you, and it wasn't me. Never tell me Ralph—"

"I'd never do such a thing," Ralph declared. "Evan and I get along very well."

"Who were you fighting with?" Lord Mountjoy demanded.

Helen looked at the embarrassed Evan with mild interest.

"I did it!" Angel said haughtily. "And I would do it again."

"This is the outside of enough," his father said. "It's one thing to pay court to a girl, but to be forcing yourself on her such that she must defend herself so desperately..."

"But I didn't," Evan claimed, looking at his father in horror. "Angel is the one who—"

"It was all your fault!" Angel retorted. "You should never have said that about me."

"What did I say? I can't even remember."

Lord Mountjoy stared hard at him. "That is always your defense. You can't remember. It's wearing a little thin, Evan."

Evan looked around the table in disbelief. Everyone except Judith assumed the worst about him, and she was biting her lip to keep from laughing outright.

"And then," Angel said, "he laughed at me."

"Really, Evan," Terry admonished. "It's just not done. Maybe you are used to looser manners in the army, but in England women must be treated with respect."

Ralph was looking at his plate, embarrassed for Evan's sake.

Helen said, "I think we should speak no more about this. I'm sure it won't happen again."

Evan looked with renewed horror at his unlikely defender, who met his confusion with a satisfied little smile. He had been a soldier long enough to recognize an indefensible position. If he said nothing, they would all think he had taken some liberty with Angel, fondled her or some such thing. If he protested, he ran the risk of the girl leading them, albeit ignorantly, to assume he had compromised her more seriously. He might even be forced into marriage with her. Angel's triumphant, self-righteous look sealed his fate. He was beaten. He would never have surrendered to the French, but against such women he was no match.

Judith was coughing into her napkin and excused herself with a red face. Evan looked at her accusingly as she fled the room, and he had an impulse to go after her. She should not be able to closet herself somewhere and laugh herself silly at his dilemma. Even as he pictured her laughing, heard in his mind that rich laughter, he began to see the humor of the situation and had to bite his lip to keep from laughing himself.

"Ow," he said, and dabbed at it again.

"Very well," said his father, after turning the decision over in his mind. "We will say no more about it, but I do not want Angel to go with you unaccompanied anymore. If Judith doesn't wish to ride with you, one of you two—" he motioned to Terry and Ralph "—must go with them. We cannot have Mad Mountjoy giving the family a bad name."

Evan winced. He winced most of the way through the meal for one reason or another. He was surprised that his father accepted as a reason for his supposed lapse that he was a soldier, or insane. He had a feeling it was an excuse he could not fall back on again. He vowed never to be alone with the unstable Angel if he could help it.

There was one consolation. He might be able to use this as a lever to get Judith to ride with them again. She rejoined them for the second course, remarkably composed. He sent her a vengeful look, which she countered with a satisfied smile. If she intended to punish him for taking advantage of her, she was succeeding. Sometimes she was too much like Helen.

Terry had seemed quite composed at dinner, even amused by Angel hitting Evan, but after several glasses of wine during the meal and two of port after the ladies had retired from the table, he was sending Evan nasty looks that boded no good for the evening's peace. Evan interrupted his father's discourse to Ralph on Milton to say he thought he would retire early. His father glared at him as he left.

He was still crossing the hall when Terry came after him. "I'm warning you, Evan, keep your hands off Angel. She's just a child. She doesn't know the first thing about the sort of affairs you are used to—"

"I did not touch her!"

"You liar!" Terry took a swing at him, but missed, and Evan got him in a very effective armlock.

Terry's shirt ripped as he wrenched himself out of Evan's grasp.

"Good Lord! Who shot you?" Evan asked.

"No one." Terry pulled his coat possessively over the fresh scar high on his shoulder.

"I know a bullet wound when I see one. Who did it?"

"I don't know."

"That's what you meant when you asked, 'Do *you* mean to kill me, too?' You laid the emphasis wrong—on the *you* rather than the *me,* and I didn't catch it."

"Terry, we have to tell him," Judith said from the stairs. "What if it happens again?"

"It won't happen again."

"Terry, it's not fair."

"Tell me what?"

"Angel shot Terry," Judith said bluntly.

Evan stared at her for a moment, unseeing. He was picturing the woman who had fired at him. It could have been Angel—but why?

"What?" he said stupidly, to fill the growing silence.

"It was a lover's quarrel, I tell you. And she bitterly regretted it." Terry kneaded his scarred shoulder with his hand.

"But really? She shot you?" Evan asked, coming back to his senses. Still, Angel could have no motive for shooting at Evan himself, not one he could think of, anyway.

"Just a scratch...to teach me a lesson. Truth to tell, I had it coming."

"Seems a little desperate, doesn't it?" Evan asked, then caught Judith's look and remembered Angel's kiss that had gone so awry. But that led him to remember Judith's kisses, which he did like, no matter how impetuous or ill judged. She colored as he stared at her, and he knew she was thinking of their lovemaking. These Wells women were dangerous.

"She's a very headstrong girl, which is why..." Terry faltered.

"Why he doesn't think he can marry her, after all," Judith finished for him.

"You were going to be married, then?" Evan asked.

"I had not actually asked her. She was only sixteen. But I suppose I had courted her. She had every right to be angry when I started calling on Lady Sylvia."

"If Angel loved you enough to shoot you, is it possible she loves you still?" Evan asked numbly.

"Enough to kill for him, you mean?" Judith flashed Evan an offended look.

"What are you talking about?" Terry looked confused.

"With me out of the way, and at her hand, you might be grateful to her," Evan continued. "You would certainly be the heir."

"That's absurd! She's just a passionate child. And she clearly prefers you now to me."

"She may have changed her mind about me, but I—"

"Of course not! What am I thinking?" said Judith, covering her eyes. "Having once shot someone and fainted at the sight of her handiwork, having seen the awful effects of a bullet, she would never do such a thing again."

"I expect you are right," Evan said lightly, but without conviction. "I do hope this propensity for shooting people does not run in the family." He stared at Judith, but it was Helen he was thinking of.

"Don't even joke about it," Judith said. "Angel was truly sorry. You should have seen her. She wept for days."

"What did Father say to all that?"

Terry glanced at Judith. "We didn't tell him."

"Didn't tell him! However could you keep such an injury secret? It must have laid you up for weeks."

"Oh, no," Judith replied hastily, "we had to tell him Terry was shot. We just didn't tell him who did it."

"I told him a pistol discharged while I was cleaning it."

"I see," Evan said, shaking his head. "And he believed you?"

"I don't know that he ever believes me, even when I am telling the truth."

"And how do you feel about Angel now?"

"I don't know," Terry answered in some confusion. "I thought I had quite got over her, but the thought of you manhandling her makes my blood boil."

"But he didn't," Judith said. "Angel leapt at him to kiss him and knocked him down on the steps. He's lucky he only got a split lip. He might have hit his head."

Terry stared at Evan openmouthed, playing the scene out in his mind, then bent double in a guffaw. Evan looked accusingly at Judith, who was laughing again in turn.

"I think I liked it better when everyone thought I was a profligate."

"I really thought—I thought . . ." Terry started laughing again.

Evan never found out what Terry thought, for Lord Mountjoy came out of the dining room, Ralph trailing behind, and demanded to know what was so funny.

"Nothing, Father," Evan said automatically as Terry buttoned his coat.

"What did I tell you?" Lord Mountjoy confided to Ralph. "My own sons conspire against me. They won't tell me what they fight about. They won't even tell me what they laugh about."

"Oh, sir, don't blame Evan," said Judith. "Sometimes he can be so droll without even meaning to."

"I suppose I do not have a proper sense of humor," Evan conceded.

"You never did," agreed his father. "Come tell your story in the library so we can all have a laugh."

"It is not, I think, a story for ladies' ears," said Evan desperately, trying to think of something passably funny to fill the void, while pinching Judith's arm for shifting the blame onto him.

"Then why did you tell it to Judith?"

"We did not know she was eavesdropping on the stairs," Evan said smugly.

"I was not eavesdropping. I went up to get my shawl. I couldn't help overhearing you."

"Well, if Judith thought it was funny, I'm certain Helen will not be shocked and, to be sure, Angel will not even understand it," Lord Mountjoy said, leading the way into the library.

"What won't I understand?" Angel demanded from her seat by the library table.

"About the colonel's daughter," Evan said smoothly.

"Which colonel's daughter?" Helen asked.

"I'm not at liberty to use her name, but she is something of a legend. She engaged in all manner of support to the troops—no, I do not mean that," he said, sending an accusing look at his father. "She nursed the wounded mostly, even drove them back from the front when she could get a wagon to carry them."

"How many horses?" asked Judith.

"What?"

"How many horses did she drive?"

"Four, why?"

"Do you think I could drive four horses?" she asked, to try to make him lose his concentration.

"My dear Judith, I'm sure you could drive a team of six if you set your mind to it, but you are not going to drive me off my train of thought."

"Let him get on with it and stop teasing him, Judith," Lord Mountjoy admonished kindly.

"She was captured by the French. The battle lines had moved and a troop of French cavalry surrounded her wagon. She could not get it back to her own camp."

"Did they let her go?"

"Another officer might have, but this French captain took a fancy to her, at least that's what we suppose. Anyway, he accused her of being a spy."

"And was she?" Helen asked.

"She hadn't set out to be, and she defended herself quite vehemently in very broken French, extracting a promise from the captain that the wounded would be exchanged for French wounded no matter what happened to her."

"And what happened to her?" asked Angel, fascinated.

"The captain took her back to his tent to question her."

"Are you sure you can—" Judith began.

"Oh, don't stop me now. Remember how humorous you thought the story was." Evan was satisfied to see a blush steal into Judith's cheeks.

"But you're not telling it the same way," Judith protested.

"Of course he is," Terry said, to add to the confusion. "And did he question her?"

"All night, apparently. It took a long time, you see, since he had little English and she had less French."

"And was her French so very bad?" Judith asked suspiciously.

"Oh, no, she spoke French quite fluently, but she saw no profit in letting him know that. She understood completely everything he said and everything that she overheard, much of it useful information for us."

"So she was a spy?" Helen concluded.

"She was a loyal Englishwoman."

Judith looked at him and smiled. "Did she fancy this French captain?"

"We never found out, but I rather think not, or not that much, anyway. About dawn she rode out of camp in his dress uniform and on his second best horse."

Ralph snickered.

"That's extraordinary!" Lord Mountjoy said. "She would have been shot if she had been caught. Why didn't he stop her?"

"He couldn't."

"Did she kill him?" Angel asked, with what Evan thought was unnatural relish.

"No, she merely knocked him out."

"That's not very exciting," Angel said.

"He did get demoted though, for they found him next morning, gagged and tied naked to his camp bed."

Terry howled again in a good imitation of his previous mirth, and Lord Mountjoy chuckled, too. "But not the sort of story you should really tell the ladies," he conceded.

"Well, that's what I thought, but you wouldn't listen to me."

"It was funnier the first time," Judith said primly.

"It was you, wasn't it?" Angel asked obliquely.

"Me?" Evan asked in a puzzled voice.

"The young officer, and the girl was really French," she replied.

"Whatever gave you that idea?"

"It's the sort of thing you would do, you and your metaphors."

"It is not!"

"So you never made love to any women during the war, then?" Angel baited him with a look that was only superficially innocent.

"Well I—well I . . ."

Judith stared at him with prim interest. They all stared at him.

"I don't remember," he said hopelessly and quite untruthfully.

This did send Lord Mountjoy off into a roar of laughter.

"It is hardly a laughing matter," admonished his wife.

"I think I am going to bed now," Evan said, making a hasty exit and fairly leaping up the stairs.

Bose was smiling for once. "I heard your father laughing wholeheartedly. Things must be going well."

"Bose, I have been routed twice in one evening. I can never recall being so badly defeated during an entire war. What is it about women that makes them put their own twist on your words? I absolutely never know what they are thinking."

"Just because you are not having any luck, do not condemn women in general. You must learn to manage a little better."

"I think the safest thing for me to do is stay in bed all day tomorrow."

"Coward!"

Chapter Seven

Evan awoke to rain lashing against the window and knew there would be no riding that day. It did, however, mean Judith would be trapped in the house, too. Even she would not go out on an errand of mercy in this weather.

As Evan had supposed, she was up and occupied even at this early hour of the morning. He ran her to ground in the library. She was toiling over some plans when he entered, but she immediately rolled them up and made as if she were leaving, with such a look of impatience that he decided there would be no reasoning with her today.

"I don't mean to scare you away from your office. If my company is so unwelcome, let me just find a book to read, or else the elusive *Times,* and I will take myself off."

"You wretch! How am I to answer that? Tell you that you are not welcome in your own house?"

"Well, no, I was hoping you would not be that unkind. But after the thrashing I got last night—mostly at your hands, I might add—I just hope the rain ends before everyone else gets up."

In spite of the pain she had caused both Evan and herself by repeatedly refusing him, Judith was proud of standing firm and was feeling a little superior at having bested him so easily. She could not help but chuckle in memory of the previous night's sport, and hoped that they could deal together as companionable antagonists, if no other way. "I was not very fair to you, was I?"

"You were downright cruel."

"But you set yourself up for it. The temptation was overwhelming."

"You are not the only one to suffer overwhelming temptations. I manage to exercise a deal of control over myself that you do not even appreciate." He sidled around the desk toward her.

"I don't know what you can mean, Captain Mountjoy," she said as she got up and put the chair in his way, almost tripping him.

"Don't show me that prim mouth. It makes you look far too much like Helen, and you are not, no matter how much you pretend to be so straightlaced."

"What do you mean by that?" she challenged.

"So, nothing of moment happened that night? You have a damned cutting tongue for such a sweet beauty, and you wield it like a saber. Nothing could have sent me away so effectively as the thought that I did not measure up to your expectations."

"Perhaps you didn't." Judith moved to the table.

"You wouldn't care to expand on that, I suppose? No, I thought not. I don't know what it is about Meremont, but it seems to drive everyone who lives here into intrigue or madness."

"Perhaps the damp air," she suggested with a rueful smile.

"The what?"

"The damp air that seeps up from the barrens at night."

"Of all the absurdities..." He thought he had her cornered behind the long table, but she slipped around the end near the bookshelves, where he thought not a mouse could get through. Two strides brought him up to her, and she chuckled deliciously in spite of her honest attempts to evade him.

She had a hunger she had never felt before, certainly not with Banstock. There was a delicious pulling deep inside her, but she knew what it was now. Even as she kissed Evan, probed his mouth as he did hers, part of her knew that she was vulnerable, that he could do anything to her and she would let him. He paralyzed rational thought with that mouth and those intent brown eyes. It had not been the wine; she had been drunk on Evan. She had him by the lapels now, and he had thrust a leg between her thighs, causing her to moan amidst their desperate kisses. But she heard something—the door opening. That recalled her to reason, and she cursed herself for letting Evan seduce her again.

"Damn!" he said, whirling guiltily to meet his next embarrassment. His eyes dropped to Thomas. "Lad, wherever did you get that pistol?"

Judith gasped. "Thomas, put it down, child. Don't—"

Evan turned and carried her to the floor under his weight as the gun went off. She was breathless for a moment, then smelled the gunpowder. Evan was heavy on top of her, his face turned away. He groaned.

"Evan, say something. Are you hit?"

He turned his face to her, raising himself on one elbow. "Are you all right, Judith?" he gasped, his eyes desperate.

"Of course I'm all right. You shielded me. Where are you hit?"

"In the heart," he said, lowering his head to kiss her. And for a brief moment she let him, returning the kiss desperately, as if it would be his last, as if he was going to die in her arms. An instant later Evan opened his eyes with a sigh and again raised himself over her. "Sorry, it's just being so close to you, feeling you under me made me give in to one of those overwhelming temptations."

"Evan!" she said warningly. "You had better be shot or I will kill you myself. Now let me up." She grasped him by one ear.

"Ow! I surrender." He rolled off of her, and helped her to her feet just as Lord Mountjoy came into the room with shaving soap still showing under his chin.

"What the devil? What's going on here?"

"It seems—it seems Thomas has got hold of a loaded pistol somehow," she said, wringing her hands.

Thomas was still staring at Evan, who was now standing.

"Thomas!" Lord Mountjoy snapped.

The child's face crumpled into tears, and Lord Mountjoy relieved him of the pistol. "Where did you get this?"

Judith knelt by Thomas and held him, but there was no getting anything out of the weeping child. "I kilt him. I kilt him," he sobbed.

"Good Lord, no," said Evan, coming and bending over the boy. "You missed me entirely. Now tell us where you came by the pistol."

Thomas stared at Evan as though he were a ghost and started a new binge of crying.

"What are you doing to him?" Helen demanded, coming into the room and kneeling, with some difficulty, by the boy.

Thomas threw himself into Lady Mountjoy's arms, and she stroked his back to ease his sobs. "No doubt you are responsible for scaring him half to death."

"Yes," confirmed Judith, rounding on Evan. "If you hadn't pretended to be wounded, he wouldn't have been so frightened."

"So it's my fault he almost shot me?"

"You made it worse," Judith declared.

Evan opened his mouth to defend himself, but three accusing stares and a sobbing child were too much for him. He retreated in poor order, almost wishing the boy had winged him. Then he would have gotten a little sympathy.

As he climbed the stairs, he pondered where Thomas could have got a loaded pistol. Even drunk, Terry would not have left one lying about, and Ralph was entirely competent when it came to shooting. Evan almost turned back to see if he could tell whether it was the same pistol that had been fired at him by the stream. But the woman had been too far away. If he could not recognize her, he certainly would not be able to recognize the gun. It had not been Thomas who had done that, but it did occur to him that Helen might have kept the pistol loaded and ready in case she had another chance at him.

But Helen had been incensed, genuinely angry at the incident. Was she a good enough actress to fool him on that? Or could Angel, in spite of what Judith and Terry believed, have been keeping a loaded pistol in her room, a room she shared with Judith? Unlikely. And if Angel had now determined to marry him, why would she be wanting to kill him, however much he provoked her? It had to be someone else.

He threw himself down morosely on the bed. The only compensation for the entire episode had been feeling Judith succumb to him again. Her fires might be banked, but they were most definitely still burning. He ran through in his mind what they might have done if they had not been interrupted. The library would have been no good for such a tryst. The dower house was best. The trick was how to keep her passionate until he got her there.

Then it hit him that he was thinking like a soldier again, planning strategy, concerned only about the act, not about Judith and how she felt. The only way he had any right to her was if he could convince her to marry him. Anything else was completely unfair. Still, he replayed the kisses in his mind, and the soft feel of Judith under him, until breakfast.

The stir had not died down by then, and Lord Mountjoy passed the pistol around the table with the bread, demanding to know whose it was. Evan stared at it in disbelief, for it was his. He almost owned up to the fact, then bit his lip. He would rather lose the pistol than admit that either he or Bose had been so careless. He would talk to Bose first.

But Bose, when confronted about letting the pistol out of his control, was stunned by the knowledge, and threw open the trunk to discover that not only was the pistol and holster gone, but the ammunition as well.

"Can you get Joan to search the rooms? If we can find the rest of the stuff, we'll know who took it. And Bose—no one but you and Joan are to know it was my pistol he had."

"Yes, sir. How long do you reckon it's been gone from your trunk?" Bose asked.

"I should think at least as long ago as the day I went fishing."

"That's what I was thinking, too."

Their search had barely been instigated when the geometry lesson in the breakfast parlor was interrupted by Lord Mountjoy, carrying the missing cartridge belt. "Yours, I believe," he said to Evan, dumping it on the table with an ominous thump.

"Ralph, would you excuse us a moment?" Evan turned to ask. If one was about to be raked down by a superior, it was always best to rid oneself of privates.

"Yes, yes, of course," Ralph said, exiting as fast as possible.

"Why didn't you own up to this an hour ago?"

"I wanted to talk to Bose first."

"He hadn't missed it?"

"No, not until I mentioned it. It was left in an unlocked trunk, and it wasn't loaded. But we don't know how long it has been missing—possibly since the day I arrived. Where did you find it?"

"In the nursery."

"Good Lord!"

"I entertained the possibility that the child might have wandered into your room and made off with it, thinking it was a toy. But Thomas could never have loaded it."

"Not unless he is an exceptional child. Besides, he could never have cocked it. Feel the pull that hammer takes."

"Yes, I already did."

"What does Thomas say to all this?"

"Only that he must never tell who gave it to him. That was all I could get out of him before Judith bundled him away. He's shielding someone."

"Would a child have any concept of that? I would have thought he would tell the truth to share the blame."

"What do you know about children?"

"Not much. I was extrapolating."

"He also said you were hurting Mother. That you must be killed."

The words sent a certain chill through Evan, but his face remained impassive. "A six-year-old has no concept of murder, either. Someone told him that."

"Who?" his father demanded with despair in his eyes. "Who would want you dead?"

"Not you, apparently," Evan said with a nervous laugh.

"Will you be serious for once? Answer my question."

"I don't know."

"You do know, but you won't say. I can tell when you are lying. I always could. You are just like Thomas."

"Except that I don't have a Judith to bundle me away."

"Tell me!" his father demanded.

"What if I should be wrong? One does not level such an accusation lightly," Evan said desperately.

"Is it—"

"Don't say it! Do you think I like to lie to you? I will handle this in my own way."

"You will get yourself killed."

"Nonsense. Didn't I make it through an entire war? I have only to be more careful."

"You, careful? Out of the question. You have never been careful."

"Well, I shall be more observant then."

"It's not Helen," Lord Mountjoy said on his way out the door. "Helen would never use Thomas in such a way."

Evan looked at him and smiled. "Of course not. I know that." The smile faded when his father had left. He now wished he had let his father speak that other name that was not Helen. Whom did he suspect? Surely not Angel, for he knew nothing about her shooting Terry.

Of course, just because Terry had been wounded did not rule him out. He had the most reason... No, Evan could not believe that. Even if he died for the belief, he would not believe that of his brother. And he was sure about Ralph. He sensed already a budding case of hero worship in the lad that could become quite bothersome. That left only the servants or Angel. It would do none of the servants any good to get rid of him. In fact, their lot must have gotten considerably easier since Bose had been entrusted with hiring more help to clean the dower house. It had to be Angel or someone else.

Talking to Thomas he ruled out. He had only to be caught bullying the boy by Helen or Judith, or that dragon of a nurse to turn them completely against him. Where the devil was Miranda when she would be of some use? He would be lucky if Thomas did not run at sight of him after this.

Could Helen be poisoning the boy's mind against him, as she was attempting to sway Judith? In spite of the events of the day, Evan was convinced Thomas had not killed his pup. Somehow he had to prove it. He took the pistol to his room and this time locked it in the trunk.

Both Judith and Terry went riding with Evan and Angel the next day, and Evan had the feeling one would not have come without the other. They seemed to be on such easy terms with each other that he found himself wondering from time to time if there was not something between them, but their familiarity was more that of siblings, the kind of relationship Judith claimed she wanted with him.

Perhaps she was simply one of those strong women who did not need men, who did not even want them. But then he remembered that night and the smoldering desire in her eyes, and he knew that wasn't so.

Angel had dropped her hat in the mud on the way back and had already rushed this creation into the house to try to save it when a female rider and her groom appeared in the stable yard.

"Sylvia!" Terry called, and went to help her dismount. The groom led the horses to the stable.

"Allow me to present Lady Sylvia Vane. My brother Evan."

"Hello. It was such a beautiful morning I simply had to take a ride even though James is in Bath—his doctor, you know."

"How have you been keeping?" Terry asked, smiling.

"I have been very lonely, sir." She tapped him with her whip as though it were a folded fan. "I recall a time when you would have visited me or brought your charming sisters over. I have scarcely seen you for weeks. I thought perhaps someone was ill."

Jolted from admiring her fair complexion and gold ringlets, Evan claimed, "That is my fault. I have been keeping Terry busy with the surveying."

Terry grimaced at Evan, who wondered what he was trying to convey to him.

"Really? And what have you been surveying?" she asked as Terry took her arm possessively.

"Just the—ouch!" Evan gasped. "Judith, you stepped on my foot."

"Oh, I'm sorry. I didn't see it."

"A new road," Terry said triumphantly. "Evan was an engineer in the army, so Father is having him survey a new road."

"A new road? It must take a great deal of knowledge to do such a thing."

Evan, limping, had by this time surmised he was not to mention the canal, and wondered how he had been so dense as not to realize it immediately. "I think it's just Father's way of keeping me from feeling useless."

"Come now, a war hero, useless?"

"There are no heroes in the engineer corps. We leave that to the cavalry boys. I fancy I have met your cousin once or twice."

"James speaks glowingly of your exploits."

"He must have me confused with someone else."

"No, Mad Mountjoy is what he calls you," she said over her shoulder.

"We were all mad, if it comes to that. War is a mad business. Would you care to join us for breakfast, Lady Sylvia?"

"Oh, I am not at all dressed for it."

"Lord Mountjoy won't regard that," Judith said. "Besides, we are all so late I will not have time to change, so you will not be conspicuous."

Lady Sylvia did not seem to care for the assurance that she would not be conspicuous. "Oh, very well."

"How's the hat?" Evan asked Angel as they all sat down at the table.

"Past mending, and it was all your fault, Evan. You would gallop down that great hill."

"We were barely trotting," Judith said, "and I did warn you to pin it on better."

"Never mind," said Evan, "we will buy you a new one next time we go shopping. I never fancied the other, anyway."

"Oh, will you? Thank you, Evan."

Lord Mountjoy cleared his throat. "So our Terry has been neglecting you, Lady Sylvia?"

"Yes, I feared there had been a death in the family."

"We should have brought Evan to call, but he is still recovering from his injuries."

Evan hesitated with a forkful of ham suspended over his plate.

"And you said you were not a war hero," Sylvia cooed in an annoying way.

Evan noticed that Helen was looking impatient and realized she was waiting for him to pass the butter. "Just some cracked ribs and a twisted knee," he said, handing over the dish.

"You make it sound paltry, but I have it from my cousin, James, that you were trampled by a troop of cavalry at Bordeaux. Now I call that heroic."

"Had they been French cavalry, where I could have got a lick back at them, it might have been heroic."

Lord Mountjoy looked confused. "But whose cavalry was it?"

"Alas, they were our own boys, and rather drunk, so I could only swear in their wake and listen to them laugh at me."

Terry and Ralph chuckled.

"Surely not your cousin, though, Lady Sylvia," Judith said innocently.

"Of course not. James would never ride over his own troops. Besides, he was wounded in February and has been home on leave all this time."

"Please convey my sympathies," Evan replied.

"I suppose you will settle down here now?"

Evan's hesitation was real, as was his reluctance to commit himself. A negative shake of his father's head helped him out of his dilemma. "I can't say that I've thought much about it."

"Keeps talking about going off to America," Lord Mountjoy interjected critically. This made Helen and Angel stare at him, since Evan had never mentioned America to them.

"Such a barbaric country," Sylvia said.

"It can hardly be worse than Spain," Evan countered.

"Tell me about it."

"Spain?"

"No, silly, I have had my fill of Spain from James. Tell me about America."

"I don't know a thing about it." Evan vigorously chewed a bite of biscuit and swallowed.

"You never said anything to me about America," Angel said, pouting. "I don't think I would like it there."

"Can't say that I blame you," Evan agreed. "They don't like the English much. There's a war on, remember. There's bound to be a need for us veterans there."

"But you might be killed in America," Lady Sylvia protested.

"I might be killed in Devonshire. What's the difference?" Evan asked irreverently.

"You see what I have to put up with?" Lord Mountjoy asked. "No more sense than when he first left home. I don't know about your cousin, but I find these soldiers to be irresponsible scamps."

"They have perhaps a knack for minimizing danger so as not to worry us," their visitor said perceptively. "I should call that very responsible."

Evan stopped chewing abruptly and glanced at her with a frown. So she was not an empty-headed beauty. Why then did he not like her? Perhaps because Judith did not.

"I should be going, but first my errand. I should like to invite you to an alfresco party next Saturday. Please say you will come."

Evan took a large bite of bread so that he could not be expected to reply and glanced toward Lord Mountjoy.

"I'm sure you young folk will have a jolly time, but I am past—"

"But I particularly need your advice on some farm matters. It is not easy since Father died. Please come."

"Yes, yes, of course we will come, my dear. You had only to ask."

It bothered Evan that his father, even though wary of this woman, could be manipulated by her.

"You will come, too, won't you?" she asked, turning to Evan.

"I know nothing about farm matters, but I should be happy to attend."

Terry and Angel saw Lady Sylvia out, Angel walking with her the whole way to the stables to ascertain from her what would be proper attire for the picnic.

"'Surely not your cousin, Lady Sylvia,'" Evan quoted in a singsong voice when they had gone. "How am I supposed to keep a straight face when you come out with comments like that, Judith?"

Judith laughed outright, and Lord Mountjoy chuckled.

"She acts like such a silly goose, I can't blame Judith for baiting her," Lord Mountjoy said.

"*Acts* is the operative word," Evan warned as he drained his coffee cup and looked hopefully to Judith, who decided to refill it for him.

"What do you mean?" Ralph asked. "I thought she was charming."

"Yes, of course she was," Evan said. "I doubt if she found out anything she came for."

"The Lord knows. She was sharp enough to snap up those fifteen acres I need."

"And I almost blurted out something about the canal. It's a good thing Judith and Terry have their wits about them."

"The canal," Helen said. "I almost forgot."

"Helen, you don't suppose Angel will say something about it?" Lord Mountjoy asked his wife.

"I shouldn't think it would come up. They talk only of fashions."

"I did warn her it was private family business, but I will speak to her again," Judith said.

"Threaten to step on her," Evan advised. "That should bring her into compliance."

"I'm sorry," Judith said, but without contrition. "I couldn't think how else to get your attention."

Evan smiled at her, then caught sight of Helen frowning at him and hid behind his coffee cup.

"We can't keep it quiet forever, you know," Lord Mountjoy said. "So Terry had better get a move on. That's why I was agreeable to this party. Perhaps he can pop the question then."

"I don't like it," Helen said.

For the first time, Evan nodded in agreement.

Evan was returning from the canal site when he came across Thomas more than a mile from the house. He could not in good conscience leave the boy to his own devices. He had no idea how far the lad had leave to wander, but he would bet it was not past the edge of the yard.

"Would you like a ride home, Thomas?"

Thomas looked torn, and Evan realized it was only the temptation of riding a horse that kept the boy from fleeing. "I can ride your horse with you?"

"He can carry two. Scramble up here and I'll show you how to steer." Evan pulled Thomas up by one arm and seated him in front of him on the saddle.

"Now when we come to the turn in the lane, give a little tug on the right rein and make sure to loosen the left one."

"How can I make him go faster?"

"Tell him to trot."

"Trot!" Thomas commanded, and laughed in delight when Taurus obeyed him. "May I ride your horse someday, since I am not to have a pony?"

"Not by yourself. Perhaps Father will relent about the pony, if you tell him what really happened."

"No. I am not to have a pony and not another puppy, either."

"You wouldn't want another one for a year, anyway."

"Why not?"

"It takes a year to get over losing one, at least that's what I've heard—that you must mourn through four seasons until you are ready to move on."

"A whole year?"

"Father is a tough old bird. It takes a long time to prove yourself to him. It's taken me half my life. Eventually he will come to trust you again, the way I trust you."

"You do?"

"Who told you I must be killed?"

"I must not tell that. I promised."

"And you have never broken a promise, have you?"

"No, never."

"Did you promise Father you would take care of the puppy?"

"Yes, and I did."

"Do you know who killed Toby?"

"You did!"

"I did not. I liked Toby. Who told you that?"

Thomas fell silent.

"It was the same person who said I must be killed, wasn't it?" Evan asked.

Thomas nodded. Evan wondered how a mother could poison her child's mind so, unless she believed it herself.

"I did not kill Toby, and I want to be your friend, Thomas, but you must trust Father and me."

"Tho-mas! Tho-mas," the nurse called, as though she were calling in sheep. Evan was on the point of evading her when she popped around the side of the house and caught them jogging toward the stable.

"How dare you put him up on that great horse!" Miranda pulled the boy down and held him tightly. "He might have been thrown to his death or trampled. My poor Thomas. No one cares about you but me."

"I should think you could keep better track of him, as you have nothing else to do all day," Evan said in annoyance.

"What?" she gasped. "He could have been killed, and it would have been your fault."

"He will have to learn to ride someday," Evan shouted after her as she carried Thomas off, stroking his back and muttering endearments to him. The boy waved a forlorn hand at Evan over her shoulder.

"Never!" Miranda hugged her baby, interrogating him as to whether the nasty beast had bit him or stepped on him.

Evan shook his head and turned Taurus over to a stable boy.

Evan went to the dower house, as was his custom now. He could remember his grandmother more clearly in the garden than anywhere else, he realized as he leaned against a tree. It was as though she was still here. It did not disturb him that she haunted the place, for he had only good memories of her. He had always come here when he had been in trouble, which was often. He could not remember exactly what had sent his father shouting after him, but he was sure it was nothing he'd ever done on purpose. All boys were careless or thoughtless, he supposed. Gram would hide him and feed him until the worst was over. They would read together and discuss great literature. She'd been his only friend.

"You're thinking of your grandmother, aren't you?" Judith asked, coming up to him.

"How did you guess?" He turned to her.

"You were smiling."

"Surely that is not the only time I smile."

"Well, in that particular way. She was a memorable character. I brought the rest of the newspapers downstairs for you."

Evan stared at her and wondered if she tortured him like this on purpose, or if she really could forget what had happened over those newspapers. "I shall get though them eventually. Thank you."

"I'm not sure it's such a good idea. I know you want to forget the war."

"I think I have, to some extent. That's why I want to read up on it. I sound such a dunce when someone asks me something. It's all gotten rather muddled."

"Your letters were very clear and precise," said Judith, seating herself on the bench beside him. "You usually disposed of all military matters in two or three short paragraphs that sounded very like a newspaper report. Then you recounted anecdotes about food and the lengths to which you and your comrades went to get the most absurd things."

"Food becomes very important to you when you haven't any.... What have I said?" he asked when her expression became bereft.

"Nothing. I know what you mean."

"I wish you did not know what I mean. Was it very bad, your time in Bristol? Ralph told me a little, very little. I suspect he tripped over the worst of it as lightly as he could."

"Helen and I tried to shield Ralph and Angel from our desperation, but Ralph was hard to fool. Angel is good at pretending nothing is wrong so as not to worry anyone else."

Evan stared at Judith, trying to squash an uneasy feeling he had about Angel. Like Sylvia, there was more to her than met the eye. Could Angel's innocent face hide a desperate nature? Still, why would she take it out on him? Unless...unless his spurning her had made her decide she wanted Terry to be the heir again and marry her.

"Evan, are you ill? You look so bleak."

"Sorry. Was I away for long?"

"Yes. I know my conversation is rather dull, but I do not usually put people to sleep with their eyes open."

"I just got lost in a memory."

"The war."

"Uh, yes. The most bitter thing about it is I can't remember even when I'm awake who's alive and who's dead. And I should be able to, except there were so many of them—men you draw close to for a time, then never see again. I wish I knew if I might expect to run into some of them somewhere."

"That's why you want the papers," she whispered.

"Yes. Perhaps I should just let it all go. If I remember them, I have to remember the French, as well. Do you suppose there is any absolution for a soldier?"

"I don't know," she said, then remembered her sham religious vocation. "I am not an expert, but I'm sure if you asked for forgiveness it would be granted."

"God might grant it, but I don't think I ever could. It was murder pure and simple, no matter who condoned it, no matter the necessity for it, no matter that they had done worse to us."

"You are too hard on yourself. After all you have been through you should not torture yourself in this way."

"Should I rather blot out all the mistakes I have made? Cut them out of my mind like bad spots in an apple?"

"If it were possible, I would do so—pretend that I had no past, that this was the beginning of my life. But we can't do that, Evan, can't pretend nothing happened before today," Judith said sadly, "for I would go on making mistakes and hurting people. I should have to cut myself off from every single day of my life, exist only for the moment. It would mean I had learned nothing and would go on making the mistakes over and over. Are there people who can live so shallowly?" she asked with tears in her voice.

"I don't know," Evan said. "Not us, apparently. I wish I had not gone away. I would have been here. I would have known you these seven years. Then I would not be too late and we could be married."

"It would have been too late already."

"Whatever do you mean? You can't have had the church in mind for longer than that."

"Yes, I—I must get back to the house." She rose abruptly.

"Is there no turning back from this?" He stood and took her arm. "Can you not serve God in some other way?"

"Do not tempt me," she said bitterly, looking at his hand, the warmth of which drew forth the hunger from her deeper self. She stared at his fingers until he removed them, but did not meet his eyes. She dared not, for she would have been lost again.

He let her go, and she was both happy and sad that he was reconciled to her decision not to marry him. She could talk to him quite normally now without even blushing, but always there was that tug of desire in her. What she suffered did not matter, she thought as she strode back to the house. The important thing was to convince Evan to turn his love elsewhere, to be no more than the friend she had been today.

Chapter Eight

On Saturday the carriage conveyed the ladies in their muslins and shawls. The men chose to ride. Wendover was not a small house by any means, but certainly did not run to the size of Meremont. It was better kept, Evan decided, regarding the neatly planted flower borders and clipped hedges surrounding the building of beige sandstone. Perhaps it was too well kept. It had not that careless grandeur of Meremont that would have led one to excuse the untidy lawn or an undusted windowsill.

Sylvia met them in the hall and immediately conducted them through the house to the backyard, where her cousin James was watching the laying of a cloth on the luncheon table and shouting something to Sylvia's very deaf Aunt Tess, who was sitting nearby in a chair. James lounged toward them to be introduced and shook hands with the reserve, Evan decided, of a man who has been wounded somewhere in the torso.

"Which of you is Lady Mountjoy again?" James asked playfully. "None of you can be old enough."

Judith and Angel laughed at this sally and went off with him as Helen pursed her lips and hesitated at the back doorstep. Lady Sylvia took Lord Mountjoy, Terry and Ralph off to show them her orangery. Evan disclaimed any interest in it.

Judith looked at the blankets and gay coverlets they were expected to sit upon and sent an appealing glance toward

Evan. Suddenly it hit him: Helen could not possibly sit on the ground in her condition, or if she did, she could not get up again.

He picked up a wooden bench and moved it to the vicinity of the blankets and food table as gracefully as though he were pulling out a chair for a lady at dinner. Helen sent him a resentful look but sat down promptly. Evan wondered if Sylvia did not know about her pregnancy or was going to make her ask for a chair like the aged aunt. He was surprised at how much he disliked Sylvia for such a slight.

He sat beside Helen on the bench rather than kneeling on the coverlet, where he would have liked to be with Judith. It was really safer here, for Angel was also reclining on the blanket, as was Captain Farlay, in what looked to Evan like a brand-new uniform. Somehow Farlay made the act of lying fully clothed in public seem indecent. Perhaps it was his bulging thigh muscles or the casual way he leaned on his left elbow, Evan thought. He must have been hit on the right side. Why was that important? Evan suddenly realized he had been studying Farlay as though he were an opponent, an enemy in whom one sought a sign of weakness to take advantage of in any fight that might occur. But this was not a war, and he would have to stop thinking like a soldier.

What on earth was he if not a soldier? Evan realized with a mental start that he was a very jealous man. And he was not only jealous of Judith, whom he loved, but of each time Farlay drew a laugh from Angel, however childish, and of each slight offered to Helen. She had looked about the hall as they passed through the house and perhaps wondered why they were not good enough to be entertained inside.

Lady Sylvia came back, trailing Lord Mountjoy, Ralph and Terry, all discussing breeds of apples, Evan supposed. He rose momentarily, but once Sylvia had knelt on the blanket, he sat on the bench again with an air of protectiveness that confused Sylvia and Lord Mountjoy.

After reciting all the delicacies she was having prepared for them, including her homemade cheeses, Sylvia said, ''I was just going to show everyone my milch goats. Would you like to come?'' She directed the query at Evan.

"I think I'll stay here, thank you,'' he replied. "I did say I wasn't a farmer.''

Angel and Judith, who had seen the orangery before, dutifully trailed after the group to the goat shed, holding up their new dresses. Judith threw him a look of gratitude, but the gaze Helen turned on him was one of irritation.

"If you are sitting here merely to discompose me, you may go with the others.''

"Actually, I am sitting here because I am in the same state as you. I have a very creaky knee, and if I ever get down on that blanket I shall need help getting up again.''

Helen smothered a laugh. "So you are not sitting here just to keep me from looking singular?''

"Why no!'' he said in mock surprise. "I thought you were sitting here to keep me from looking singular.''

"You are very bad to be making game of me. I cannot like you. I shall never like you, no matter how charming you may be.''

"Can I not, at least, make a truce with you, so that we do not distress Father so much with our dark looks?''

"When have you ever cared about your father, running off to the army like that? You hurt him, Evan, you hurt him badly.''

The accusation came like a slap in the face, and it surprised Evan that Helen cared so much for his father.

"Then you never wrote to him,'' she continued, seeing she had made an impression on him. "I don't see how he could bring himself to forgive you, let alone make you his heir rather than Terry or...''

"Or Ralph or Thomas.''

"I can never be at peace with you.''

"But other than deserting my family and then coming back to cut up everyone's expectations, what have I done? Surely we can put aside our differences—''

"No! Because you have not given up the idea of marrying Judith.''

"Oh."

"And you are so extremely provoking. You don't even deny it."

"Not since you have rumbled my lay. What gave me away? I have kept clear of her not because of you, but because she is very good at keeping me at arm's length."

"Your eyes."

"I keep thinking perhaps she may relent, give up these religious convictions. People so often do, you know."

"Yes, I'm quite sure any people you know would do so, but not Judith. She will stand firm no matter how sad eyed you look."

He turned his sad eyes upon her.

"And so will I," she said with a resentful tilt to her chin.

He could see the resemblance between Helen and her two younger sisters when she was like this. Angel still had her baby fat about her face, but she might mature into the same subdued beauty as Judith—well, perhaps a shade less subdued. And Judith in ten years would resemble this vital, extraordinary woman, who looked much too young to handle a husband such as Lord Mountjoy, much too delicate altogether to have borne two strapping sons and to be carrying another child. He could see why his father loved her. No matter what happened Evan would not come between them, even if it meant leaving.

"What are you thinking?" Helen asked. "I never know."

"I was thinking we are at an impasse."

"Spoken like a soldier. What do you mean to do about it?"

"I don't know."

"You're not really going to America, are you?" she asked.

"I suppose that would solve everything for you."

"No, for Hiram would not get his canal."

"You want me to stay then?"

"I want you to build the canal and marry Angel."

"Not a chance. She is far too dangerous for me."

"As you said, she is just a child. Surely you can manage her."

"Pray never tell her so," he whispered, for the others were coming back. "That is what makes her so very dangerous."

Helen sent him a reproachful glance that prompted Lord Mountjoy to wonder if Evan had been toying with his wife.

"I think they are bringing luncheon out now," Lady Sylvia announced, settling herself on a comforter beside Angel and Judith and commanding Terry to bring her a plate. When it appeared that James would volunteer to do this for Judith, that young woman rose and said she would like to see the table for herself, so he had no choice but to serve Angel, who was looking pointedly at Evan and getting only the blankest of stares in return.

"Shall I bring you a plate, ma'am, since it seems to be the custom?" Evan asked Helen.

"I will get it myself," Helen vowed as he helped her up. Evan watched in amusement as Lord Mountjoy solicitously served his wife and escorted her back to the bench, claiming the seat beside her with a glare at his oldest son. Evan saw no place he would like to sit, since James was between Judith and Angel, so he got a plate of food and leaned against a tree to observe the party as he ate.

He regretted he didn't have Bose to talk to, for he could imagine what his batman's judgment of Lady Sylvia would be. He would say that she was everything Angel and Judith were not, insulting her without seeming to. Evan would agree with him.

Sylvia saw him watching her and smiled at him. Those merry blue eyes seemed to suggest an intimacy, a sharing that did not exist, should never exist if she were about to be engaged to his brother. One had to like her, it seemed, or pretend to like her. One had to be charming, as Terry was being. Evan could see how she could turn anyone's head. She had certainly captivated Angel, drawing her out of her pout about being ignored by complimenting her new outfit.

But Terry was not in love with Sylvia. He was merely doing his duty to the family as he saw it. He looked handsome, with his smoky eyes and long sideburns. Evan felt inordinately proud of his brother that day, to sacrifice himself for the good of the family.

A gurgle of laughter escaped Judith, and Evan transferred his gaze to the mustachioed Farlay, who was flashing his white smile at her. Evan felt a little queasy and thought it might be the cake. He put his plate down on the table and wondered what to do with himself. Angel came to his rescue as she got up and took his arm, saying he must see the baby goats.

"He's very handsome, isn't he?" she asked as a little goat nibbled Evan's fingertips.

"The handsomest goat I have ever seen, Angel."

"You pretend to be so dense. You are just like Judith. Of course I did not mean the goat."

"Who, then—Terry? I was just thinking that myself. I am very—"

She gurgled with laughter. "No, silly, Captain Farlay. I think Judith likes him."

"Who, the goat?"

"If you don't stop it this minute, I shall slap you, Evan."

"Then don't let your personal pronouns dangle so precipitously, my dear. Just say what you mean."

"Judith likes James Farlay and you're jealous."

"I wouldn't be much of a man if I wasn't jealous, but I promise you I do not intend to call him out over it."

"That seems very poor spirited of you. You are jealous, but you won't show it by more than a frown. How far would he have to go before you would call him out?"

"Pretty far. It's against the rules to be fighting duels. Both the winner and the loser could be court-martialed."

"Really? So your rank is more important to you than—"

"Certainly not, but I think you exaggerate the danger of Judith laughing at James Farlay's jokes. A soldier is bound to pick up a lot of amusing stories. Judith has a lively sense of humor in spite of you all. I see nothing wrong in her enjoying herself."

"Have you never told her any of your amusing stories?"

"Not more than one, and you remember how that went down. Also, she says she will never marry. That doesn't just apply to me, I take it?"

"No, she means it. Seems an absolute waste to me."

"Yes, try as I might I cannot see her as a nun."

"As a what?"

"As a nun, in a convent."

"What absurdity is this?"

"For some reason she has decided to convert and go into religious life. I suppose it is the kind of calling—"

Evan's musings were interrupted by Angel's peal of laughter.

"What is so funny? I think it's a damned waste, too."

"She's having you on," Angel gasped. "Judith has the drollest sense of humor. She has me going all the time. You couldn't possibly have fallen for that or you are not as smart as Terry. I promise you he would never have believed it."

"It wasn't she who told it to me, but Helen," Evan said with some heat. He was not at all used to being laughed at by Angel.

"Well, if it comes to that, who do you think Judith learned such joking from?" the girl asked, drawing her shawl up over her head and putting on a somber face. When she got to the point of pressing her hands together, Evan lunged after her with an oath. For the moment she was much faster than he was, but it did not make a good impression on anyone that he was caught chasing her back to the yard, with her screaming gleefully. They all glared at him, except Sylvia, who looked speculative, and her cousin, who grinned at him.

James rose and came over to him with a glass and an open bottle of wine. "Having a problem?"

"I must be getting old. Time was when I could have caught her and rubbed her face in the mud."

James chuckled as he poured Evan a glass. "Time was when you would have wanted to, but not anymore, I think. Not when her little face is so kissable."

"You think so? Don't try it. You will find yourself with no end of trouble. I would still rather rub her face in the mud."

"I guess I was forgetting. You are an engineer. You lead a grittier life than the rest of us."

"A more necessary one, perhaps," Evan said with a challenge, but took the glass from him, anyway.

James laughed, his eyes glittering with amusement. "Are you saying the cavalry is de trop?"

"You boys have your uses, when a feint is required." Evan looked at Judith.

"I don't know what you mean. I like Judith. She is a charming companion and not too dangerous to kiss, I think."

"I wish you would try. She has the most punishing right."

"Warning me off?"

"Not at all, since I have not been able to make the slightest impression on her. She is fair game, and a most desirable game, to be sure. But even living under the same roof, I cannot get inside her defenses. How will you, a stranger, manage to capture her interest?"

"That is the thing about the cavalry. We move fast," said James, strolling back to the table.

Evan wondered if he had taken the right tack with James. To have claimed Judith, when he had no real claim on her, he instinctively thought to be fatal. To back off and leave the field open might either cool James's ardor or get him the slap in the face he deserved. On reflection, there was no other way to handle the situation. That was what Evan usually concluded after a trying mission. Why did this capering about on a lawn seem so like warfare?

Lady Sylvia rose and came over to him. "I have scarcely had a word with you and I so wanted to get acquainted. Why don't you come with me to the house to order the tea tray?"

"You mean you haven't got a bellpull strung out here?"

"No, silly," she said, appropriating his arm as James chuckled slyly in the background. "I wanted everything to be rather informal. One does not get to know people while sitting primly in a drawing room. I find the open air much more conducive to conversation."

"Then why are you taking me inside?" he asked provokingly.

She spun to look at him as they got through the doorway. The scar below his lip crinkled as he grinned.

"Do be serious for a moment. I must speak to you about Terry."

"What about him?"

"Is he—is he drinking again?"

"Hadn't you better ring for the tea?"

"Yes, I had forgot." She led him into a small office inside the back door and pulled a bell rope. "Sit down," she said then. "I cannot talk to you while you are looming over me like that."

He sat on the windowsill, where he could be seen from the garden. "Lovely view," he said, as a maid appeared and Sylvia ordered the tea. "You can see nearly all of your property from here, can't you?" he asked.

"Yes," she said, feigning satisfaction. "Is he drinking heavily? Answer me."

"First you answer me. What do you mean by 'again'?"

"It happened last year about this time. You must know he broke up with Angel last summer."

"I expect that accounts for it then."

"You don't suppose he means to break up with me, do you?"

"Oh, no. Is that what you are worried about? It's because of me. My coming home alive threw everyone into a pelter, including my father. They don't know quite what to do with me, don't you see? I mean, I haven't even seen the place in ten years. It has them in a bit of a worry. But I expect things will settle down again when I leave."

"You are leaving then?"

"I am still a soldier, and my ribs are almost healed. I can't malinger here much longer. I'm sure Terry will be himself again as soon as I'm gone."

"Until you come back again."

"I've flouted death too long. My luck cannot hold forever."

"They say—they say it's because you're mad that you can't be killed, that you blunder into danger with no thought for your own safety, but someone watches out for you, some dark angel—"

"They must mean Bose. Truth to tell, I would not have survived so long without him. Here comes the tea. Shall we go out?"

"Yes, I suppose we must," Sylvia said in frustration.

Evan took his tea leaning against the tree again and was glad when Lord Mountjoy, nudged by his wife, said they must soon call for the horses. Judith was still laughing at James, but so were they all. Evan tried to concentrate on what James was saying, but he could not. He did not think he could trust James any more than he could Sylvia.

As they mounted up, Terry asked, "What did Sylvia want to talk to you about?"

"She was pumping me again. I told her I was still planning on leaving. I didn't know what else to say to her."

"We saw you in the window," Terry confirmed.

"After Angel, I'm becoming wary of being alone with any woman."

"I'm sure you had nothing to worry about from Sylvia."

"Yes, but being a soldier I am so very gun-shy now that I did not want to take any chances. She's very charming, but do you really like her, Terry?"

His brother stared at him and shrugged.

Lady Sylvia came around to the front with James to see them off. She was sure of Terry; that was a point in his favor. But what good was Terry now that Evan had come back, unless Evan didn't mean to stay? The title didn't come into it; she was already Lady Sylvia from her father. But she wanted to control Meremont. Terry would let her do that, but Evan she did not know about. He was crude, perhaps even stupid. He'd said he had no interest in farming. That was a point in his favor, if it were true. She really must discover how things were to be left when Lord Mountjoy died.

The second son was never as good a catch as the first, which Evan now was. That business over his elder brother she could ignore. If Evan had killed him to get the title, he had paid for it by being banished. It now looked like he had been forgiven, but perhaps he was only needed to build the canal.

How could Lord Mountjoy hope to keep such a project secret with Angel running tame at Wendover?

Evan might be sent packing after that. And what was the good of being his widow if he went off and got himself killed in another war?

She had best wait. It would not do, anyway, to leap so quickly from one man's arms to another's, especially as they were brothers. Then there was the grandmother's bequest. Sylvia knew Mrs. Pellham had been wealthy, but not how her estate had been left.

And that's where Angel came into it. Such children spilled family confidences as though they were idle gossip. Once Angel told her how things stood, Sylvia would know if she wanted Evan or Terry. If she gave Judith a passing thought, she dismissed her as a bluestocking and of no consequence. There wasn't a spark of competition in her. If Angel was meaning to have Evan, and with her sister's blessing, as it appeared, dear Angel might be in for a rude awakening.

Not yet, though. Sylvia must get to know the Mountjoy affairs better before she made her move. All this passed through her mind as she smiled pleasantly and waved to the carriage.

"Did the day live up to your expectations, dear cousin?" James asked in his familiar way.

"I haven't decided. They are an odd bunch, the Mountjoys."

"How so?"

"Evan is not at all as you described him. He seems awkward, clumsy, especially around me."

"Awed by your beauty, no doubt. He didn't seem overly shy of Angel. He's very much as I remember him, but you know such crude behavior is not particularly remarked on the battlefield. Recollect I have never seen him in female company before."

"What did you think of Judith?"

"A mere country girl. Less wile and guile than her young sister, who would provide a pleasant romp, I think, but not Judith. She is amusing enough to talk to, but there is no flirtatiousness there."

"That would leave you out."

"I could charm her if I wanted to."

"And Angel?"

He snapped his fingers.

She considered for a long moment. "Angel, I think, for the time being. Can you manage that?"

"That isn't even challenging. You are going to marry me in the end, aren't you, not this Terry?"

"Isn't that what we've planned?"

They had surveyed a line the last distance to the edge of the river and come out pretty much as Evan had predicted, smack in the middle of Lady Sylvia's ground. It was a straight line of sight from the gap down the middle of a gradually sloping watershed.

"Are we done for today?" Ralph rode up to ask. "Terry wants to know if he can come in now."

"If he's finished measuring that last stretch, which it looks like he has."

"I'll tell him," said Ralph, as he collected Terry's horse and led it down to the riverbank for him.

Evan heard hoofbeats and turned in the hope that Judith had ridden out to meet them, as she sometimes did. It was Lady Sylvia and James. He forced himself to smile, cursing in his mind at the mischance that led them this way at this particular moment.

"So this is your road?" she asked provocatively. "Why does it lead to the river?"

"That's where the dock goes," Evan said.

"You do know that you have gone straight through Lady Sylvia's land?" James declared indignantly.

"What?" Evan asked, achieving a blank look that would have fooled anyone but his father.

"My land begins at those scrub trees and continues to that cottage above." She pointed with her riding crop and smiled.

"No! Really? How could I have made such a mistake?"

Terry and Ralph rode up, none too pleased.

"Hello, Sylvia," Terry said guardedly.

"Terry," Evan said, staring up at him, then dropping his head in embarrassment. "I don't know exactly how to tell you this, but I must have been off a degree or two from the start."

"A degree or two?" Terry asked. "Well, what's that, when all things are considered?"

Ralph winced or gave a good imitation of it.

"You've planted your stakes right through Lady Sylvia's land." James pointed with his whip.

"You don't say!" Terry gasped.

"Sorry, Terry, we shall have to do it all over again."

"Evan, how could you have been so stupid," Terry chided. "Father is going to be very displeased."

"I know. I can't seem to do anything right. I suppose I should not have started the survey until I was quite sober."

"But really, can we be off by that much?" Terry seemingly grasped at straws.

"A degree or two would change the whole course of the road." Ralph was warming to the ruse. "We have no choice but to start over."

"I don't suppose you would like to sell us a right-of-way, Sylvia," Terry suggested. "You could make use of the road."

"I'll consider it," she said playfully, "if Evan will ride home with me. James will show you where the property lines run."

"I think perhaps I had better go with James then," Evan said penitently.

"Are you afraid to talk to me?"

"What? No, but I have my gear to gather up."

"James will help them."

Evan rolled up his maps and handed them to Ralph. He mounted Taurus as though he were riding to slaughter, then mumbled figures to himself for the first mile, putting Sylvia in a temper.

"Would you attend to me?"

"Pardon. I was trying to figure out how I was going to explain this to Father. You see, he gave me another chance and I have failed him again. I don't know what he will say."

"Perhaps it's not past mending."

"You mean you would consider selling a right-of-way? I should be eternally grateful, and I promise we would not spoil your trees much."

"Damn my trees! I won't sell a right-of-way. I might consider a trade for shares in the canal."

"In the what?"

"The canal. They have been using you to survey a canal."

"Well, I thought—I thought it was stupid place to put a road."

"You do need looking after. He plans to build a canal down that valley."

"Wait a minute. A canal makes even less sense than a road and would be enormously costly. Where's the money to come from?"

"I'm sure Lord Mountjoy has a plan. He must mean to sell shares in the canal, and I want some."

"Is that how these things are done?"

"Well, of course it is. Don't you know the first thing about business?"

"I never had to deal with it. In the army they just tell you to put a road there and give you the men to do it with. It doesn't really matter how much it costs. It only matters how long it takes."

"That would be your view of it. Wake up, Evan. They have tricked you. They were using you to do the survey. Once they don't need you anymore..."

"Father wouldn't do that...again," Evan said with the most hurt look he could muster.

"Oh wouldn't he? Listen to me, Evan. I can be your friend, the only friend you have around here."

"But Terry—"

"Is as grasping as the rest of the Mountjoys."

The shock on Evan's face was genuine, but it was there for a different reason than she supposed. If she could see through Terry, she was sharper than he had thought.

"Evan, don't look at me like that. I know why Terry has been playing up to me. He wants to marry me for that land."

"No! I don't believe it. He wouldn't do something like that."

"Why not? He means to cut you out, too. Mark my words."

They had arrived at her lane by this time, and Evan was looking genuinely dejected, merely walking Taurus now.

"Come inside with me," she commanded.

"I can't. I have to get home before Terry and explain to Father what I've done. Maybe it's not too late."

"It won't do any good. Terry has had his ear all these years. Do you think he will listen to you now? When they throw you out, come to me. I can help you."

Evan looked doubtfully over his shoulder as he rode off.

What the devil were they to do now? He hadn't thought she would swallow that road story. The amazing part was that she believed a surveyor could be duped. Oh, well, so long as she considered him an outsider in his own family, there was a chance she would let him know what she was planning. First he had to know, once and for all, what this canal was for and where it was going.

* * *

He strode into the library and into a meeting oddly like a council of war. He pulled up abruptly at the serious expressions on the faces of his father, Judith, Terry and Ralph. He grinned sheepishly, closed the door and ambled in.

"Well, what the devil happened?" Lord Mountjoy demanded.

"Nothing much, except that she's convinced I'm a gullible dolt."

"That probably required little artifice," Lord Mountjoy snapped, causing Judith to giggle.

Evan smiled. "She thinks you all have duped me into surveying a road where you really mean to dig a canal, and that then you will set me adrift again."

"So she does know about the canal," Lord Mountjoy said.

"Really, how could she think you would not know the difference between a road and a canal?" Judith asked.

"Well, there is also my drinking problem...."

"He was good, Judith," Terry said. "You would not believe how doltish he can act."

"Yes, I would," she countered.

"Thank you very much, brother." Evan seated himself.

"What is the upshot of it?" demanded Lord Mountjoy.

"She wants shares in the canal."

"Never!" He thumped the table for emphasis.

"I'm dumbfounded," Evan said, matching his expression to the words and drawing a chuckle from Ralph. "You are willing to offer her your son."

"It's not the same thing at all. If Terry marries her, he will own her property. She won't have anything to say about Meremont."

"That's not what she has in mind."

"Evan's correct," said Judith. "Lady Sylvia would never agree to a marriage settlement to her disadvantage. Women have some rights now, you know, especially if they are in control of their own assets."

"Whose side are you on?" Ralph asked with a grin.

"Doesn't it seem to anyone else as though we have been trying to victimize Lady Sylvia?" Evan asked uncertainly.

"She started it by buying up that land," Terry claimed. "Now she thinks if she marries me she will wind up with Meremont. Well, she is wrong, for now you are thrown into it."

"Ah, but she doesn't know that. As far as she is concerned I am an ignorant soldier, kept here as long as it is convenient to you. She thinks I am being victimized, used by my own family."

"Such nonsense!" Lord Mountjoy blustered. "Why ever would she think you are not a member in good standing of this family?"

Evan pulled a blank look, and Judith laughed at him. "I suspect it is because that is what Evan has led her to believe. If only we could think of a way to use that against her."

"I am, so to speak, *in her confidence*," Evan drawled, scrutinizing his fingernails. "She certainly divulged things to me that she would never tell any of you. I might almost fancy myself a spy in her camp if I had the courage to pull off such a role."

"Such a role, as you call it, would not take courage, but effrontery, of which you have more than enough," Judith assured him.

"I have not. She did, in fact, invite me in when I rode home with her, but I thought it safest not to take her up on the offer."

"Why ever not?" demanded his father. "If she thinks to prey on you, we might find out something useful to us."

"Father, please! Consider Terry's feelings in the matter."

"What feelings?" Terry demanded.

"The quite natural feelings of a man almost affianced to a woman. To have his own brother—"

"You dope. I haven't a single particle of feeling for Sylvia. It would have been a marriage of convenience only."

"I begin to think it would have been a marriage of inconvenience," Ralph interjected, "if she is as mercenary as . . . as—"

"As we are?" Evan supplied.

"Well, yes," Ralph agreed. "Now that you mention it, does it seem quite fair to her?"

"If it will ease your conscience," Evan said, "I'm pretty sure Sylvia hasn't a particle of feeling for Terry, or anyone else."

"We are agreed then," Judith concluded.

"What?" they all asked.

"Evan is to romance Sylvia and see what he can get out of her, and also keep her busy until our plans are finalized."

"Your mind leaps ahead of mine," Evan said. "I can see no end of problems. How am I to keep Sylvia busy if I am to get any work done?"

"I can do much of it for you," Ralph volunteered, "if we go over it at night. It's not as though it is all that complicated."

"Thank you very much," Evan replied, shaking his head.

"Evan, it would be useful," Lord Mountjoy suggested.

"You needn't have any qualms on my account," Terry assured him, "and truth to tell, if one of us has eventually to be sacrificed to Sylvia, I'd as soon it was you."

"What?"

"No one is being sacrificed," Lord Mountjoy insisted. "Haven't we just agreed a marriage probably won't get us the land? Evan, you must convince her to sell you a right-of-way."

"I'm pretty sure the price would be too high. Why don't we take the easy course, give her the shares she wants?"

"If I know Lady Sylvia, she wouldn't settle for anything less than a controlling interest," Judith stated. "If she ever got control of the canal, she would control everything."

"Have you thought that perhaps we need her?" Ralph asked.

"Need her?" Judith demanded.

"By what calculations we have made so far, and this is a guess," Ralph said, "the canal could cost upward of ten thousand pounds."

"It's true, but if all goes well, we may do it for less," Evan replied.

"Well, of course we will have to sell shares," his father conceded. "I was hoping that Evan would buy most of them."

"With what?"

"Your grandmother's fortune, of course."

Evan started laughing that hysterical laugh of his. "You can't be serious. She never left me that kind of money."

"Well, no, it is mostly in the funds," his father said. "I shouldn't think the income would run to more than thirty-five a year."

"Thirty-five pounds?"

"Thirty-five hundred," Judith retorted, and was well satisfied with the stunned look her news produced. "I suppose you could sell some stock if we got desperate, but if the canal does take two or three years, as you say, we might just be able to swing it without dipping into your capital."

"So you really do need me! Now it all makes sense." He laughed a little dryly.

"Evan," his father said, "that isn't the only reason I wanted you back."

"Yes, I was forgetting. I am an engineer who will work for free."

"You are my son. You belong here. That is the only reason that matters. If you don't believe it, you may take your inheritance and leave. You were always free to do that."

Evan looked from one to the other of them, not enjoying their hanging on his decision. In the army he had always taken his direction from above. He knew how to do things, but he needed someone to tell him what to do. He needed his father.

"I don't want to leave," he said quietly.

"That's settled then," Lord Mountjoy said with relief. "We have only to decide what to do about Sylvia. Can we begin work on the east end of the canal?"

"Yes, of course. Clearing the ground, anyway, if Bose can recruit work crews around here."

"Let's do that then. Keep her wondering, anyway."

"I'm not so sure Sylvia wasn't right about you," Evan said with a return of his ingenuous smile.

"What did she say about us?"

"That you are using me. You haven't, after all, told me what this whole canal project is in aid of."

"Well, I don't know, either," Ralph said.

"Our plans are not final yet," Lord Mountjoy said gravely. "All could still come to naught if anyone finds out."

"And being the oaf that I am, I might blurt it out to Sylvia. I see your point. I agree then. Don't tell me. I suppose spies don't know everything."

"The more I think of it," Judith demurred, "the more I begin to realize it may not be wise to foist Evan on Sylvia. He really is no match for her."

"Now see here!" Evan protested.

"When you look at how embarrassed he gets with only his family roasting him, I don't see how he can keep his composure in such a role. We had better forget—"

"You can trust that to me, at least," Evan claimed as he rose. "I don't want to hear any more about it. And don't tell Angel anything you're not willing to tell me. She is much too close to Sylvia to suit me. God, look at the time, and I am still covered with mud. I must change for dinner."

He rose and left, followed by Ralph, who also bore the signs of the day's activities.

"I think you have done the trick, Judith," Terry said, "by telling Evan he would be no good at it."

"Yes," Lord Mountjoy agreed. "He fell for that, hook and line. My compliments, my dear."

"Thank you, gentlemen. I just hope we are not squandering Evan's fortune to no purpose. Everything could still come to naught."

"We have only to fight a delaying action until the purchase of the factory lands is complete," Lord Mountjoy said. "So long as Sylvia does not find out about that, we can worry about her riverfront later."

"I wish I had your confidence," Terry said. "It seems we only increase our risk, to own one end and not the other."

"Would it—would it bother you, Judith, if Evan did end by marrying Sylvia?" Lord Mountjoy asked.

"No, why should it?" she asked blankly, as she rolled up the map. "I suppose he must marry someone."

"You have nothing to fear from Sylvia," Lord Mountjoy answered.

"She does want this house. Haven't you seen how she looks at it, as though she is ripping down draperies and changing the wallpaper in her mind?"

"Yes, yes, I know, but it is always wise to know your enemy, my dear. Remember, even if she were to marry Evan she would live in the dower house, not here."

Judith stared into space. She had been decorating the dower house with particular care, decorating it, she now realized, to her own taste. What had she been playing at?

"Helen? What is it, dear?" Lord Mountjoy asked as the door opened.

"It is nearly the dinner hour," Lady Mountjoy replied.

"Good Lord, there's no time to change. We will have to sit down as we are."

Evan and Ralph returned, looking superior at having cleaned up when no one else had. It was difficult for the conspirators to sit through an evening of sewing and cards without talking about the canal when it was uppermost in everyone's mind. Angel read to them until she tired of it. Then they took turns until it was time for bed. Even Terry refrained from drinking and took a turn at the ritual.

"Oh, Helen," Lord Mountjoy said, almost as an after-thought. "I wish you would invite Lady Sylvia and her cousin for dinner soon."

"You do?"

"Yes, we must reciprocate for the delightful meal she gave us."

"It was not delightful."

"I know that, but I hope no one in this family is ungracious enough to say so."

"I thought it was fun," Angel said defensively.

"That's because your knees don't creak when you try to sit on the ground," Evan informed her.

"Oh, I hadn't thought of that. Captain Farlay didn't seem to be having any problem."

"He hasn't done anything except lounge around camp and take an occasional ride across the country, which he would be doing anyway if he had been home."

Angel glared at him. "I think that is very unhandsome of you, Evan, when he has been at pains to tell us how brave you were."

"But it's tradition for soldiers to abuse each other. I am puzzled as to why Farlay would bother to say anything good about me. Before Saturday I had not met him above twice."

"It's because he's a gentleman," Angel said. "He could hardly tell me you were a coward, even if that were the case."

"Well, that's found me out," Evan said with a laugh. "I'm not a gentleman, and probably a coward into the bargain."

"I wish you would not joke about such things," Angel argued passionately. "People might take you seriously."

"Angel is right," Lord Mountjoy said gravely. "You treat the whole war far too lightly, almost as though it made no impression on you at all."

"I wish it had not."

"Regardless of what you say inside the family, I expect you to conduct yourself with more prudence in the presence of company."

"You mean try to act normal?" Evan taunted.

"If that's possible!" Lord Mountjoy said with a demolishing glare. "Now, Helen dear, you will invite them, won't you?"

"Of course, I will, including Sylvia's Aunt Tess. I know my duty. But I don't like it, I tell you. I don't like it at all."

With that Helen gathered up her sewing and left them. Angel followed her out, looking superior at having Lord Mountjoy confirm her views.

"I don't like it much myself," Evan said. "God, I have taken to agreeing with Helen. What is happening to me?"

"You are becoming one of us," Judith vowed sanctimoniously.

Evan shot her a shrewd glance, but could not get her to blush even by staring at her breasts. And that was dangerous, for he could feel himself hardening merely at the thought of kissing her.

"I trust," said Terry ponderously, "that you will disgrace yourself during this little dinner enough to stay in Lady Sylvia's confidence."

"What? Oh, I feel sure I shall be presented with no end of opportunities to do so," Evan agreed, crossing his legs and cuffing Ralph, who was laughing at him.

"Tell us, sir, what you are planning," Judith asked, leaning forward with interest.

"I think not," Lord Mountjoy said.

"But I want to enjoy the anticipation of it," Judith said with a gleam in her eyes.

"You can anticipate all you want, Judith dear. You simply have to wait until the appointed hour like everyone else."

Chapter Nine

Evan found himself riding into Bristol at his father's insistence, in the carriage with Lord Mountjoy, Judith and Angel, who could not pass up the chance to go shopping.

It would have been a tiresome day, except for sitting across from Judith and watching her breasts bounce. Once Evan noticed this, he could not keep his eyes off of her. She tumbled to what he was thinking and, rather than being embarrassed, merely squirmed in her seat and pulled her shawl about her.

"Are you cold, my dear?" Lord Mountjoy asked.

"No, I am fine. Evan seems to be a bit hot," she said, directing Lord Mountjoy's attention to the sweat beading his son's brow.

"It's that uniform. You order yourself some suits today. You aren't a soldier anymore."

"Some new boots would not come amiss, either," Judith noted.

"That's only because I have been trod on so much lately."

Judith smiled victoriously. She was pleased to know that she could arouse him, but the ripple of desire in her stomach that had answered his look was somewhat disquieting. She would have thought she was now above such passions, since she had kept Evan at bay for some weeks now. But she did enjoy the anticipation of what he might try next. Even though there was no future for them, she did enjoy fencing with him in this private way. And if she could bring him to his knees, so to speak, in the presence of others, knowing he could give no excuse for his inattention or blunders, she enjoyed that as well.

Men were so stupid. They did not enjoy dalliance at all, only the end product. Whereas women thought only of seduction, not of the result. How could they ever both be satisfied? Her rational mind told her she played a dangerous game. The compassionate side of her counseled that she was being cruel, but she suffered, too. It was Evan's fault that he was so tempting.

Still, an intelligent woman should have more control over herself, should not give out little sighs in the middle of sewing a seam just because she had thought of him. She could not even keep her mind on the shopping. All she could think of was whether Evan would like this particular shade of blue.

Evan was having an equally hard time keeping his mind on what his father and his grandmother's lawyers were saying. He listened to the legal droning, resisting with difficulty the urge to let his mind wander to Judith. He signed the necessary documents and was given his quarter-day money, feeling rather odd about taking it.

As they descended to the street, he said, "May I ask you a very prying and personal question, Father?"

"Put that way, I'm not sure I want to hear it."

"Could you make use of this money for your household, as I have no particular need of it?"

"Whatever for? Is anything amiss?"

"Only that you seem so short of help."

"Oh. When Helen came, she weeded out all the dishonest servants, and we find we go on very well without so many."

"Dishonest?"

"Cook, especially, was stealing me blind. That's why I was looking for a housekeeper."

"And found a family."

"Think what an economy it was to marry Helen rather than hire her. If Helen knows one thing, it is how to keep house."

"I think she also knows how much the canal means to you and is doing everything in her power to save you money."

"Shall I tell her to stop?"

"No, that would only offend her and make her feel small, as though she isn't helping, when actually I imagine she has saved you a considerable sum."

"What then?"

"A present, I think, and a promise that things will be better some day. Sacrifice can become bitter medicine if it is not acknowledged."

"For a rough soldier you have got a thought or two in your head. You pick out something nice for her. Take Angel with you. Judith must come with me for a few hours."

"Where are they off to?" Angel asked.

"I've no idea, but we are to meet here at four o'clock. Can you advise me on a tailor?"

"I know where Terry goes."

"And then a present for Helen."

"Only Helen?"

"You may pick out something for yourself, so long as you get Judith the same."

They made several forays about the town, to return with packages for the coachman to guard. Most of the clothes Evan ordered for himself would not be ready for a week, so all the packages accumulated today were frivolous.

When Judith and Lord Mountjoy returned to the carriage, Angel was eating a bag of peppermints and Evan was lounging inside, almost dozing.

"You look worn to the bone," his father said.

Judith turned a critical eye on Evan. "I should think you would be able to keep up with one small girl."

"I'm old, Judith. There's no getting around it. I'm old."

"Poor baby."

* * *

Evan slipped off from the havoc in the hall to restore himself with a brandy in the library. He noticed some of the books that were scattered about. There were three on porcelain, and one new one on steam engines. He sat down and leafed through one of the porcelain books and realized there was a lot more to it than he'd ever thought. The book on steam engines was more to his taste. They were mostly used for mining work.

His father entered, in an affable mood. "You did well. I haven't had such a smile from Helen in weeks."

"Angel gets all the credit. She picked everything."

"So are you going to marry her?"

Evan choked on his brandy. "No, I'm not!"

"Then I take exception to you leading her on like this."

"Leading her—if anyone is being led, it is me." Evan stood up. "I feel the trap yawning at my feet a dozen times a day. I have no intention of marrying Angel."

"But all the presents. Why do you do it?"

"Because I think she hasn't always had a lot of presents. And I never had a sister to spoil. It's rather nice."

"If you think of Angel that way, you have two sisters now."

"I can never think of Judith in that way. I buy her whatever I buy Angel. It just doesn't send her into raptures. It is gratifying to know that her affection can't be bought, that it must be earned."

"Her affection you may earn, as you say, one day. I warn you not to aspire to anything higher." Lord Mountjoy poured himself brandy.

Evan looked at him and saw that he meant it. "Why not?" he asked with a frown.

"It is the only thing you could do that would make me send you away."

Evan turned to stare out the window and finally understood. Judith and his father. He felt as though he had been shot through, that there was a gaping hole in him that could never be healed.

* * *

He had no stomach for dinner that night, would far rather have kept to his room, until he realized that what cut him the most was not that his father might be having another affair; he was used to that. It was that there still was no stability. No matter how much they had shared in the past weeks, he could still be sent away like an unruly boy being shoveled off to school to get rid of him. And once he analyzed his reaction, he saw that it was that of a boy, afraid to enrage his father and prepared to step aside.

How could he have considered it? He loved Judith even if she did not love him, or love him solely. That was why she was keeping her distance. She was trying to prevent herself from falling in love with him. What a dilemma that would place her in! Poor Judith. That's what she'd meant when she'd said he was too late.

It was Judith who had advised him to grow up, and he was determined not to be cowed. He would make a push to win her in spite of his father. He could not offer her Meremont, not if he had to defy his father to marry her, but she could have anything Gram's fortune could buy. And he could offer her his love. It was brand-new, having never been used before.

So he sat through the meal, trying not to stare at Judith too much, and responding to conversation as it came to him. Angel was once again enumerating all the things she had got that day, as though merely thinking about them gave her pleasure. Evan smiled at her childishness, as did Helen.

"I chose the pink ribbons because they match my lips, but Judith got the blue ribbons to go with her eyes. Do you like the pink ones or the blue ones, Evan?" Angel teased.

"Very much," he said absently, grateful for an excuse to really look at Judith. "But you know me. I would be just as happy if Judith wore nothing."

Helen and Angel gasped, but Ralph and Terry started laughing, and Judith looked outraged.

"That is the outside of enough!" Lord Mountjoy asserted.

"What did I say?" Evan asked in some confusion, and it took a full minute before he groaned and put his hand over his eyes. Unfortunately, this did nothing to quell the hilarity.

"I'm sorry. That came out badly."

"Helen, I begin to share your qualms about this dinner Saturday unless we can shut this lout up in the basement," his father said.

"I warned you it would be a disaster," Helen declared.

One would not have thought a dinner planned by three women with different aims would have much chance of success, but Angel's desire to impress Sylvia did not conflict with Helen's intention of keeping Sylvia from finding any fault with the meal. And Judith's distracted advice about the menu was not even attended to. She spent part of her time speculating on what Lady Sylvia was planning and part on what Lord Mountjoy had up his sleeve.

But there was a vast deal of her attention taken up by those soulful brown eyes that undressed her at every opportunity. She found herself wanting Evan more now rather than less. What if she had been wrong? Was it possible for her to live in the dower house without feeling that she had abandoned her son? She shuddered at the temptation.

It was too late, she told herself. She had made her intentions plain to everyone, including Evan. He had already given up trying to seduce her. Now she longed for the warmth of his hand on her bare skin. She knew she went out of her way to be near him on the off chance he might touch her. Whenever she was near him she felt a thrilling contraction in her stomach that almost made her gasp. If just thinking about Evan turned her into a hotbed of desire, she was afraid to consider what another actual encounter would be like.

She also spent a good deal of time thinking about Evan and Sylvia. He had seemed adamantly against the woman, but if it was the only way to achieve their goal, would he marry Sylvia to please his father? She decided that if Evan

was fool enough to be trapped into marriage with Sylvia, so
be it. Sylvia would never rule the roost so long as Lord
Mountjoy was alive. After that, of course, anything could
happen.

What a gloomy view. They had better try to pry a right-
of-way out of her by some other means.

Even though Helen acquiesced to her husband's desire to
put Sylvia next to Evan, she perversely seated Angel on his
other side. Evan sent frequent persecuted looks across the
table to Judith, making it difficult for her to eat without
choking. James, from his seat beside Judith, was not obliv-
ious to Evan's grimacing, but put it down to ill manners.
The cavalryman used every opportunity to exchange confi-
dential smiles with Angel. In due course the ladies rose and
retired to refresh themselves, while the gentlemen lingered
over the port. Terry was drinking judiciously; Evan was
pretending to overimbibe. Having to fend off both Sylvia
and Angel made him so jumpy he did seem like an outsider
at Meremont.

James excused himself to smoke one of his cigars in the
garden. He discovered Angel and Sylvia walking there, and
adroitly made off with Angel to view the flowers. When the
men were ready to retire to the long drawing room, Evan
went to see what had become of James. Sylvia pounced on
him like a cat on a mouse.

"Well?" she demanded.

"Well, what?"

"What have you found out about the shares?"

"Father has finally admitted he means to sell shares in a
canal. If I will build it, I will have some, but only if I get a
right-of-way across your land. I don't suppose you want to
sell me one? It would please Father very much."

"It is not my aim to please your father, and it should not
be yours, either. They are using you. They cannot build the
canal without you. Big of them to give you some shares.
Find out how many. What about Meremont?"

"What about it?"

"Who will get it?"

"I have no idea."

"Is it entailed?"

"No, I don't think so."

"Evan! It's most important that you make sure how things will be left. What are you to get when your father dies?"

"I can't see that it matters. He might very well change his mind later. I am sure to do something to upset him. There's no point in even thinking about that. I may as well leave when my time is up." Since this was very much how he really was feeling this night, his speech had the ring of truth to it.

"Don't be a fool, Evan. All is not lost yet. What is it for?"

"What?"

"The canal, silly."

"Just to carry the crops and fleeces downriver. Oh, and he did speak about opening up that old quarry again. I don't know much about such things. Does it strike you my father might have slipped a cog?"

"Slipped a what?"

"Gone off a bit daffy in his old age?"

"I hadn't even thought of that."

"I think about it every day. What if I dig this stupid canal only to have it become a laughingstock? Where is James, anyway? They will be waiting to play cards in the drawing room. I should have warned you about that. Do you play whist?"

"Yes, of course. We had better go in, then."

Evan's gawking at the hunting prints and polished furniture was enough to convince Sylvia that the long drawing room was infrequently used. Evan led Sylvia to the card tables. Helen and Sylvia's aunt declared themselves content to sew by the fire. So they were to be Evan and Sylvia against James and Angel at one table and Judith and Lord Mountjoy against Terry and Ralph at the other. They planned to switch pairs midway through the evening.

Lord Mountjoy sat facing the other table so that he could see almost everyone's face. Evan was content so long as he could see Judith. The play was bantering and jovial in the way games can be, until James brought up the matter of the war.

"It confounds me how you survived Badajoz. We were told the French shot all the engineers down to a man."

"They did," said Evan, slapping down a discard during the resulting silence. Sylvia shot James a speaking look.

"So you were shot?" Angel asked, filling the conversational gap.

"Yes, but not seriously. It was that press of bodies falling on top of me that saved me at first, then nearly suffocated me."

"Why were you in on the attack?" demanded Lord Mountjoy from the other table. "As an engineer your job should have been finished by the time they stormed the walls."

"It was so dark you couldn't see your hand in front of your face, and we were trying for a bit of surprise. We engineers were the only ones who knew where to place the scaling ladders."

"You shouldn't have had to go up the ladder first," said Sylvia.

"Actually, it was down. We had ladders down into the trench, which the French had filled with all manner of broken stuff. Then it was move the ladders and crawl up them again to try to get past their chevaux-de-frise—nasty logs spiked with broken sabers."

Sylvia's eyes were large and luminous as she regarded Evan.

"You didn't go there, surely?" Angel asked with parted lips.

"No. Bose managed to find me during the night and bandage me up."

"But you were in the city," James insisted. "Someone told me you were. He said he would know your wild laugh anywhere."

Evan frowned at James. "There was such a howl coming from inside the city even at dawn that I thought the battle must still be raging—your deal," he said, leaning back and taking a long drink of wine.

"And was it?" Angel asked.

Evan saw Judith looking anxiously at him, and he gave a faint smile. "It was our own men carrying on like a pack of mad dogs. I never saw such a rabble in my life. It fair gave me the shivers." He drained his glass.

"You were afraid?" Sylvia asked in disbelief.

"Yes, and with good reason."

James waited for Evan to continue, and when he did not, explained, "Several officers were shot by their own men, when they tried to enforce discipline."

"They should have obeyed you," Lord Mountjoy vowed.

Evan stared at him. "They were not, properly speaking, my men, but infantry given me to get the job done. With the walls breached, they took their rights as they saw them, to plunder and rape."

"Didn't you try to stop them?" Angel demanded.

"I did try," Evan said, rubbing the scar below his lip.

"Did a Spanish wench give you that for your pains?" James asked.

"No, I caught two fellows raping a nun and interfered." Evan ignored the hiss of shock from the women. After all, he was supposed to be disgracing himself. "It was one of our men, but as he was dressed in a Spanish grandee's clothes, I could not tell what unit he was from."

"What did you do then?" Angel asked, leaning forward with no regard to exposing her cards.

"I can't exactly remember. I rather think Bose knocked me out, although he has never admitted it. When I woke up, he was bandaging me up again and dribbling some of the best wine I had ever tasted down my throat, but mostly all over my uniform."

"That's when you started laughing," his father commented.

"Yes, for we had been drinking sugar of lead, and here he was wasting this stuff. Speaking of wine, this isn't bad, either. Is there any more?" Evan asked, lounging toward the sideboard.

Sylvia stared after him, entranced, her lips parted. Lord Mountjoy studied her as she watched his son. If ever a woman wanted a man, Sylvia wanted Evan. He cleared his throat. "The Spanish were our allies at that time. What did Wellington have to say to all this?" he demanded.

"That if he had put the entire French garrison at Ciudad Rodrigo to the sword three months earlier he might have saved five thousand English lives at Badajoz." Evan returned to the table. "Hindsight is never much use—I've forgotten what was led."

"You're drinking too much," his father said, rising from his table at the entrance of the tea tray. Their rubbers had ended, with Lord Mountjoy and Judith the clear victors. Evan's table played out the rest of the hand before Sylvia and Evan conceded defeat to James and Angel. It had been difficult for Evan to lose with such a skillful player as Sylvia for partner, but she had been too preoccupied with James's probes and Evan's offhand answers to pay much attention to his clumsiness over the cards. Evan had the feeling that war was not what James was supposed to be talking about—that he was acting without orders, so to speak. Evan also had the uncomfortable notion that Sylvia had found out something about him in spite of his low-key answers. He would give much to know what it was. For effect, he refused tea and let on that he was half-drunk.

"You are drinking too much," his father repeated urgently, in an undertone that everyone could hear.

"I shall be sober by tomorrow. Wouldn't want to make another mistake," Evan mumbled under his breath, as he seated Sylvia at Lord Mountjoy's table.

Sylvia looked sharply at James.

"Ah, yes, are you still surveying that . . . road?" James asked. "What do you mean to do with it, anyway?"

"Oh, we have given up on the road," Lord Mountjoy said blithely.

Evan was startled enough to drop the cards and had to gather them up from the floor and table and start his deal over.

"You give up too easily, my lord," Lady Sylvia said indulgently. "I did not absolutely refuse to sell you a right-of-way across my lands."

"Oh, really, my dear?" Lord Mountjoy said, sorting his cards. "I rather thought you had."

"You've never even made me an offer."

"I could offer what I paid for the land around it. Of course, it's no good for farming, being so close to the river."

"I might consider five thousand an acre."

"Hah, hah, such a wit. You are most charming when you are teasing, my child." He patted her hand indulgently, and she withdrew it.

"I assure you I am not—"

"Spades!" Lord Mountjoy announced.

Evan jumped. He was finding it difficult to follow the play and the conversation.

"As I said, I have a new plan," Lord Mountjoy said proudly.

Sylvia looked at Evan, who shrugged and grimaced to indicate he had no idea what was going on.

"What plan?" she was forced to ask.

"Wouldn't you like to know, my dear?" Lord Mountjoy said, as though to a child.

Sylvia quietly steamed.

"Oh, well, may as well let the cat out of the bag. You will see it sooner or later. I've decided against the road."

Evan hesitated over his discard.

"I'm going to have a steam railway instead," he declared, as though he were a child relating what new toy he was going to be treated to.

Evan stared at him, then made a quick audit of the room. Terry's eyes were fairly bulging and Judith was gaping.

"Forgive me, Father," Evan said slowly, "but did you say a steam railway?"

"Yes, you know, one of those steam engines that run on rails. I saw one demonstrated. It is just the thing for us and quite economical since we have our own wood. I have been assured it will be cheaper. No horses to maintain, you see. What could I have been thinking of? No, the steam railway has it all over the road."

"But I don't know anything about steam engines or railways."

"You won't have anything to do with it. You aren't even needed."

Evan fell silent and threw away the wrong card.

"Aha, you didn't remember that spades were led."

The evening fizzled after that. Sylvia was so deflated she did not even offer to dicker with Lord Mountjoy over the land. She and James escaped as soon as was possible.

"What an extraordinary evening," James said. "I don't know how I endured it." He was regarding Aunt Tess, settling down for a nap in the corner of the carriage. "Except for the fun of baiting Captain Mountjoy, and that announcement about the steam railway, I should have fallen fast asleep."

"Perhaps Evan is right."

"About what?"

"Perhaps Lord Mountjoy is demented."

"My dear, the whole family is demented. Now I know where Evan gets it. They are all Mad Mountjoys. What shall we do now? It appears you have wasted your money."

"I don't know, except that Evan is the key. He is very unhappy, and he will, I think, do what I suggest from now on."

"Which will be?"

"I haven't quite decided yet. Do you know he killed his brother?"

James glanced sharply at her. "I heard some such tale, that he was sent into the army because of his brother's death. How did it happen?"

"He overturned the curricle and broke Gregory's neck."

"You make it sound as though he did it on purpose."

"We don't know that he didn't."

"You are a strange woman."

"Why did you bring up the war?"

"I was curious about him. I mean, you hear things about a man, that he is cold under fire, and you wonder why. My blood is fairly on the boil before a battle. But Mountjoy trudges about his duties as though the French snipers cannot even see him."

"And what conclusions have you drawn? That he is insane."

"I think he is too dull to have any nerves. All he thinks about is wine and women. He cannot even concentrate on his cards."

"He is not much of a planner, is he? He needs someone to look after his interests."

"You, I take it."

"Don't say it like that. They are taking advantage of the boy."

"My dear, he is scarcely a boy, though he does act like it in his father's presence."

"You noticed that, did you?"

"What are you planning?"

"I haven't quite decided yet."

"Rather late for a walk," Evan commented as Judith crossed the yard, pulling her shawl about her.

"I saw you from my window," she said, then reflected that it was stupid to let him know she was seeking him out.

"Father enjoyed himself tonight."

"Yes, he spiked Sylvia's guns. Did she believe him?"

"Sylvia may finally concede that Father has gone around the bend, so to speak."

"Evan, you didn't."

"I did, luckily, say something to that effect even before his startling announcement."

"He enjoys it, you know—the challenge of it all."

"He would have made a great general."

"Generals destroy things. He is building something here."

"I know. Soldiers destroy things, too, though Wellington usually had us put the bridges back on our way out. It kept the men occupied."

"Wellington never said anything about what happened to the civilians?"

"Not that I heard."

"That proves he could not have stopped it, either," Judith reasoned.

"I hadn't thought of that."

"Now I understand what was too horrible to speak of."

"Those who suffered were not the French, nor even the Spanish who held out against surrender. What has a nun to say about a battle? She would imagine her cloth would protect her from the worst that can happen to a woman, but it didn't." From the tail of his eye he caught her cringe. "Judith, I'm sorry. Surely you understood what I meant when I said the city was sacked."

"I had originally thought you meant looted. In person you are very much as you are in your letters. You talk and talk without saying anything of importance, then you drop these conversational bricks."

"You look so pale. Oh, I was forgetting about your vow," he said belatedly. "Such a thing could never happen in England. You have nothing to fear." He disliked keeping up the pretense, but if she needed this lie to keep him at arm's length, he would not take it away from her.

She sighed as though she were trying not to cry. "What made them do it? Would they listen to no one?"

"It was too late. They had crossed the line between men and animals. There is an end to honor, to compassion, to any real emotion. Even hatred ceases to have any meaning. There is only hunger and need—the need to destroy something only because it is weaker."

"I still don't understand," she said, trying to ignore the hunger she felt for him.

"Neither do I."

"I'm glad you don't understand. I don't know how you stood it."

"There was no time to think about it when it was happening. Afterward, well, time takes the edge off it. You know how dicey my memory is, anyway. I expect I have conveniently forgotten the worst of it."

"You're only saying that to make me feel better."

"Do you doubt me? I don't remember this house, not really. All I remember is what Gram told me of it. I have blotted out nearly the whole beginning of my life. What I haven't obliterated, I've distorted without even realizing it. What a waste!"

"No, what a talent!" she said richly. "I wish I had it."

"What could you possibly wish to forget?"

She drew in a breath, as though she would say something, and turned those brilliant eyes on him.

"No, don't," he said, pulling her to him and kissing her forehead. "See, it's gone now. I've kissed the hurt away like a bad dream."

"If only it were that easy," she said, sheltering in his embrace.

"It is," he said, holding her close. No matter how much he wanted to transfer that kiss to her lips, he knew it would be a mistake at this point. "You're shivering with the cold," he said. "Come to the dower house and I will make a fire for you."

It was what Judith was expecting from him, that he would try to make love to her again. A refusal rose to her lips, but she bit it back when she realized it was what she wanted from him. He took her hand and pulled her in that direction. She followed him wordlessly, mindlessly. She felt warm and moist between her legs, and in no need whatsoever of more heat.

By the time they were inside he had forgotten all about a fire, as well. He shut the door with finality and leaned her against the wall as he stripped off his coat and shirt. He could not get his neckcloth untied, and she laughed at his desperation. His mouth covered hers, and she joined him in a devouring kiss. He pulled her toward him as he worked the fastenings on the back of her gown. She stood throbbing as he rapidly stripped her of clothing, except for stockings and shoes. These she stepped out of herself. He picked her up and carried her to the sofa in the sitting room.

Some small voice was talking inside her head, but it was too faint to get her attention above the throbbing in her veins. Evan teased at her nipples while she ran her hands though his long dark hair, glorying in her conquest. Perhaps she understood more about war than she realized. This was the only war that mattered, and it was one they both could win, if only... What was the one thing she had to do to win? She could not quite remember, though she did try, as Evan desperately struggled out of his boots and the rest of his clothes, except that ridiculous neckcloth. He hovered over her, and she reached up with a laugh to unknot it for him. He buried his face between her breasts again, and she arched her back, bringing her legs up. He hooked his left arm under her right knee and took hold of the sofa back so they should not fall, then plunged into her.

It was as though they were running together, as though they were one, but in some other place than Devonshire. They were united in their mindless desire to keep up the rhythm of moving against each other. She knew where they were; they were inside her. She felt at that moment like the vessel for all the love in the universe. Her internal muscles grasped him, trying to milk the love out of him. She heard gasping and moaning but could not tell anymore which of them was making the sounds.

Then he grew larger, and she jerked in a spasm again, locking on to him, willing him to stay inside her forever, to never leave her. What had he said about shutting off the past and living only for the moment? Surely she could do that. She was doing that. If she never had another joy in life, this would make up for it. Her hips and stomach felt warm and cozy. Evan grabbed a sheet and pulled it over them as he lay down precariously on the edge of the sofa beside her. A delicious lethargy overtook her and she slept.

* * *

There was a loud thump, and Judith opened her eyes to bright sunlight. Evan sat on the floor, rubbing his naked knee and making no pretense to cover himself as Judith was doing. She gaped at him. Why was he so much more startling to look at in the sunlight than in the dark? She stared at the taut muscles, the scars, and those so apologetic eyes as he went to gather up her clothing.

"I suppose there will be the devil to pay for this," he concluded, glancing out the window. "Shall I help you to dress?"

"No, I can do it myself." She watched in fascination as he shrugged haphazardly into his clothes.

"What is it?" he asked, bending over to kiss her. "Have I hurt you?"

"No, but I think it must be contagious."

"What?"

"Your madness. By all that's reasonable it was an act of utter folly and stupidity for me to follow you here last night."

"No, it was an act of courage and honesty. Now my father has to give me leave to marry you."

"What has he to say in the matter?"

"Why, nothing," Evan said lamely, cursing himself for almost revealing that he knew about the affair. "But we must tell him, at any rate."

"Tell him what?"

"That we are to be married."

"But I can't."

Evan hesitated and looked at her in disbelief, and she cowered behind the sheet.

"Do what we agreed, Judith. Cast off yesterday and start new, just the two of us. It doesn't matter if he throws us both out. He needs us more than we need him."

"Just the two of us? But that's impossible. I cannot leave Meremont. I cannot leave . . ."

"Who? Who can you not leave?" he demanded.

"Oh, Evan! I have ruined everything! I must be insane to love you like this! I cannot afford to love you. I have no room in my life for you."

"You had last night," Evan accused, pulling on his boots and scowling in his disappointment. "Is this all I am to have, an occasional midnight tryst, when what I want is to be your husband?"

"You will not even have this again. What if this insanity has produced a child?"

"But... but you said you could not have any." He sat beside her and pulled her hands away from her tear-stained face.

"I said I would never have any. I did not count on you driving me mad."

"Oh, my God! You took that risk for me? Then we must marry, don't you understand that?"

"No, I took that risk for me. Last night was what I wanted, at least that part of me that has taken leave of her senses. If there is a price to pay, I will carry it alone."

"No, we are in this together. If you are with child, tell them I raped you. Father would believe that, and I will not deny it."

"Hide behind another lie?"

"What do you mean, another lie?"

"There is someone else I must consider."

"Who? Never mind, I think I know."

She wept then. How could she tell him about Thomas? Evan had said he did not want children, he had hated his own childhood so much. But being Evan, he would no doubt shoulder the responsibility for another man's bastard. She could not foist that on him. She raised her head to confront him and discovered he had gone.

Evan had no idea how Judith got back to the house or how she explained her all-night absence to Angel. If confronted about it himself, he would tell the truth—that he loved her and wanted to marry her. It rankled that she still preferred his father to him. And he did take a moment to wonder how they managed such an affair under the noses of both Helen and Angel, let alone Terry and Ralph. It had been easy enough for him and Judith to slip off. Perhaps Judith and his father even used the dower house. His stomach tightened at the thought. If he had hated his father, it would have been easier to bear. But he had come to care about the man, and the whole twisted affair was tearing him apart.

He did not bother to go to bed, but got a mug of coffee from the kitchen and went to the library. He fetched the *Times* out from under the blotter, but his father had been through it, of course, which rather ruined the pleasure of it for Evan.

A half hour later Judith found him still sitting cross-legged on the floor in the library, trying to put the paper back into some semblance of order.

"Am I in the way here?" he asked resentfully, looking up at her. "I can just as easily read elsewhere."

She cleared her throat. "Not in the way so much as a distraction. I find it very hard to concentrate on my ledgers when I know you are staring at me."

"I don't stare at you. At least I won't anymore."

"Yes, you do stare and it makes me feel . . ."

"Desirable?" he asked hopefully, wondering how she could complain about such a thing when she had been so desperate for him to love her only a few short hours ago. Perhaps she had taken his advice and now lived only for today. Perhaps for Judith, last night had not really happened.

"Uncomfortable," she corrected sternly as she put her papers on the desk.

"Well, there is not much joy to be had from the *Times* today anyway," Evan grumbled as he got up. "Father has been at it like an overzealous terrier, confusing the pages, clipping great holes in them and leaving it a shambles. I don't know why, but a used paper seems almost like a ruined woman. There simply is not as much pleasure in it, for it being so shopworn."

Judith gasped and stared at him.

"What is it?" Evan asked.

She ran from the room.

"What have I said?" he called, getting up to run after her, but her door slammed before he reached the foot of the stairs. He did go up and knock at her door, but the weeping from within would have deterred a more valiant soldier than Evan. He returned to the library, grumbling. "Women. They are inexplicable."

"What did you say to Judith?" Helen demanded as she thrust the door open.

"That's what I would like to know. We were having an ordinary talk and she suddenly looked stricken and ran from the room."

To Evan's surprise, Helen nodded. "I will speak to her. I need you to do something for me."

"Me? What?"

"You must go with Angel. Captain Farlay has called and means to take her riding."

"He won't be wanting me along then."

"I want you to go along. Otherwise I have to send to the stable and order a groom to go."

"Oh, really now."

"You are always saying how you want to be Angel's brother. If ever she needs a brother, she needs one now."

"I think we can trust Farlay to hold the line—well, cavalry. . . Perhaps you are right."

"Of course I am right. Now get down to the stable before Angel is finished changing."

Evan had a right to be angry with her, Judith thought, after the shock had waned a little and she had dried her eyes. It should have come as no surprise that he would lash out at her after she had teased and tempted him, then actually lain with him again. Much as he acted the buffoon, he was not stupid. But the cut was a shock for being so underhanded, so subtle. Why hadn't he come right out and said he wanted nothing to do with her, since she was such an easy mark now? Did he imagine she would blame him if she were pregnant? She had not thought him capable of such cruelty.

But she knew she had done worse to him. She had gotten his hopes up and then dashed them again. She had to stop seeing him alone, stop wanting even his comradeship, or they would continue to torture each other for the rest of their lives. She had expected a confrontation when she went into the library. She had been ready for it—defenseless, but ready. She had not been looking for such a backhanded blow. How could she face him again? She knew the answer to that: by being as cold and distant as stone.

It was obvious to Evan that Angel's ride with James would have gone far differently had he not been along to guard her. As Angel walked toward the house, looking back once at Evan, James made ready to remount. Evan grabbed his reins at the bit.

"If you ever lay a hand on her..."

"What? What will you do?" James demanded with a sneer.

"There won't be enough of you left to spread on toast!"

James's eyes widened for a second, then he laughed. "Big words from someone who can't even stay sober."

"Yes, but I know how to kill people, and being an engineer, I can think of a hundred places to plant your remains where no one would ever think to look for them." Evan let go the reins and walked toward the house. He didn't know if James had believed him, though Evan thought he'd sounded pretty convincing. Then he realized that if James ever did harm Angel, he would indeed have no qualms about killing him.

Evan's heart was still thudding from his altercation with James when he returned to the house. He took a chance and opened the door to the library. Judith was there, writing. She looked at him coldly, then went back to her work. Evan had the strange feeling he was treading dangerously in trying to talk to her, but he was in a dangerous mood. And much as he tried to deny it, he wanted her still. He closed the door.

Judith looked up again, obviously displeased. "What do you want?" she demanded.

Evan sighed. "I want to know what I said to hurt you so. I do it all the time and I am always sorry, but this time I am mystified." He started to approach the desk.

She snapped her head up, stopping him in his tracks with a look so piercing he almost doubted it was the same woman. Her blue eyes were open wide and very dry, as though she had cried all the tears she possessed, or as if she was seeing him for the first time and not liking it.

"Judith? If you cannot tell me, I understand. Just believe me when I say I didn't mean it, whatever it was."

So he hadn't meant to hurt her. He had merely used an uncommon simile, and she had taken it as though it were an accusation. Because what he'd said was true. She looked away, unable to face him. "It was nothing," she lied. "I am fine now. It was simply a headache. It's gone."

"But should you see a doctor? What caused it?"

"I don't know, but if you keep interrogating me, I shall have another very soon." She pronounced the words with so much venom that he turned and left, without knowing it was not his fault.

If only he had stayed. If only he had asked one more question, she would have dissolved in tears and told him the whole of it. It would have been over instead of going on and on. If she'd thought it was bad to have him hate her, she now realized the incident provided a relief of sorts. It was twice as hurtful to think that he still loved her and that she could do nothing for him but hurt him again. This had to end.

Chapter Ten

Evan struggled with his faulty memory throughout the night. Perhaps she had merely lost her composure when she'd found him in the library and had run out because she could not bear the sight of him. But she had seemed to regain her footing easily enough after their first tryst. It must have been something else. He had been still wrestling with the paper and ranting at his father for ruining it.

Then it hit him: he had likened the *Times* to a ruined woman. That's when Judith had looked stricken and had run out. What a fool he had been to blurt out such an unfortunate comparison when she was caught in the dilemma of being mistress to the father and in love with the son. But he did not think of her as ruined. He found her to be a particularly courageous girl snared in an impossible situation. Somehow he had to help her out of it, even if it meant confronting his father with the truth.

But what was he to do now about Judith? There was no way to apologize for such an offense. If he attempted it, he would only make matters worse and cause her even more pain.

To Evan's surprise, Judith agreed to ride with them before breakfast. She was coldly composed now rather than angry, but he knew there was no approaching her about yesterday. He took the coward's way out and dodged a confrontation by talking only commonplaces. Even if he was to know Judith merely as an ally until this damned canal was finished, that was better than having to leave her now.

He had been riding behind the girls, in a brown study over what he could possibly do. Judith was in the lead, and he suddenly realized that Angel was not bumping and bouncing, but was rocking in time to her mount as they cantered down the hill.

"I did it, didn't I?" she said when they pulled up at the bottom.

"You certainly did," he said, as pleased as she was. He was happy that he had noticed. "You should have seen her, Judith. I think she may ride as well as you someday."

"Well done, Angel," Judith said with genuine delight.

"And I like this new hat Judith picked out for me," Angel added. "The wind doesn't seem to carry it off."

"It looks well on you," Evan said, and Judith nodded.

He had such a sense of well-being suddenly, now that Judith was talking again. Then he realized nothing ached. He had left off having his ribs taped, and his knee felt as good as ever. What more could a man ask? Well, he could ask a woman to marry him, but not just yet. He would have to gentle her again first, as with a horse that had been spooked too often. In time he would get back in her good graces.

Evan was still afraid that if Judith were so involved with his father and the management of the estate, she might not be willing to give that up. But at least she was not going to take up the cloistered life. He had been angry when Angel told him, but had laughed about it later. It even occurred to him that he had suggested the excuse to Lady Mountjoy himself.

They paused at the dower house so Judith could measure some windows for draperies. Evan and Angel walked the horses while she went in to perform this errand. They could hear hammering inside.

"Do you really think I will ride as good as Judith?"

"Yes, why not? You do like it now, don't you?"

"I like riding with you, anyway."

"Who have we here?" Evan asked of the imp who appeared from behind the hedge. "Thomas! Have you escaped your nurse again?"

The boy nodded shyly.

"Would you like to ride Molly?" Evan offered.

"Oh, yes, please."

Evan boosted him up and showed him where to hang on to the sidesaddle, then grinned at Thomas's giggles as the horse moved underneath him.

"Evan?" Angel asked as she walked Bart. "Do you think I could ever be of any use?"

"What do you mean?"

"Do you think I would make someone a useful wife?"

"I don't think men look for usefulness when they decide to marry," he said as he led Molly and Taurus along one of the garden pathways, looking back at Thomas's smiling face.

"What do they look for?"

"Unfortunately, money."

"Which I haven't got."

"Oh, I think between Father and me, we shall be able to put together a respectable dowry for you, if you have the patience to wait a year or two."

"I don't want a dowry."

"Nonsense, what do you want if you don't want—"

His speech, and indeed his breath, was stopped by her kiss, all the more so because she had a grasp on his coat collar that he could not shake off, trapped as he was between Taurus and Molly, and worrying about Thomas. Bart stood watching placidly from where Angel had dropped his reins.

"What are Angel and Evan doing out there?" Terry asked Judith.

"Walking the horses. I can't be too long about this or they will go on home without me. Are the carpenters—"

"They are not! They are kissing!" Terry shouted from his vantage point on the ladder.

"So they are," said Judith, stepping to the window and looking down on them. "And Thomas is in the middle of it. How stupid!"

"Well, I won't have it!" Terry came partway down, but she stopped him with a hand on his arm.

"Don't! We have no right to interrupt."

"Yes I have—I have the right of a—of a brother."

"Terry, no," she said as she ran out of the house after him.

"You can't do things like that with horses about," Evan was saying. "Terry, tell her—"

Once again Evan was cut short, but by Terry, who thrust Angel rudely aside and planted his fist in his brother's face. Evan went down, forgetting to let go the reins and pulling the horses' front hooves dangerously toward him. Judith gasped, and Angel screamed from her sitting position on the ground. The noise made Molly start and Bart run for the stable. Taurus danced uncertainly beside Evan for a moment, waiting for his master to jump up and for them to be off.

Braving Molly's nervous attempts to rear, Judith snatched Thomas from the saddle. Terry dived in and grabbed the reins, forcing the fidgeting horses away from his still-prone brother.

Evan looked quizzically up at him, then raised an arm to fend off another expected blow. Instead, Terry grabbed his hand and pulled him to his feet.

"I like fighting you a lot better when you are drunk," Evan said ruefully. "Then I can beat you. Otherwise I think not."

"God, Evan, what have I done? I almost got you trampled. All because—all because..."

"Because of Angel," Evan stated. "I thought you didn't—"

"Because of me, is it?" Angel raged, getting to her feet. "I suppose it's my fault you had a fistfight and nearly got trampled."

Just then the distraught nurse burst through the hedge and snatched the wide-eyed Thomas from Judith's arms. "How dare he hurt my baby!"

"He's not your baby," Judith said, but had to give Thomas over or hurt him by struggling with Miranda.

The nurse gave them all an angry glare and ran off with Thomas—no small feat, Evan thought, since the child had to weigh four stone.

"This is not my fault!" Angel insisted with a stamp of her foot.

"But you can't be throwing yourself on people when there are horses about," Evan said reasonably. "They spook at anything odd."

"Odd? Odd, am I? I'm sick of all of you, always laughing at me behind my back. I hate you all!" she cried, and finally ran away.

Finding himself near the stone bench, Evan slumped down upon it, looking a little warily at his brother.

"I think you could have managed that better," Terry said.

"Me? What have I done?"

"Nothing, absolutely nothing to have them falling all over you—first Sylvia and now Angel."

"Fickle, aren't they?" Evan asked as he fingered his bruised eye tenderly.

"Just because you are a soldier. I don't know how much of a soldier you are if that's the best defense you can offer."

"I have no defense left," Evan said, holding his head.

"Even when you had nothing, you had everything. It will always be that way. I'll always end up playing the fool." Terry turned on his heel and left the garden.

Judith recaptured Molly and Taurus and led them up to Evan.

"Haven't you got anything awful to say to me?" Evan asked, squinting up at her, his eyebrows furrowed.

She relented. She could not be unkind to him again. "Poor Evan, that eye will be black in a day or two."

"Thank you very much for those words of comfort. What a whirlwind Terry is when enraged. So he still loves her?"

"Apparently. I had thought he was over her."

"You would think a piece of hot lead would discourage any man."

"Can you walk?"

"Oh, yes. At least I'll try," he said, getting gingerly to his feet. "Just when things were healing. But then, I'm not used to having nothing hurt. This feels more normal."

"Poor baby," she said, without knowing how much comfort those words gave him. He knew she had forgiven him in her heart. That was all that mattered.

From his father he got no sympathy whatsoever.

"What the devil have you been up to?"

"Nothing, Father," he answered tiredly.

"Nothing again?"

"I hit him," Terry said.

"I'm not even going to ask why. I don't want to know. So long as you settle it between you before mealtime, it's none of my concern. But if either of you endangers our enterprise with this stupid competition, I will have something to say."

Both sons eyed him warily and ate in silence. The meal was endurable only because Angel was not there.

After lunch Evan, Ralph and Bose rode out to the site, followed reluctantly by Terry, who cooperated in the new survey but did not resume friendly relations. It was worse than when he was drunk, Evan thought, for Terry did not hold a grudge after those episodes. Evan sent them home in good time for dinner and, with Bose, rode again to the village, where half a dozen cottages recently rented by his father were being cleaned out for the use of the canal builders. Bose went inside to inspect the progress.

There had to be something other than the porcelain factory to interest them here. Evan stared at the brick edifice. It had as many windows and doors as a gentleman's house, but he assumed these were to release heat and fumes, which would be more of a problem than keeping the place warm in winter.

Even allowing that breakage was a factor when shipping by wagon or packhorse, porcelain was a small commodity and could be better handled that way. Evan considered what sort of thing was normally shipped by canal in Europe—not small, valuable stuff, now that he thought about it, but bulky, heavy cargo that could not be sent any other way, either because of the expense, or because of size or weight. Nothing large and bulky loomed up at him here to give him a clue, however. He would discover their intentions himself, he resolved, rather than having to be told, like a child clamoring to know the solution to a puzzle.

The past caught Evan a glancing blow as he remembered how his father had given him riddles to work out when he was little. In his mind he suddenly heard him laughing, and not in an unkind way. So his father had played with him as he now played with Thomas. Evan simply had not remembered. Why shut that out—a good memory? There was someone else in it, but before he could determine who, the curtain came crashing down again. He stood trembling by his horse, knowing now that it was all still there somewhere in his head and not being sure if that was a comfort or not.

"What the devil is the matter with you?" Bose demanded.

"Nothing. I'm fine."

"You look to be coming down with the ague."

"I think we can begin digging as soon as we can round up a crew."

"I've already canvassed the farms hereabout, but without much success. What say I see how many I can round up in Tiverton and send them on here? Then I'll ride downriver to Exeter. I shouldn't think we want more than twenty or thirty to start with. Once word gets about that we are hiring, we shall have vagabonds from all parts of the country falling in on us."

"Well, hire them as they show up. We can make use of just about everybody. There is plenty of money in my trunk. Make sure you take enough with you."

"You want some water boys, I suppose. As long as the rest can wield a pick and shovel..."

"No, hire them all. We can use them as cooks or whatever."

"I shall set out tomorrow."

They rode back slowly, Evan letting his mind drift, hoping to stumble on another memory. Instead they almost rode straight into Captain Farlay in the beech wood.

"Out reconnoitering?" Evan asked.

Farlay whirled his horse around as though they were one. "Actually, I'm lost. I was working my way back from Sylvia's river property...."

"Wendover is that way. You can ride past Meremont." He waved Bose on with a gesture. Evan had not believed the lie and Farlay knew it, but it was necessary to both of them. They rode through the woods side by side.

"Any fish in that stream?" James asked.

"I don't know," Evan countered. "I never had a chance to find out—that is to say I don't remember." He wondered for a moment if Farlay could be the figure in white, weighing the honor of a soldier against the ruthlessness of anyone who had fought in the late conflict. He shook his head.

"What's the matter?"

"Just trying to remember where I saw you last."

"It was yesterday," James said in some surprise.

"No, I meant during the war."

"Salamanca. I took a ball in my shoulder at Orthez in February."

"So you have been home since March. Isn't your leave up yet?"

"I can ride, as you can see, but not wield a saber to any purpose. I shall ask for an extension."

"But you do mean to stay in the army?"

"Unlike you, I am a second son. I have no choice."

"Well, don't go murdering your brother. It's no fun being the eldest."

Farlay rolled a shocked eye at him and Evan burst into one of his harsh laughs when he realized the import of what he had said.

"I suppose you mean to stay," Farlay said belligerently.

"We engineers never get much credit in the army. And life here does have its attractions."

"Including Sylvia? I've seen the way you look at her. You are attracted to her."

"One would have to be dead not to be."

"That can be arranged."

Evan laughed again. "You're warning me off! What would Sylvia have to say to that?"

Farlay stared at him in impotent rage.

"No, I won't tell her," Evan promised. "It should be interesting to see if you can pull it off."

"You don't care about Sylvia."

"Whereas you really do love her. My deepest sympathies, Farlay. Good day to you."

Evan dismounted in the stable, still trying to fit Farlay with the assassin's role, but it did not wash. Farlay would have made sure of his kill, for one thing. But more important, he was not a sniper. James would have made it a fair fight, at least faced his opponent. Plus, at the time it had happened, Evan had not even met Lady Sylvia. "It's just not possible," he mumbled to himself, then said, "Thomas, is that you hiding there?"

"He's the most like my pup." Thomas put the puppy back with its mother. "I know I can't have it. I only come to hold it when I get lonely for Toby. You won't tell, will you?"

"Of course not," said Evan, leaning over the wall of the stall. "What kind of brother would that make me?"

"But you're not my brother. Nurse says so."

"Not the way brothers usually are."

"Still, I'm sorry I shot at you."

Thomas crawled between the rails, and Evan knelt to talk to him. "And I'm sorry I almost got you thrown off my horse. It wasn't very smart of me getting all tangled up with Angel when I should have been minding you. You weren't hurt, were you?"

"No. I just pretended I was going to get stuck with a pin."

"A pin—oh, I remember, a surprise, like falling off a horse."

Thomas nodded. "Besides, Aunt Judith grabbed me. She will always watch out for me."

"You two are very close, aren't you?"

"She is my favorite, and I am hers. Nurse says she spoils me, but I don't mind that."

"I think a child needs a little spoiling and a guardian angel like Judith. But you will want to learn how to take care of yourself. I remember Father telling me it was more important to know how to fall off than how to stay on, since staying on did not hurt. Would you like to practice falling?"

"Oh, yes. Which horse shall I fall off of?"

"We won't use a horse, but a mound of hay to start with."

Evan stood and raked up a pile of fresh hay. "Watch how I roll." He did a somersault, hitting the mound with his head tucked. "I'll help you through it a couple of times."

After three tries, Thomas somersaulted onto the mound by himself. His cries of delight attracted Judith, who had been waiting for Evan. She knew she owed him an explanation, at the very least an apology, for her odd behavior, but she could not talk to him in the presence of a stable lad. Exactly what she meant to say to him she did not know— perhaps that she was sorry she led him on, knowing she would never risk leaving Meremont. If only he could promise to stay here forever, she could wed him. But those particular vows should not have conditions attached. That was the problem. Everything had happened backward.

"I thought I heard you playing in here," she said with a smile as she came in the doorway. "You're not allowed, are you, Thomas?"

"We're not playing, Judith. Evan is teaching me how to fall."

"Perhaps I should teach Judith, too," Evan said, grateful for an excuse to come and take her arm. "It's something she should know how to do."

"Come on, Judith," Thomas said, his eyes round with excitement. "It's not as surprising as a pin."

"Oh, no. I have no intention of getting all covered with hay like you two. You will both be in trouble, for it is almost time for dinner."

"But I want to fall off a horse now," Thomas pleaded, jumping up and down.

"Perhaps tomorrow," Evan promised. "Come, I will give you a ride back to the house." Evan stooped, and Thomas leapt onto his back.

"Trot!" Thomas commanded, giving Evan a kick, while almost strangling him.

"Well, Evan, why don't you trot?" Judith asked.

"Oh, no. One thing you must learn is that you walk your mount the last half mile home to let him cool down."

"Very well, then. Walk on, Evan."

"If only Evan were so obedient to his father, he would get in less trouble," Judith said.

"Less trouble than me?"

"No, Thomas," Evan said over his shoulder. "I will always be in more trouble than you."

Evan did trot up the stairs, to the delight of the bouncing Thomas. His giggles were infectious, and when Evan knelt to let his rider dismount, he got a genuine smile from Judith.

"I suppose I had better help you wash up," she said to the little boy, "then deliver you to Cook if we cannot find Nurse."

"Where is Miranda?" Evan asked. "I keep expecting her to leap out of the woodwork and snatch Thomas away. It isn't like her to lose track of you for so long, is it, Thomas?"

Judith knelt to pick some hay off of the lad's coat. "I suppose that depends on where you ditched Miranda, you naughty boy." Judith shook her finger at him, then hugged him anyway. Thomas grinned and winked at Evan.

"Confess, Thomas, where is Miranda?" Evan knelt to show that his sternness was only in jest.

"Well, I think she might be . . ." Thomas laid one grubby little finger against his cheek and rolled his eyes as if deep in thought. "I think she might be locked in the little house."

"The privy?" Evan stood up and looked at Judith. She gaped at him, and they both burst out laughing.

"I can't imagine how the outside catch could have slipped," Thomas said, shaking his head sadly.

"Oh, you can't? Well, I can," said Evan as he ruffled the boy's hair and headed back down the stairs.

"You won't tell on me, will you, Evan?"

"Tell what, you imp? Just remember, Thomas, such a joke is only funny once."

"Yes, Evan."

Evan shook his head as he went to rescue Miranda. He suspected that as Thomas grew, his fertile imagination would be a sore trial to the poor woman. He could only hope that when the new baby came, Miranda would transfer her attention to it and give Thomas a bit more freedom. A boy should have a year or two when no one knew what he was up to so long as he showed up in time for dinner. Evan was quite sure that was what it had been like for him. He simply could not remember it all. Probably that knock he had taken on the head when the curricle flipped had fogged his memories, but they were still there.

He arrived at the privy to find the door off the hinges. Resourceful woman, Miranda. He only hoped she would spare the rod with Thomas. But the way she coddled him, Evan guessed that Thomas had only to turn that innocent look on her to have her petting him again.

* * *

It rained the next day, hard enough to discourage pleasure riding or surveying. After spending a frustrating morning trying to get Judith alone, Evan rode to Wendover to call on Sylvia. She was with James, but sent her cousin packing when she saw Evan's bruised face.

"What happened to you?"

"Nothing much, had a run-in with Terry is all," he said shyly, as though it happened every day. He looked uncomfortably around her elegant sitting room, as though he had never seen a place like it before, and said nervously, "You were right. They were planning to cut me out. You must think me quite stupid not to have guessed."

"Sit down and drink this," she commanded. "Of course you are not stupid, but they are taking advantage of you." She stopped a moment behind his chair, her hands on his shoulders possessively. "You do see that?" She pulled a stool up near his chair and spoke confidentially, as though she were persuading a child.

Evan was tempted to smirk, but remembered Judith's lack of confidence in his acting ability and frowned instead as he sipped the potent whiskey. "I thought it was the price of getting to stay."

"What has your father promised you?"

"Nothing really. I shall have Gram's money, of course." He recklessly downed the rest of the whiskey in the glass. "They can't keep that from me, but I am expected to use it to buy shares in this railway."

"How many?"

"I think he said I would get forty."

"Forty out of how many?"

"I—I don't think he said."

"Evan, you must pay more attention, love." She stood up and took his jaw, turning his face and inspecting his eye. "This is important. If it were forty out of a hundred, you would have almost half."

"That's good, isn't it?" he asked with a vague smile.

"That's very good," she said, sitting on his lap and coiling her arms around his neck, "but fifty or sixty would be better."

He went quite red in the face and his heartbeat picked up. He tried to tell himself it was the whiskey, but he knew the feeling. There was an animal attraction here, one that embarrassed him because he couldn't help it. He scarcely dared look at Sylvia, because all he really wanted was Judith.

"I can help you, Evan." She kissed the side of his face and was working her way toward his mouth when he stopped her.

"But what about James?" He glanced anxiously toward the door.

"James will do what he's told. You must find out how many shares there are, where the railway is to start and why they are building it. Do you understand?"

"They'll never tell me that."

"They will if they think they can trust you. Let them think they can have the money...no. Demand to know more about it before you agree to sign the papers. You have power, Evan. You must learn how to use it. I could teach you so much." She did kiss him on the mouth then. He stopped shrinking from her and took control of it, for he did not want this intimacy. He gripped the back of her neck and kissed her hard enough to make her draw back, but he wouldn't let her go. Being lunged at by Angel was bad enough, but this was a disgusting business. He knew he could have her for the asking and he didn't want her. He simply could not let her know that.

She broke it off, breathlessly. "Evan, you're hurting me," she said, a shade of fear in her eyes.

It was what he was playing for, a delay. "I'm sorry. I'm not used to women like you—breakable ones." He took his hands from her shoulders and stared at his fingers.

"I'm not that breakable, but you have much to learn," she said, getting up and straightening her dress. She swallowed hard as he got up and walked toward the door. "Don't go," she commanded.

"I must. They will miss me."

"You won't forget what you must learn?"

"I won't forget." He walked out the back door as if he owned the place.

Lady Sylvia went to the window in the office to watch Evan stride toward the stable on his muscular legs. He was neither as elegant nor as gentle as James. Evan had, to her mind, a brutishness about him that made her stomach recoil with desire. She had been so close to capturing him that she almost regretted pulling back. He had frightened her and she had liked it. Evan was powerful enough to truly hurt her, but he would only do so out of ignorance or anger, unlike some men, who did it simply because they were more powerful than women. Evan was dangerous. James, on the other hand, was completely safe and rather boring. One day Evan could be truly powerful, if he let her make the decisions. James had thought to put her off by telling her Evan was incompetent. That only made Evan more desirable in her eyes, for he would be entirely dependable once his loyalty was won.

Evan nodded to James in the stable.

"That was a short visit."

"Long enough," Evan murmured, meeting Farlay's stare with a satisfied smile.

"I bet it was. Remember what I said."

Evan merely raised an eyebrow at him, then mounted and rode back toward Meremont, congratulating himself on a narrow escape and wondering what to do next.

Dinner was a quiet affair, with Angel still absenting herself. Evan thought about apologizing to her, but decided to wait until she emerged from her bedroom. He was getting to be so wary of women anymore that he felt jumpy all the time.

When Judith and Helen had retired from the dining room, his father asked abruptly, "What did you learn?"

Evan, who had been following Judith out the door with his eyes, gave a start when he realized he was being addressed.

"You did ride over to see Lady Sylvia today," his father prompted.

Evan glanced at Terry, but instead of a jealous glare, met once again that businesslike intensity.

"She wants to know if I will have a controlling interest and what the railway is for. It's my guess she won't make a move until she knows whether the venture is likely to be profitable."

"Would she sell the land to you?" Ralph asked.

"Only at an exorbitant price, but possibly not even then. Judith is right. She wants Meremont."

"Has she suggested an alliance between you two?" his father prompted.

"She's suggested a lot of things," Evan said uncomfortably, glancing at Terry. "What do you mean by an alliance?"

"Could you get control of the land if you offered her marriage?"

"No!"

"Come now, Evan," Terry prodded. "I concede that she prefers you to me. Don't you think you can manage it? I had almost talked her into marriage when you interfered."

"She does not prefer me," Evan said, jumping up and pacing the room. "She is a calculating beauty who will prefer any man who can give her what she wants."

"Really, Evan," Terry gibed, noting his discomfort. "I know you say you don't like her, but it appears someone must marry her."

"No, I won't do it. I would do anything for you but that."

"Don't you think you can handle her?" Terry asked.

"I know damn well I can't. And I—I don't want her in this family." Lord Mountjoy stared at him thoughtfully.

"That subtle tongue of hers would have us at each others' throats for the rest of our lives," Evan continued.

"Even if she had no real power, she would be here, cutting at us."

"But we need her land," protested his father. "We can't continue without it."

"Maybe we can. I want to ride out tomorrow and take another look. Until then I don't want to discuss it."

Numbly, Evan moved with the others into the library. He knew that what he would propose tomorrow would meet with opposition. It would add a year to the project at least, but he would not be a party to duping a woman, even one he disliked, for gain. He would rather frustrate her by leaving her with nothing.

Calculations spun through his head the whole evening, as he added up the pounds and days. He was roused from his mathematical stupor by his father, telling him to go to bed. To Evan's surprise they were the only two left in the room. He rose stiffly, his bruised eye pounding as he walked toward the door. His father was still pouring over his plans, those same plans that Judith had been looking at in the library the day Thomas fired at them.

Evan took a candle from the hall table and carried it to his room. He would simply have to sell some of Gram's stocks. That should raise enough money to make up for his change in plans. And if they hired more men, they might not even be delayed that long.

Chapter Eleven

Evan set the candle on the small table by the bed and was undoing his neckcloth when he heard it—breathing.

"Bose, are you asleep in here? I didn't even know you were back."

A noise by the door made Evan turn that way, and that was fortunate, else the whistling saber would have caught him in the neck or head instead of a glancing blow across the shoulder blade. He crashed onto the edge of the mattress, knocking the candle out, and with the instinct born of battle, slipped down and rolled under the bed.

He could hear his own breath, rasping now, and sharp footsteps. Then it came, a stabbing thrust that caught him in the thigh. He yelped, rolled again and listened, holding his breath.

The saber slithered under the bed once more, and this time he rolled onto it, grabbing the hand that held it, a strong hand. A booted foot crushed his fingers, but he grabbed at that persistently enough to bring his assailant crashing to the floor.

He felt a qualm over Helen's unborn child and held on until the other foot had stomped his hand numb. He gave up then and let go. He had lost again, he decided, as the footsteps scuttled out of the room.

Evan laughed at the absurdity of being killed under a bed, and not even a woman's bed. He laughed hysterically, even as the blood saturated the back of his coat. His leg was bleeding, too, and he knew that was potentially the more dangerous wound, since the leg arteries were so much bigger.

He must stop laughing and get some help or he would die like a rat under his own bed. That thought made him laugh even harder, but he forced himself to roll until he was near the door. There was a very faint light coming up from the hall, where one candle still burned. What if she were waiting there?

He got to his knees, then his feet, and made one lunge toward the banister. Resting on it with the left armpit, he staggered and slid down the stairs, still not managing to silence his insane laughter.

"What the devil is going on? Evan, I had not thought you were drunk." Lord Mountjoy was holding the candle now, but Evan could scarcely see anymore.

Your vision goes first, he told himself. He was fainting, and he had not the strength left to ask for help to save his life.

"Evan, what is the matter with you?" His father's voice reached him vaguely as the roaring in his ears overwhelmed him and he fell down.

He woke and stirred, then regretted it. Another battle? Vaguely he tried to remember what the damages were, but when he opened his eyes he was not in a tent or a hovel, but his room at Meremont. Then he remembered. He saw a classic profile by the window and said, "Judith?"

"Of course not," said Helen.

Evan jerked so hard a groan escaped him. He watched with fascination as the woman he assumed to be his assassin rose awkwardly from the small chair by the window and came toward the bed. His heart was racing and he was breathing as though he had been running.

"Your fever is getting worse," she said, touching his forehead with a hand that seemed to singe him. "And you have been babbling this past hour about gabions and logs and all manner of things."

"Where is Bose?" he asked with dry lips.

"He isn't back yet. Are you thirsty?"

"No," he said, eyeing the water glass she offered with terror.

"Are you all right?" she asked.

"I don't know. Are *you* all right?" he countered distractedly.

"I am now. The sickness usually goes off by midmorning. I had forgotten everything you had to go through to have a child, it has been so long."

"Only six years," he said, staring at her delicate hands. They did not look strong enough to have done what had been done here last night. He knew he had to see her ankles, no matter what it cost him, so he tried to raise himself on his elbows.

"Are you mad? You will tear open your wound again."

"Was it you?" he asked in his half-delirious state.

"Was what me...? My God! Did you think I did this? I know I said I would shoot you, and I still will if you do not keep away from Judith, but—but..."

"But you would hesitate before hacking me to death. That's a comforting thought."

"Evan, I am sorry this happened, but how could you think it was me?"

He was laughing again and it was making his shoulder ache, but he was past caring. He wanted so much to believe her, for his father's sake, but what was his alternative? Terry or Angel?

"Don't laugh like that. People think you are insane."

"What is he doing now?" Lord Mountjoy demanded, appearing at the door.

"He is trying to get up," Helen said in despair.

"Be reasonable, lad. If you get up you will undo all those stitches the doctor installed with such care. Look, I have brought you the *Times*. I will fold it for you."

"The *Times!*" Evan gasped, and gave another ripple of laughter.

"Helen, you may leave us now. I will sit with him." When Helen had closed the door behind her, his father asked, "Who was it?"

"Most likely a housebreaker who grabbed the first weapon at hand when he found himself trapped in here."

"It wasn't Terry. He may get drunk, but not that drunk. Besides, he says he was in his room."

"You asked him?"

"I had to call for help. I've never seen such a gory mess. He also told me you'd been shot at in the woods."

"Yes, when I was fishing."

"Why didn't you say something to me?"

Evan chuckled. "I guess it's such a normal thing to happen to me that I didn't regard it."

"Normal?"

"There were always French snipers about."

"Not in Devonshire and not in your own house. You should be shocked."

"I was, I assure you, for I thought I heard Bose in here."

"But you might have been killed. You should be outraged, and what do you do but laugh?"

"I never learned to handle disaster any other way. I could either laugh at having the very worst happen to me or die."

"But it's almost as though you expect the worst."

"It's all I have ever known."

"School could not have been so bad. You took all those walking holidays, went to stay with your friends."

"I saw a lot of the country, that's for certain."

"Not once did it ever occur to you to come home?"

"I didn't know if I would be welcome."

"Evan, don't be absurd. And you never wrote me, either."

"I did try. What could I have said? There was something so awful in the way. You can't exactly ignore a death. 'Sorry about Gregory. By the way, could you send me an extra five pounds?' That would have been absurd. Why didn't you write to me?"

"The same reason, I suppose. Your grandmother let me read your letters, after a few days or a week, whenever she thought I had suffered enough."

"What?"

"It was as though she was punishing me. She would tell me quite carelessly that she had gotten a letter from you and let me stew about it before she finally gave it to me."

"Even after I went into the army?"

"No, she stopped being quite so cruel then. If she had dropped the news that you were wounded and not given me any particulars, I would have gone mad myself. After Judith came, we read the letters together."

"It was Judith who brought you together?"

"Remarkable girl."

"Yes, I know. Judith can love anyone. I'm sorry now I didn't have the guts to face you, even on paper."

"So am I."

"We have wasted a great deal of time, the two of us," Evan said sleepily.

"Yes, I know, but from now on we will talk. There will be no more secrets between us?"

"But what about Judith?" Evan asked, wondering if his father meant to confess that she was his mistress. Then consciousness slipped away.

"Judith . . . ? Ah, delirious again."

Lady Sylvia called that afternoon, and when Angel informed her of the attack, she forced her way into Evan's room against Ralph's protests. Ralph was no match for her, but threatened to come back with reinforcements. Her patently genuine concern embarrassed Evan all the more since he was involved in a conspiracy against her.

"This is monstrous!" she raged, pacing the small room in agitation. "You must not stay in this place another night. You could be murdered in your bed."

"Now there's a quieting thought for a man to carry to sleep with him," Evan joked, to try to ease her distress.

"I shall not leave you. Don't you see that you can't trust them, any of them?"

"I shall be fine as soon as Bose gets back."

"Who was it?"

"I couldn't see in the dark."

"It had to be Terry. It's just the sort of thing—"

"It was not!" Evan retorted. "If Terry wanted to beat up on me he would do it in broad daylight in plain view of everyone."

"That Ralph, then."

"Never. Why would he?"

"Evan, you must face the fact that it could be your father. Who gets your grandmother's money if something happens to you?"

He was groggy enough to let this take hold of his mind for a moment, and he looked at her in shock. "I would rather fight the French," he said numbly. "At least I can see them."

"My poor Evan," she said, kissing his brow. But she did not say it like Judith would, and it was not comforting. Besides, his father had been downstairs, and he would not do such a thing, Evan knew.

"What are you doing here?" Judith demanded in a hard-edged tone Evan had heard her use only at their war councils.

"I am comforting him."

"You are upsetting him. Last time I checked he was asleep. Five minutes with you and he is sweating and thrashing."

Evan laughed weakly, not his desperate, hysterical laugh, but the one he used when genuinely amused. He didn't mind if they fought over him so long as they did not fall onto the bed.

He listened with pleasure as Judith routed Sylvia mercilessly from the house. Sylvia threatened to send James to guard Evan, and Judith threatened to send James packing, too, if he dared show his face.

"The nerve of her!" she said as she straightened his bed. "Sending James to guard you."

"Poor James. I wonder what he would say to such a notion. He does not like me overmuch," Evan said, beginning to feel comfortable now that Judith was with him.

"Why ever not? You are both soldiers."

"Jealous of Sylvia's affections. He thinks I am cutting him out with her."

"How jealous is he?"

"Very. He even threatened to—well, you know what soldiers are. They talk a lot of nonsense."

"Evan! I have been trying to think who could have attacked you. It could have been James himself. A saber is just the sort of weapon he would choose."

"Now Judith, that's absurd. James would not come at me in the dark, attack me from behind."

"Perhaps not sober, but drunk or enraged? Besides, who else could it have been?"

"A housebreaker. Recollect I am suddenly rather wealthy, and I do have money in my trunk."

"Is any missing?" she asked, glancing toward the trunk under the window.

"I've no idea what Bose took with him, so I cannot say. I imagine he will clear that up when he gets back."

"I still think James is the most likely suspect," Judith said, pulling the small chair toward the bed.

"You forget his shoulder wound."

"He looks perfectly healthy to me."

"Oh, he can sit a horse," Evan quoted sleepily, "but he cannot yet wield a saber to any effect."

"How do you know that?" She sat down and took his hand.

"He told me so."

"When?"

"Yesterday."

"Which is why he did not manage to kill you outright. Did you tell your father this?"

"No, but it is only a coincidence I had that particular conversation with James yesterday."

"We shall see what your father says."

"Judith, there is no proof. You must not accuse him."

"Go to sleep," she ordered, pointing a commanding finger at the bed.

"Yes, ma'am," Evan agreed with a chuckle. It was the best thing for him. Besides, if Judith still cared for him, perhaps he could persuade her to marriage. For the first time since the attack he went to sleep with a quiet mind.

Judith watched over Evan, as she had the first day he had come to Meremont. She marveled at his trust in James when they hardly knew each other. Or perhaps she simply did not want to consider the alternatives. Evan's story of a housebreaker she dismissed. But the thought that one of their household could be capable of such an act was highly upsetting. She tried to weigh the probabilities logically, but could not in Evan's case apply logic. All she felt was a passionate desire to protect him from whatever danger was coming. And it was still coming. He might shrug off the fishing incident, but she could not. Yet there was no one she could bear to suspect of this crime, except James. That was passion again, not logic. And passion would not keep Evan alive. Well, if James showed his face here he would have her to deal with. As for the rest, she had only to keep Evan safe until Bose returned.

To Judith's surprise, James did show his face, as a reluctant escort to Lady Sylvia. He did not look like reinforcements, if that was what he was supposed to be; he looked embarrassed. Judith received them coldly in the hallway, since Lord Mountjoy was dozing in the library over the newspaper and her sisters were occupying the morning room.

"We want to see Evan," Sylvia demanded, removing her gloves and folding them.

"He's asleep," Judith said, taking up a position at the bottom of the stairs. "Your first visit was disturbing enough. I would not let you see him again even if he were awake.''

''But he is in danger, and must we stand talking in the hallway?''

''Yes, for you are not staying.''

Sylvia looked surprised. ''I have brought James to watch over Evan. You cannot comprehend what danger he is in.''

''I comprehend it quite well, which is why James is not staying, either.''

''What are you saying?'' James asked suspiciously.

''Miss Wells is no doubt overwrought,'' Sylvia said placatingly. ''She can't know what she is saying.''

''I know very well what I am saying. Evan was attacked with a saber after being threatened by someone expert in its use. You now expect me to let—''

''That is absurd!'' James asserted. ''I was not here last night, and if I were I would never do such a thing.''

''That is what Evan says, not that I place any reliance on either one of you.''

''I have never been so insulted!'' Sylvia said.

''It is not you who have been insulted, cousin, but me,'' James said with a gleam in his eye.

''But she accused you of the most vile thing, just because she does not want to face the fact that it is one of the family.''

Judith's color flared under the lash of the truth, and her dislike for being discussed as though she were not there.

''Yes, and if she were a man I would call her out for it,'' James answered. ''But as she is only a woman I have to take it.''

''Only a woman, am I? I warn you not to try to go up these stairs. You will see what I am capable of.''

''Yes, Mountjoy warned me about your punishing right,'' James said with a smile.

''I will go to him then,'' Sylvia offered.

''What impropriety is this?'' Judith asked. ''An unmarried woman going to a man's bedchamber?''

''She's right, you know,'' James agreed.

"But Evan is in real danger. Besides, you go to his bed-chamber," Sylvia said accusingly.

Judith flushed, but stood her ground. "But I am his—his aunt."

"You are nothing of the sort."

"It is perfectly proper for me to look after him."

"There is nothing proper about you."

"That is only your opinion," Judith said staunchly.

"I think you will find that my opinion carries some weight in this district."

"You may throw your opinion and your weight around as much as you like. You are not going up these stairs!"

"She's got you there, Sylvia," James said, his voice crackling with laughter.

Sylvia turned on her heel and marched out of the house.

"Well done, Judith," James said, lifting her hand to kiss it. She stared at him in shock.

"You should have been a soldier's wife. I do believe you would have stopped me, but indeed, I did not attack Evan." He turned and left with a bemused smile. Far from comforting Judith, his parting shot, which was too genuine to be mistaken for other than the truth, left her more disturbed than the encounter with Sylvia. If not James, then who?

Angel came out of the morning room in tears. "Judith, I will never forgive you for offending Lady Sylvia. She was only trying to help."

"She was interfering."

"I hate you. I hate all of you."

"You always say that. You know you do not mean it."

"I do mean it."

Angel ran up the stairs, and Judith found herself watching her to make sure she did not go into Evan's room. At least she could keep track of Angel at night. That was a plus to sharing a room.... God, what was she thinking? Not Angel!

"You got rid of them," Helen said flatly as she, too, came out of the morning room.

"Yes. How did you manage to restrain Angel?"

"I pretended I was having pains and got a good grip on her wrist. I find I am quite accomplished at playing a part if I am desperate."

"Well, thank you. Angel would only have added to the confusion." Judith turned to go up the stairs.

"Judith, I don't want you nursing him, either. You know the danger you run. It was your express wish to keep him at a distance."

"Yes, but he needs me now," Judith argued.

Her sister turned to go with a shake of her head.

"Helen?" Judith called from the stairs.

"What is it? Do you want me to sit with him again?"

"No. You don't really dislike Evan, do you?"

"Dislike him? He is exasperating. He provokes Hiram on purpose. We went on quite well without Evan."

"But surely you don't hate him."

"No, of course not. He's just terribly inconvenient." Helen disappeared then, and Judith went up the steps with her head in a whirl. Such a cold word, *inconvenient*. Was it just her sister's dry wit or would she really like to be rid of Evan? Judith buried her face in her hands. What had he done to her that she could suspect her own sisters? She was most definitely not her usual calm and organized self. Much as she was still determined never to marry Evan, the thought of losing him was driving her mad.

"Judith?" Lord Mountjoy called from the hall.

"Yes, what is it?" She composed herself and leaned over the banister to talk to him.

"I thought I heard voices. Who was it?"

"Just Lady Sylvia and Captain Farlay calling to see about Evan."

"I thought she was here this morning. She must really like him to call twice in one day."

"She was rather concerned. I assured her we are doing everything that is necessary."

"When he is better, he must return her call. Who knows where her concern might lead." He went back into the library, rubbing his hands together.

Tempted

222

ther entered and cocked an eyebrow at him. "Come to think of it, what are you doing up?" "It's better to be walking around a bit ... ening up. And I do know what I ... case." "Lord ... "Don't get up.

Bose ...
men in the co...
by what had happe...
managed to get Evan to c...

"You saw nothing?"

"It was pitch-black," Evan said be...

"You are the limit, Evan. I coddle you ...
through Portugal and Spain, only to have you ... -
dered under your own bed."

"Sorry, Bose. I didn't do it on purpose."

"Well, I am sleeping in here tonight, but what am I to do
with you in the daytime? Someone has to oversee the workmen."

"I shall be safe enough during the day," Evan said without conviction. "You should get some rest now yourself.
You look ragged."

"Not bloody likely."

Evan woke up feeling stiff and hungry, but not particularly wretched. His back didn't even hurt much unless he
breathed too deeply. He began to shuffle slowly into his
clothes, and not even Bose's threats could keep him in bed.
"I shall feel very much better where I can keep my back to
a wall somewhere. You don't know what it's like lying here
helpless."

"Stay at the house. If you even think about getting on a
horse I will tie you up."

"Don't worry. I shall follow your orders."

Evan retired to the empty library and retrieved the latest
edition of the *Times* from under the desk blotter, spreading
it out to savor. He was not halfway through it when his fa-

Mountjoy looked skeptically at the arm in the sling, but merely sorted through the mail. "Here's one for you."

"Ah . . ."

"Shall I open it for you?"

"Please."

Lord Mountjoy slit the envelope with his penknife, sniffed the enclosure appreciatively and handed it to his son.

"What is it, Evan? Why are you laughing? If you are getting hysterical again I shall—"

"It's from Lady Sylvia. Seeing as she's been thrown out of our house, she is inviting us to hers. A dancing party in two weeks. I can only assume she thinks I will be up to dancing by then."

"And will you be?"

"Of course. We engineers aren't layabouts like some of those cavalry boys. But I wonder what she means to accomplish with this. She says it's by way of an apology for the unfortunate incidents of yesterday."

"I should have liked to have seen Judith in action."

"She was magnificent. According to Ralph, Lady Sylvia returned with James, and Judith routed them both."

Lord Mountjoy chuckled.

"I need to ask you something," Evan said to his father.

"About Sylvia?"

"Forget Sylvia. I can take care of her."

"That's not what you said two days ago."

"That was before I had decided what to do about the canal. Now I have decided, so she is no longer a problem."

"What about the canal?"

"Oh, hang the canal. I'll build it for you. I don't care if it does ruin us."

"It won't, not if you mean to invest in it."

"I know very well the money for the canal was supposed to come from Gram. That must have given you a turn when she left it to me."

Lord Mountjoy conceded this with a toss of his head and lift of his eyebrow.

"You did plan on using the money for that, didn't you?"

"Yes, I suppose I did."

"Haven't I already said I would build it?"

"But why, if you don't believe in it?"

"I've done other things I don't believe in. I've decided if I wait to fully understand things, they may pass me by. Which brings me to Judith." Evan knew his father could not send him away in his present condition. If ever there was a time to press his suit it was now.

"What has Judith got to do with the canal?"

"Absolutely nothing, but I love her and I want to marry her." He waited for the explosion, but it did not come.

Lord Mountjoy sat down slowly in a chair. "I'm afraid that's impossible."

"Why is it so impossible?" Evan demanded. For once his father was going to own up to his sins. "She isn't already married. We are not related by blood. We are not even cousins. I know Helen is against me, and that may sway Judith, but she is certainly not on the verge of going into a religious order."

"A what?"

"Never mind that. Something holds her back. What is it?"

"I can't tell you. She made me promise I would not. Does this mean you'll withhold the money for the canal?"

Evan stared at his father thoughtfully. If his father had a guilty secret about Judith, he was not revealing the fact either by anger or embarrassment. Evan was puzzled. But then he realized that an affair with her brother-in-law would make Judith feel very guilty, and might not even phase a man as experienced as his father. Evan sighed. "No, of course not. Not out of any love for your schemes, though. I am only thinking of keeping hundreds of veterans gainfully employed for a few years. Even if no cargo is ever floated on the canal, having those men here spending money will give the local economy a boost."

"Yes, yes, of course, it's the patriotic thing to do."

"Will you speak to Helen about Judith?"

"Now, Evan, if you mean to be trifling with Judith, I won't have it. She has been through quite enough. She doesn't need—"

"What do you mean? What has she been through?"

"It doesn't concern you."

"It concerns me greatly. I love her."

"After a few weeks acquaintance?"

"I know it seems unlikely, and she has tried to keep me at a distance, but it is all so unmistakable."

"If you indeed mean it, I shall put in a word for you...if you think that will help."

"Why did I even ask you?"

"That's what I was just thinking. Your brain must be addled. I begin to believe you are in love. And to agree to the canal..."

"Yes, even without knowing about the porcelain manufacture."

"How did you find out about that?"

"Judith has been studying about it, hasn't she? Have you any hope of buying it?"

"I was trying to keep everything quiet, to keep people thinking I was buying up farmland."

"Well, if I could figure it out, I'm sure Lady Sylvia will have no trouble with it. You should have gotten hold of her ground first."

"It wasn't hers when I started this scheme. She bought it from a farmer."

"She bought it on speculation, thinking she could hold you up for it."

"I thought so myself. Then, when she seemed inclined to accept Terry's offer, I thought perhaps it was Meremont she was after. Finally you came along."

"Me?"

"You. She really wants you, I can tell."

"No, you must be mistaken."

"There is something about you. You have . . . potential."

"Potential what?"

"The potential to be dangerous, I suppose, plus a reputation."

"I have not."

"Stop. It is not unknown to us here—the risks you took, how you laughed the heartiest when the fighting was the worst."

"I was not alone in that," Evan said defensively.

"Yes, but compared to Terry, you are certainly the more intriguing character. You should have seen her face that night we were playing cards. You had her hanging on your every word."

"I had no intention of interesting her. I was merely trying to convince her of my stupidity."

"Perhaps that is one of your appeals."

"What?"

"You are reckless, potentially dangerous—that appeals to her—and you have, she thinks, no imagination for using your considerable power."

"She thinks she would control me?"

"Yes, and controlling you—a loose cannon, so to speak—would lend her a great deal more credence than controlling Terry, who is still unproven."

"Which is to say he has not done anything spectacularly stupid yet."

"Yes, that's it. That's why she wants you."

"Well, I think you can disregard what Lady Sylvia wants. She won't get it."

"Then I won't get my canal."

"Haven't I already promised that you will? I may not put it where you want it, but I will build it." Evan left on that note, with his father shouting after him to explain himself.

Chapter Twelve

"Before we begin with these letters, Judith dear, there is something I have to ask you." Lord Mountjoy folded his hands to still their tremors. "Evan has come to me—for the first time in his life, I think—for help. I fear I am powerless to do anything for him. Are you adamant about not marrying, or is there a chance...?"

"I cannot. It seemed an easy-enough decision when I made it—to stay here as Thomas's aunt. But Evan tests me on it every day." She got up and paced the library. "I did try to tell him about my past when he first came here. I thought it best he knew, but my courage failed me. I am a sad disappointment to myself. After all he has faced, I could not make a simple statement that would have spared him all this agony."

"You are afraid Evan would leave someday and you would have to take Thomas away," Lord Mountjoy said in despair.

"I will not risk that possibility, not when you and Helen love Thomas as much as I do."

"I am rather glad you have not told Evan. You are the only thing that has kept him here."

"Surely not. You may not think he loves you but he does."

"But he loves you more. Can you not marry him? We could, perhaps, agree to share Thomas if Evan promised to stay."

"I cannot marry him without telling him, and I cannot possibly tell him that I love my son more than him. I certainly cannot choose, but if I must, I will stay with Thomas."

"And you would not want me to tell Evan, either."

"No. Gutless of me, is it not? When I think of all he has been through—"

"Stop it, Judith. Do you think he went into the army out of courage?"

"What else?"

"He was running away from me, and with good reason, I might add. I was surprised he ever returned here. I had almost given up hope."

"He's here now. How long he will stay is another matter. Once he has started something he will finish it. He is like that. But when the canal is done, if I still refuse him, he will leave."

"But if you accept him . . ."

"Have I the right to tie Evan to Meremont simply because I must stay here?"

Mountjoy rose and came toward her. "You have suffered so much."

"I never expected I would regret my decision. Once made, I thought my life would be easy."

"Then you do love Evan?"

"Yes, unfortunately. I am so sensible in most matters. How could I have let such a thing happen?"

"One does not let love happen, my dear. It happens quite against your will. I do know that."

"Have you ever regretted getting mixed up in our lamentable affairs?"

"Not for a moment. My life was so empty before."

"Yes, you do know about love. At any rate, it is best Evan goes on thinking I won't marry him out of religious scruples. It will hurt him, but not as much as the truth."

"Religious scruples? What sham have you been playing at?"

"Helen told him I was going to become a nun."

"So that's what he meant about you going into a religious order. And he swallowed that?"

"Yes, my scholarly pursuits lend credence to it," Judith said primly as she seated herself at the desk and took up her pen. "Evan may be intelligent, but he is quite gullible in some ways."

Lord Mountjoy roared with laughter. "It is too bad you are not going to marry him. It would be fun to watch him being outmaneuvered by you the rest of my days."

"Oh, you may witness that anyway, if Evan stays here. I don't think he has the inclination to run a business. Don't take me wrong. If you ask him to do something, he has the energy and expertise to carry it out, but on his own . . ."

"Not the desire. That is my fault. The boy spent most of his life thinking he had no future. He has never learned to plan for himself. I nearly ruined Terry, too, by putting Evan in his place."

"If we can keep Terry away from the bottle, he is quite competent to manage things."

"And Ralph?"

"Rather like Evan. He knows how to solve things but would not on his own think of the puzzle."

"Evan always liked to solve puzzles. I kept him out of a lot of mischief that way. I'm glad you did not tell him. Part of his love for you is the intellectual puzzle you present him."

"So if I told him the truth he would lose interest in me?"

"No, I don't think so."

"More likely he would hate me for trapping him."

"I think I know him better than that. I hope I live long enough to see what you two make of this place."

"You will."

Judith went back to her room to change and sort out her sewing for the evening, well satisfied with the afternoon's work.

Evan was just thinking about changing for dinner and wondering if it was worth the effort when his father came into his bedroom with a framed painting.

"I thought you might like to have this down at the dower house. I had put it away."

"Who is it?" Evan asked, as he gazed at the portrait. "It's not Gram, though there is a resemblance."

"It's your mother, of course. Do you mean to tell me you don't even recognize her?"

"No, but then I don't remember much about the house, either, or..."

"What?"

"Not even your face. I didn't know who you were until you spoke. Your voice, now—that I remember."

"I had no idea. When you left here—"

"When you sent me away..."

"To school. You were going to school, anyway. You didn't remember then?"

"No. It's just as well."

"That's what you meant when you said you had no past." Lord Mountjoy sat down heavily, making the small chair creak.

"At least I wasn't homesick like half those young wretches. Father, what is it?"

"I always assumed you didn't come take your leave of me because you were defiant."

"It was because I was not sure of my welcome, the same reason I didn't come back for holidays or..." Evan looked at the picture again, then stood it on the floor by one wall. "I would rather have a painting of Gram."

"When your grandmother wrote you that your mother had died, the regrets you sent were so cold and formal. I imagined you were proudly masking your grief. I never imagined you didn't even remember her."

"I didn't realize it myself until I came back here. Nothing was as I remembered it because I *didn't* remember it. All I had was what Gram told me, the pictures I made up with her words...and your voice, drumming things into my head.''

Evan looked once again at the painting. ''She was beautiful, but shallow, I think.'' He turned abruptly to his father, a strange light in his eyes. ''It was Mother who didn't want me here, wasn't it?''

''I tried to reason with her. I couldn't make her see that it was an accident. She continued to think you'd killed Gregory on purpose, because you were jealous of him.''

''No doubt she infected young Terry with that notion.''

''I had not thought of that. If you were jealous of Gregory it was because she favored him so.''

''Perhaps I was. I can't remember. Worst of all I can't remember what Gregory looked like.''

''It doesn't matter now. I was thinking the picture might be some comfort to you. I see now I was wrong.''

''Why should I need comforting?''

''Judith does not wish to marry, not you or anyone else.''

''That's the answer I expected.''

''Then why did you put me through this?''

''When besieging a city, Father, one always looks for the easiest way in, but keeps two or three other possibilities in mind.''

''And what are your two or three other possibilities?''

''Wouldn't you like to know?''

''You must get one thing straight.'' His father raised his voice. ''Judith is not to be distressed. If you make her shed so much as one tear, you will be thrown out of the house on your—''

''You are sounding more like yourself now. You had me worried for a moment there.''

''I am not joking.''

''I should leave off joking, too, when you have had enough. I will not impose my suit upon Judith, as it is so unwelcome.''

''Then what was all this in aid of?''

''I'll keep my promise, but that doesn't mean I have given up. You have set me a little mystery to solve—two, really.''

"If you go digging around you will only stir up trouble for Judith."

"I don't need to dig. If I think about it long enough the answer will come to me, just like one of your riddles."

"Do you remember those?"

"Some of them. It's like finding a long-lost toy, tripping over a memory like that in the attic of your brain."

"But you don't remember your mother?"

"No. That is odd, isn't it. She seems a stranger to me."

"She said you ruined her figure."

"What?"

"Her pregnancy with you ruined her figure, and having Terry absolutely destroyed it."

Evan stared at him a moment, then burst out laughing. "I can see now why she favored Gregory, if he didn't make her gain any weight."

"It seemed a cruel thing for her to say."

"It's absurd, Father. One can only laugh at absurdities."

"I suppose."

Evan looked at the portrait and chuckled. "I think I will hang it in the dower house, after all. I remember now she said something once about wanting never to be relegated to the dower house."

"Yes, she did say that." Lord Mountjoy looked at the picture and chuckled, too, as he left the room.

Since Angel was not at table, they turned their conversation to the business of the canal, and Evan drew a model in his mashed turnips of how they would bank the removed earth to shore up the sides of the canal in the low places. They could control the level of water to some extent with locks, but the fewer of these they had to build the better.

"I wish you wouldn't play with your food," Lord Mountjoy commented. "It makes it look quite unappetizing."

"Shall I pour on more gravy to demonstrate what will happen if we do not pack the sides sufficiently?" Evan teased.

"That will not be necessary."

Helen observed this byplay with a prim smile, and Judith laughed outright at them.

They had talked themselves out by the time they moved into the library, and Ralph read some of his poems as the ladies sewed and the men sipped claret. Evan almost went to sleep listening to the lively, inflected voice and finally excused himself. He meant to ride out to the site the next day, so he decided to call it a night. He was almost to the door of his room when he felt a strange quivering in his stomach. Nothing to worry about; they were all downstairs. All but Angel, of course. He warily nudged the door open with his foot and peered in the corners, dimly lit by his candle, before entering.

"Anything the—"

"Bose! Damn you!" Evan said, whirling and wincing at the pain this caused. "Don't you know any better than to go sneaking up on a fellow like that?"

"Surely you don't expect to be attacked in your room every night?"

"No, but I own to being a little jumpy."

"You were never so squeamish when the French snipers were having at you under a bridge or down in an entrenchment."

"There was nothing I could do about them. It just rankles to get it from behind and by a . . ."

"By a what?"

"An unknown hand."

"You have some knowledge of this you are not telling me."

"Nonsense. Are you going to help me undress or not? I mean to ride out with you in the morning."

"That will add to the delights of the day."

"I must see what is going forward."

"Very well, but you are to come back at noon and stay here."

"Yes, sir."

* * *

"I was watching you sew last night," Evan said as they walked the horses after riding back from the workings.

"You always watch me sew," Judith replied. "What is so fascinating?"

"I don't know. It's comforting, somehow. Mother never sewed."

"You remember that?"

"Yes, I begin to find that childhood was horrifying only to a boy. It doesn't bother me much at all."

"I'm so glad. You will make your father very happy."

"I plan to. Have you started your dress for the dance yet? If you don't think you have time to make one, we can go into town and buy you one."

"I'm not going," Judith said, frowning at his change of subject.

"What do you mean, you're not going?"

"It's simply not worthwhile to dress me up for these events. Nothing will come of it."

"Never mind that you might derive some amusement from it."

"But I wouldn't."

"With all Lady Sylvia's ridiculous friends coming from Bath for it?"

"From..." Judith seemed speechless for a moment. "How do you know her friends are ridiculous?" she asked distractedly.

"She doesn't associate with country folk hereabouts. Her guests, outside of us, are bound to be silly chits or strutting popinjays."

"You suggest I go expressly to laugh at them?" She had regained her color and put on her haughty face.

"Why not?"

"I have not a dress that will do, and that is final."

"I'm sure Angel has two or three to choose from. Borrow one of hers."

"You expect me to wear a borrowed dress?" she chided.

"Then come to town with me and I will buy you one."

"Out of a shop? Oh, that will never do. A real lady has her dresses made for her."

"A real lady would not taunt me so."

"I shall not go."

"Then I shall not go, either. Now that I think of it I rather like the idea of the two of us dining here in lonely state. Don't look at me so uncertainly. You know I would hold the line unless you feel inclined to mop my fevered brow." He rested his head against hers and gazed merrily into her eyes. "Or unless you fell into another one of your passionate trances. Then we could always go back to the dower house."

"What is the matter with me that I lose all control?" she asked desperately.

"You love me. That's not a crime."

"It is when I torture you with it."

"We are agreed then." His lips were close to hers, almost brushing them. "It's safer if we both attend this ball. I'll speak to Father."

"What? But I thought—"

"That I would try to seduce you again? Not in my condition at the moment. Perhaps when I am more able to do it properly."

"Oh, Evan, I have ruined your life, as well as my own."

"What do you mean? My life was ruined before you came into it. I have no regrets about this, and you should not, either. I promised I would not try to sway you, but it isn't easy for me." He kissed her, and she returned his embrace with a hungry passion. He breathed raggedly, keeping her face pressed to his. "Don't move, Judith. Don't let this end."

"We must," she whispered.

"Can we not hang on to this moment a little longer?"

"It's not fair to you."

She pushed him away gently and left him swaying, with his eyes closed and his arms hanging limply at his sides. She had never seen a man look so beaten.

Taurus nudged him in the back to remind him of the apple that was waiting for him. Evan walked him to the stable and handed him over to a groom. To his surprise, Judith was still there, and she held a finger to her lips and pointed to the stall with the puppies.

In the straw the setter lay nursing her pups. Thomas was snuggled up against her, and she licked the pups and Thomas indiscriminately.

"He could be one of them," Evan whispered.

"Yes. I am worried about him."

"I must see what I can do to get him another, else he will grow up in the stable."

They started back toward the house, with Judith looking perplexed. "There are children who do such things—kill animals—without realizing it is wrong or...permanent," she said uneasily.

"Children who have not been raised right."

"It's not all in the upbringing. There is such a thing as bad blood. Not insanity, precisely, but a streak of brutality that will out in spite of—"

"Has Father done something?" He looked at her so intently she was taken aback.

"Your father? What are you talking about?"

"This is not the first time he..." Evan couldn't say it. He could accept the idea that Judith was his father's mistress. He could even overlook it. But he could not say it.

"You father is a kind and gentle man. Surely you are not suggesting he killed the puppy?"

"No, but when you mentioned bad blood, well, I myself have that shadow cast upon me, and... Don't look at me so. In spite of what Thomas says, I didn't hang his pup."

"Thomas said that?"

"Yes, I suspect that's mostly why he tried to shoot me."

"Where would he get that idea?" Judith asked as she went up the steps.

"I don't know. It set me back on my heels, I can tell you. I thought I was getting on well with him."

Evan pushed open the door for Judith, who saw the mail on the hall table, walked over and began to sort through it absently.

"At any rate," Evan continued, "I shouldn't worry about the Mountjoy brand of insanity. It seems to set upon us rather later in life."

Judith stared at him, openmouthed in a way he could not resist. He took advantage of her encumbered state to kiss her longingly. She dropped letters between them and struggled for air. "Evan, I wasn't talking about your father."

"Oh, well, if you mean your sister's little starts, I'm sure that is due only to the pregnancy. I have given up thinking—"

"What little starts?" Helen demanded from the doorway.

Evan jumped back from Judith as though he had been stung and would have overset the table had it not crashed into the wall. Helen's appearance from the breakfast parlor was worse than walking straight into a French picket.

"Don't touch that paper!" his father ordered from the library doorway, causing Evan to recoil in the other direction, staggering into the wall. In a very few moments he was reduced to a wreck.

"If you go spreading that nonsensical story about me..." Helen threatened.

"Never! I swear I will never say anything."

Judith was whirling from one to another of them, saying "What?" in a distracted way and dropping more letters onto the floor.

"Never say anything about what?" Lord Mountjoy demanded.

"Nothing, Father," Evan said desperately as he retreated backward toward the stairs.

"You stay away from Judith," Helen warned as he crept up the staircase in disorder.

"Have you been at Judith again?" Lord Mountjoy bellowed, looking up at him.

Evan fled in disarray.

"What was that all about?" his father growled.

"I don't know," Judith said. "Something about Helen being insane."

"The very idea! Sorry, Helen. You know what a clumsy oaf he can be. I'm sure he did not mean to hurt your feelings." Lord Mountjoy escorted his wife to the breakfast parlor.

Judith shook her head as she gathered up the mail. She had been so close to telling Evan the truth. Had they only walked around to the front of the house instead of coming in the back door the die would have been cast. She realized, though, that she was relieved she had not told him. Much as she thought Evan should act more mature, she did enjoy seeing him embarrassed. That's when she realized it was the boy in him that attracted her. Whatever liberties he might take, he was so very unsure of himself that it was funny. She smiled wistfully at his confusion and tried to imagine his reaction if she had said one or two more fateful sentences. She shook her head again. After all this time she could not tell him.

She stared at the letter on top of the pile and gasped, then rushed into the breakfast parlor to find Lord Mountjoy.

Evan wrestled with himself for a full half hour about whether he could face them all again. He could say he had overdone it and not go down, could even use the excuse again at dinner. But that would be acting too much like Angel. Besides, he would miss seeing Judith, and he had to face them all sometime. And Judith always had the courage to confront him after he seduced her.

Then it occurred to him that he made such stupid mistakes all the time. Most likely his family would take no notice or forget all about it. If it came to that, he wasn't so sure what he had done that was so bad, except to get caught kissing Judith. Well, that was bad enough. But only Helen had seen the kiss, not his father. Of course, she might have told him . . . Finally Evan could not stand the suspense.

He arrived at the breakfast table to find only Helen there. She appeared to steel herself as he sat down.

"I'm sorry—" he started to say.

"I don't want your apology. I want you to behave."

"Where is Father?"

"He has some business to conduct in Bristol. He will be back tomorrow or the day after."

"Oh, and where is—"

"Judith went with him to do some shopping. Is there anything else you want to know?"

Since Helen was plainly irritated, Evan wondered for the twentieth time if she knew about the affair between her husband and her sister. He shook his head. It was too fantastic to believe she would willingly condone it. But if they had been as destitute as he suspected, perhaps she would put up with anything. Or perhaps—his guts crawled at the thought—perhaps it had been part of the original bargain. Suddenly the eggs before him looked nauseating, and he closed his eyes.

"Well?" she demanded, nearly causing him to spill his coffee.

He wondered if Judith had been spirited off on his account. "Is she by any chance shopping for a ball gown?" he asked instead.

"I—I don't know. Are you going to be sick on me? If you are, I would rather you go back to your room."

Ralph and Terry shouldered their way into the breakfast parlor then, full of talk and not paying attention to anything but their food. Evan told them he would not be riding out that afternoon, and Ralph checked one or two points with him before Evan excused himself and retired to his room. He should go with them if for no other reason than to keep his mind occupied. Otherwise, he was only going to brood about Judith.

He did realize one thing: he would no longer be able to sit back complacently with the knowledge that the woman he loved was being taken advantage of by his own father. The sick feeling had nothing to do with pulling his stitches in the hall. It was all inside, and he was not sure it would go away no matter how far he traveled from Meremont. But he did know he could not stay here permanently under these circumstances. For now, he would move into the dower house, so that no one else would see how much he hurt. He would build the canal, not for his father, but for Judith, and he would ask her one last time if she would marry him. If she refused, he would leave.

At least he had a plan, albeit a rather hopeless one. The only thing to do was to try to get Judith to give up Lord Mountjoy. She might have been grateful to his father in the beginning, but that was no reason to tie her whole life to his. Perhaps she was just persuadable or too physically passionate for her own good. No, that did not fit with the rest of her character. She seemed so sensible, so determined most of the time. Perhaps she was determined to get what she wanted, first from Lord Mountjoy, then from him. Perhaps she would marry him after his father died. . . .

A chill went through him. The one thing he would definitely not do was wait about for his father to die.

And Judith. What would happen to her later? Would Terry marry her? The thought wrenched a groan from him. Were they both such good managers that they would form a union merely to strengthen a business?

"Evan?" Angel said, poking her head in the door.

He spun to face her, groaning again as the stitches pulled.

"Are you all right?"

"No—yes. What do you want?"

"I was on my way to Lady Sylvia's. I heard you moaning. I wanted to know if you are all right. And what sort of answer is that—'no and yes'?"

"Is that what I said?"

"Are you being dense on purpose? I must say I think it's stupid of you to be up if you are not fit."

He stared at her, wondering how she could have the effrontery to say such things if she had been his assailant.

"Evan, you look so odd."

"It's nothing, I just need...air." He dashed past her and down the stairs, setting off through the yard at a dead run, as though a troop of cavalry had surprised him and he was running for his life. He ran along the stream until he came to the wooden bridge. He threw himself down on the soft earth under it, sweating and dizzy from the exertion, and nearly passed out. He must have lost more blood than he'd thought. But he slid only to the edge of oblivion, then clawed his way back. When he opened his eyes, however, he sensed there was something wrong. It should be dark, or it had been dark the last time he had been here. . . .

He could remember two voices lifted in argument. He had often sneaked out of his room at night to pilfer a book from the library. The voices belonged to his mother and father, he remembered. His father had given up trying to persuade her and had moved on to demands.

"Why not?" she repeated. "Because, Hiram, I do not want another baby. I don't even want the ones I already have."

Evan had run out of the house and ended here, to cry the night through. He had gone home again, he remembered, in the early dawn, and had said nothing. But he had known he wasn't wanted. Anyone but a dunce would have understood that without having to be told.

Evan had accepted the fact more easily then than he was accepting his present dilemma. How could he blame his father for wanting the love of a woman, when love had been denied him so long?

Worst of all, there was no solution to this puzzle. No matter how he twisted it around, the situation was unworkable. He must throw himself into the canal project, ignore Judith and leave at the first opportunity. The only chance at all was if her love for him was stronger than her love for his father, stronger than her desire for Meremont and work. How could he possibly compete with all that?

Suddenly a little face peeped under the bridge at him.

"Hallo, Evan."

"Hello, Thomas," Evan said, sitting up. "I see you escaped your keeper again. Is Miranda looking for you?"

"Yes. Can I stay here?"

"Of course. This was always one of my favorite hiding places."

"What did you do here?"

"Sometimes I fished."

"I should like to know how to fish."

"I could teach you. You stay here, and I will go back to the stable for the gear. Then we'll spend the whole afternoon fishing."

Evan returned in short order with the required gear and a couple of apples, which Thomas devoured hungrily. They made their way along the bank, talking in whispers, and getting extremely wet as Evan introduced Thomas to the theory of fishing. They then settled down to await the results of a hastily dug worm dangling in the water on a hook.

"We just wait?" Thomas asked.

"Or you can jiggle the line about every once in a while. You must understand that fishing is mostly an excuse to lie about on a sunny riverbank and sleep. You can still say you have been doing something."

Thomas chuckled delightedly. They had been ignoring Miranda's approach. Her repeated calls of "Thomas!" had started at the house and were growing louder.

"Hide down there behind that rock," Evan said, rather than see the child taken prisoner.

Miranda popping out of the woods a moment later gave him a start even though he had been expecting her.

"You, sir. Have you seen Thomas?"

"Me? Why would I have seen him? I can't for the life of me comprehend how you manage to mislay the boy so often."

Thomas's smothered giggle was covered by Miranda's exasperated sigh and her stomping off in a dudgeon.

"You lied for me," Thomas said in awe.

"Well, I didn't exactly lie. And don't think it's all right for you to do it. Let's wait until she gets to the other side of the stable, then we'll head for the house. With any luck she will never see us."

When they heard Miranda moving toward the woods, they hared off toward the house on a run. They burst through the door, laughing, only to encounter a foot-tapping Helen in the hall.

"Mother, I was lost and Evan found me. I am ever so glad to see you." Thomas ran to Helen and hugged her about the knees, causing her to clutch the banister as she stared skeptically at the boy's head. Evan did not have the advantage of being able to hide his face in her skirt.

"So you were lost?" she asked sternly. "Is that your story?"

"You know, if we took Thomas about with us more he would know the place better. Then he wouldn't be in danger of getting lost when he wanders away."

"When he—" Helen started to say, but Evan made off up the stairs, abandoning Thomas to his own devices. "And how comes it that you didn't hear Miranda calling you?" Helen demanded.

"I did hear her, but she runs so fast her voice seems to come from all over. Then I found Evan and he quit fishing just to bring me home. That was capital of him, wasn't it?"

"Yes, I suppose it was. For now, come upstairs and change out of these wet clothes. You worry us when you wander off. Don't you realize that?"

From the safety of his bedroom, Evan listened to the animated conversation coming up the stairs. So Thomas had pulled it off. What an enterprising child! Whatever else Evan might regret, he now had the most delightful young protégé. That's when it hit him that he could not just abandon Thomas to the fate that had been his twenty years before. He had to stay, if for no other reason than to give the boy an ally and confidant.

And then . . . perhaps all his suspicions about Judith and his father were unfounded. It seemed such an extraordinary crime, when he looked at it objectively. But he could seldom do so, for he was extremely jealous of Judith. Once he realized that might be influencing him, he could face her absence with more fortitude.

At any rate, it would be cowardly to run. If he loved Judith, he should have the courage to fight his father for her.

* * *

When Helen rose from the dinner table, Evan left Ralph and Terry to the port and followed her into the library. They supposed he was merely being courteous, but actually he wanted to talk to her. He was a little embarrassed to come to the point, but when was he likely to get a better chance?

"It comes to this, Helen—if Judith does not go to the ball, I will not go, either. Do you really want us to be alone together for an entire evening?"

"But I thought Hiram needed you to go."

"What my father needs is not my primary concern."

"But there will be other people there."

"They won't eat us."

"But Judith doesn't take to strangers."

"Nonsense. If she doesn't like them, she needn't talk to them. Now dress her for this party and do it creditably, or I'm not going to buy Angel that wardrobe I promised her, and you will have her weeping all over the house."

"She is already moping all over the house. This ball is the first thing to catch her interest in days. She spent all afternoon at Sylvia's helping with the preparations."

"Why is Angel still upset?" he asked, then remembered with a chill the way the girl had reacted after she had shot Terry.

"She says she has been disappointed in love."

"Oh. Well, the best thing for her is a party. You have only to get the three of you ready. Send the bills to me."

"I don't like being ordered about by you and I don't like going to this ball."

"Don't distress yourself. Neither is likely to happen often. Things were simpler in the army. You told someone to do something and it was done."

"But those were men."

"Yes, that's why things were simpler. A troop of moderately intelligent men could achieve wonders."

"Destroying themselves, you mean? Do you call that 'wonders'?"

"That's not what I meant and you know it."

"If a troop of moderately intelligent women ran the world there would be no wars."

"I think you must be wrong. You have only to think of Lady Sylvia to realize that men have no monopoly on that sort of thing."

"And you hold her in contempt."

"There are men who hold all intelligent women in contempt, but I am not one of them."

"And do you hold me in contempt?"

"Certainly not. I have the utmost respect for you."

"A very apt retort to my question, seeing as I once threatened to kill you."

"Like a French shell, I could see it coming."

She laughed unexpectedly, sounding very much like Judith. "I'm sorry I sent you away that day, but I had been arguing with Hiram and I wasn't feeling well."

"I realized that later. Have we a truce then?"

"In all matters but Judith. You are to leave her alone."

"May I not even dance with her?"

"Once then."

"Twice?"

"Very well, twice, but that is all. Are you quite finished?"

"Why no, we have not even negotiated how many dances I am to have with you."

Terry and Ralph came in then, so the banter had to cease, but Evan was glad Helen was warming up to him.

Chapter Thirteen

While Evan, Ralph and Terry continued the survey, Bose oversaw the clearing of trees from the eastern stretch of the canal. That work could be started without arousing too much suspicion, since they would have done the same for a roadbed for a steam railway. But Evan worked impatiently and rode back to the house two or three times a day to see if Judith and his father had returned. He still could not rid himself of the fantastic notion that they were having an affair. The possibility hurt him enormously.

He pushed Ralph, who loved it, and Terry, who resented being roused out of bed, so they could get in half a day's work before breakfast. No matter how hard Evan drove himself, he still could not sleep without horrifying dreams. Evan had steeled himself to look upon the most ghastly relics of war without flinching. But this affair! This was alive and happening now. He felt he should be doing something to prevent it. Yet there was nothing he could do, nothing he had a right to do.

After two fretful nights, he began speaking of dashing off to Bristol to see what was the matter. Bose looked at him as though he had taken leave of his senses, and Evan subsided. If Helen could tolerate their continued absence, surely he could be patient as well.

The third day it started to rain at two o'clock, so they abandoned work and sent the men early to their dinners and ale. When Evan and his assistants rode into the courtyard,

Lord Mountjoy was just helping Judith out of the carriage. Evan looked at her in disappointment, for she was not carrying a single package. Her smile faded for a moment, but the suppressed excitement Lord Mountjoy was obviously feeling restored it as she went with him into the house, glancing back at Evan only once. Terry and Ralph followed them.

Evan stood a long time in the rain, staring at the house, feeling as much an outsider as the first day he had ridden in. He had the most childish impulse to go sit under the bridge until Judith came to look for him. But that never worked; nobody ever came to find him. He trudged wearily toward the house, turning his back on the laughter in the library and making his way up the stairs.

Judith was coming down. "Evan, what is it? Has anything gone amiss?"

"No," he said hoarsely.

"Something is wrong. I can tell by your face."

He tried to bite back the question, tried to make it an innocent inquiry, but it came out as a desperate plea. "What were you doing in Bristol?"

"I—I can't tell you," she said, her hand resting lightly on the banister.

He nodded and made as if to pass her on the stairs.

"I know it isn't fair. Your father should trust you by now. I really think he holds the truth back from you, not from any fear that you would reveal our secret, but because he wants you to puzzle it out for yourself."

"I fear I have lost my delight in puzzles," Evan said softly, with his back to her.

"Evan, wait."

"What is it?" he asked numbly.

"We bought it."

"Don't play games with me, Judith. You didn't go to Bristol on any shopping expedition!"

"No, of course not."

"You admit it?" he asked, turning toward her.

"I think you have a right to know. We bought the porcelain factory."

"You what?" he asked, shaking his head as though to clear it.

"We closed the deal on the porcelain factory. Now all we need is the right-of-way."

"Oh, Judith!" He came down the half flight that separated them and embraced her.

"You weren't worried, were you?" she asked as he held her tightly. When he eased his hold, she saw that his face was flooded with relief, the strain of moments ago replaced by a profound weariness.

"I did not know if—if I should see you again or no," he said unsteadily. He still held her hands and gave no sign of letting them go. He sank onto the steps almost as though he were too weak to stand, and she sat down with him.

"I quite see why you might expect that in the army, not to ever see someone again, but real life isn't like that."

"No, of course not." He stroked her cheek and pulled her to him for a kiss. In his fragile state she had no will to push him away. She had no will to resist him at all. He called up hunger inside her in an instant. She wanted him now and she would always want him. If he was feeling anything like the desire she felt, he must be truly suffering. It wasn't right. She was doing him some real damage, and somehow she had to stop it.

Evan did not turn up for dinner, but when Ralph was sent to fetch him, he came back with the news that Evan had thrown himself down on his bed and could not be wakened. Bose had said he would let him sleep.

"I'm so glad you are back, Father," Terry said. "That Evan is like a madman. Everything has to be done today."

"Must be the army influence," Lord Mountjoy surmised. "In a war, one day or night can mean a great deal."

"I like it when we push to finish up," Ralph said. "That makes it exciting."

"It makes dinner very late," Helen complained, "or very cold, depending on whether we have held it for you or not."

"Who cares about food?" Ralph asked as he heaped his plate.

Lord Mountjoy raised an eyebrow at him, then changed the topic. "Angel, I think once I unpack my bag I might find presents in there for you and Helen."

"Oh, can't I have mine now?"

"After dinner. Now tell me what you have been doing with yourself," Lord Mountjoy demanded jovially, knowing better than to remark on her reappearance at the dinner table.

"I have been going over to Lady Sylvia's to help with the preparations for her ball. Tomorrow we will start the flower arrangements."

"Have I got to go to this thing?" Ralph asked.

"It wouldn't do you any harm," Lord Mountjoy stated. "Since you are to be living here, you may as well meet some of the young bloods who inhabit these parts. Come to think of it, it may be damned dangerous to turn you loose with them, but there's no help for that. Is your dress ready, Helen dear?"

"Oh, yes, but Evan has said that Judith must go or he will not. So I think you must attend, Judith. I will help with the dress you started."

"Me at a ball?" Judith mused. "Now that will be dangerous."

"Why?" asked Ralph.

"Never mind," warned Lord Mountjoy.

Evan slept the night through and well into the morning. He woke with a sense of disorientation and dressed impatiently. He strode to the stable to discover that, judging from the absent animals, all the men must have gone to the factory. Because his own horses were there, however, Judith must be home. He was about to go back to the house when his father rode in.

"Why were you looking so morose when we drove up yesterday?" Lord Mountjoy demanded.

"You've never been in a battle where you didn't know if you had won or not," Evan replied as they began to walk toward the back door.

His father stopped with an abrupt gesture. "But that's part of the excitement of business—the uncertainty. That makes winning all the more golden."

"Yes, Father," Evan said with a tired smile.

"I don't see why you were worried. You didn't even know we had gone to try to settle the deal."

"Precisely. I didn't know why you went to Bristol. I only knew that Helen was nervous about it."

"Ah, you figured it out. Good lad."

"No, I was in such a state I was not thinking clearly enough to figure out anything. But while you were gone I did remember a good deal. That it was Mother I should have hated, not you, and that I was a rotten child."

"I suppose you had good reason to be. There was a time I hardly saw you. I don't like it when children are not raised by their parents. You turned seven and suddenly you had a tutor. Our paths never crossed. We lived in the same house and never saw each other."

"I have my regrets, too—that I did not face you, that I blamed you for so much that was out of your control. That I thought you..."

"What? Come now, make a clean breast of it."

"When you went off with Judith for two days, I was half-mad with jealousy. It had crossed my mind before, from things you had said, that you were inordinately close, but to go away together..."

"Jealousy? You mean you thought that Judith and I..." Lord Mountjoy looked shocked, then as though he were going to fly into a rage. Just as suddenly, he burst out laughing. "Really, Evan, I make allowance for your disordered mind, but I am nearing sixty. I don't know whether I should be offended or complimented."

"Complimented, I think. I was not at all sure about my chances of taking her away from you."

"Now see here, Evan. You may be able to coerce Judith into going to this ball, but if you annoy her I will shovel you off to the dower house whether the paper is hung yet or not."

"I promise I will never again do anything to distress her. She will have to want me. If she truly never wishes to marry, I will respect that."

"See that you do. Though I don't know how I can place any reliance on you when you show me so little respect."

"At least this time I did tell you what I was thinking."

"Yes, I grant you that, and I can see how you might mistake matters. Judith has a wonderful head for business. I don't know what I would do without her. And it was she who encouraged Terry to interest himself in Meremont, much as you helped Ralph. I wish she were my daughter."

"Well, I don't. I would much rather have her as a wife than a sister."

"But if she rejects you, you promise you will treat her like a sister?"

"Yes, but you know we fellows in the engineer corps never give up. Where is she, anyway?"

"Probably still writing letters."

Evan found Judith in the library transcribing letters and sat down deliberately on the edge of the desk and her papers, making it impossible for her to work. She stared at his muscular thigh and compressed her lips to try to still the pulse that began beating in her throat. "So you have bludgeoned them all into making me go to this ball?" she asked.

"Yes, I have been very busy on your account."

"It won't do, you know. I can't ever marry you."

"I don't recall asking you."

"Don't tease about this. You have accepted it then?"

"When the canal is finished I will ask you. If you say no then, I won't bother you again."

"The answer will be no."

"And I am never to know why?" he probed. "That is the hard part."

"I should think a soldier would be used to not asking questions, to taking orders and doing his job."

"I should think so, too, but this isn't a war. At least it's not supposed to be. You are a force to be reckoned with, Judith Wells. Don't you think that amidst all your tasks—building a canal, starting up the porcelain factory, keeping us all in line—you could find time to be my wife, as well?"

"Time is not the issue."

"You have told me all the things that are not the issue. Why can't you tell me the one thing that does stand between us? I have made my peace with Helen. I think she even likes me. Surely she was the only person keeping us apart now that—"

Judith stared resentfully up at him and toyed with the inkwell. "Not the only one," she said bitterly.

"Who then? Not Father."

"Thomas."

"Her little boy?"

"Thomas is not her little boy," Judith said boldly, staring him in the eye to make sure he got the message.

Evan stared at her blankly for a moment, then all his suspicions came flooding back and his stomach gave a lurch. He sat down in a chair, hunching over and breathing hard. "I don't believe it," he gasped desperately, willing it not to be true.

"Believe it, Evan," she said, standing up. "I have had a child out of wedlock. We have covered it up as best we could, but there are people in the world who know. That is why I must never marry anyone, least of all you. That is why I will never leave here. I have given up my son publicly, but I will never really desert him. That is the danger I would run if I married. Sooner or later I might have to choose between my husband and my son. Why aren't you laughing, Evan? If ever there was time for hysterical laughter, it is now."

"I don't believe it," he repeated with tears in his voice. "Father would never have done that to you. I know what he used to be like, but he's not anymore. He doesn't think of you that way. He loves you like a daughter. Father would never have done that to you," he chanted, looking up at her, more a boy at that moment than a man.

"Evan, of course he did not. Thomas is not his child!"

"Oh, Judith!" Evan stood up and crushed her in his embrace. "You really had me going there. I thought you meant—"

"How dare you think that about me!" she shouted, pushing him away. "Did you really imagine that your father and I—that we... Oh, let me be!" She ran from the room, and Evan sat down to recover his scattered wits.

So that's all it was! Why hadn't he seen it before? Thomas did not look like any of them.

Everything was going to be all right now. When Evan had recovered himself and downed a brandy, he went upstairs. He was about to knock on Judith's door, but heard voices and realized Angel was in there, too. He went to his room to bide his time and fell asleep with the relief of finally knowing the worst. Why had Judith not told him before?

"What do you want?" Angel demanded when she answered the door.

"I want to talk to Judith."

"You can't anymore. You can't ever torture her again. I can't believe how much I hate you." She swung at him, but he caught her arm.

"I can. Where is she?"

"She's gone!" Angel said, bursting into tears. "And it's all your fault. You had to keep digging and digging until she told you. Why did you do it, Evan, why?"

"Gone? Gone where?"

"Bristol. She's taken the gig into Tiverton to catch the stage. Once she gets to Bristol you'll never find her."

"My God, how could you let her go?"

"She made me promise not to tell." Angel threw herself on the bed in floods of tears.

"What the devil is going on?" Terry demanded of Evan, who was already sprinting down the stairs. "If you've hurt her, Evan, I will kill you."

"What's the to-do?" Lord Mountjoy asked, coming out of the library.

"I'm borrowing the curricle. I have to catch Judith. She has run off to Bristol."

"What? You can't drive, not in your condition."

Evan ignored them and ran to the stable. They found him there frantically attempting to assist one stable boy in harnessing a pair of jumpy horses. The boy looked up with relief as Lord Mountjoy came in, demanding an explanation, for Evan was more hindrance than help.

"What's this about Judith going to Bristol? If she has business—"

"She's run away and it is all my fault. I can't believe how stupid I was."

"I can," Terry said belligerently. "You've left Angel incoherent. Did you really frighten Judith away from here?"

"Yes, damn my eyes. Terry, you've got to help me find her. I can hardly drive one of these things with two arms," Evan said, making a tangle in the harness and drawing a moan from the stable boy.

"For God's sake, Terry, go with him or he will kill himself, and the horses into the bargain," Lord Mountjoy said, putting the harness right and calming the animals.

"Very well, I'll drive you, but only because I care about Judith. I will never forgive you for making Angel cry."

They tore out of the stable and up the drive, taking the turn onto the road so sharply that one wheel lifted off the ground for a split second. Evan blinked, briefly remembering another reckless drive. That was one memory he did not think he would bother to call back.

"Faster, Terry! When does the stage pass through Tiverton?"

"The stage or the mail coach?"

"Good Lord, I never thought to ask. But I'm quite sure Angel said the stage."

"That means nothing. If it's the mail coach it will have left long before we get there."

"Then we will just have to follow it, catch it and pass it. Terry, we can't let her lose herself in Bristol. She's a determined-enough woman that she would do it successfully."

"I know," Terry said, lashing the horses into a full gallop over stretches of road that called for a trot. They did not bother to stop in Tiverton more than the moment it took to ascertain that the mail coach had departed, but bowled on through the town, then increased their pace as they reached the country again.

"You drive a lot better than Gregory," Evan said, peering ahead of them. "I think I saw it cresting that next hill."

They came up on the coach, but all Evan's yelling brought no more than jeers from the passengers on top, who were used to young bucks almost causing crashes as they tried to pass. Terry saw a straight stretch ahead and made it past the mail coach, which was pressing along at a good pace.

"Pull the team across the road and make them stop."

"Are you mad? We'll just stay ahead of them until they reach Bristol."

"Terry! We don't even know if she's on board the coach. I have to know."

When Terry saw that his brother was about to grab the reins, he slapped his hands away. "Let me find another straight stretch so they can at least see us."

He brought the team to a quick halt and turned it sideways on the road, praying that no vehicle would come the other way and crash into them. Evan leapt down and walked toward the rapidly moving mail coach, holding up his good arm and waving.

"Evan, you fool. You'll be killed! They can't stop." Terry could not even leap down, since he had an unmanageable team to control, but he did not pull them off the road. The coachman might run a man down, but would think twice about crashing into a curricle and pair.

The driver hauled back on the reins and the guard braked as Evan continued to walk toward them. It belatedly occurred to Evan that he might look like a highwayman, with a pistol possibly hidden in his sling. The thought that the guard might at any moment blow his head off only made him laugh at the irony of dying in Devonshire rather than Spain. If Judith was not on the mail coach, he didn't much care.

"You imbecile! What are you about?"

"We must stop one of your passengers. There has been an illness. She must come home."

"Evan!" Judith said from the window. "Are you mad? You could have been killed."

"Judith, you're here! You must come back. I can't believe I was so stupid." He pulled the door open, and Judith got out angrily, pulling Thomas after her.

"Thomas? You here?"

"How could you think I would leave him?"

"Please, Judith, don't argue. Just come home."

"Is someone really ill?"

"Yes. Helen."

"Oh, we will come back then."

The guard threw her valise down, and Evan tossed him a coin and picked up the bag. Terry was walking the team back along the road toward them. When the rumble of the departing mail coach died away, Evan confessed, "I lied about Helen. She's perfectly all right."

"You blackguard!"

Evan was ready and ducked her first blow, but not all of them.

"Aunt Judith!" Thomas cried. "I did not know you could box!"

Once again Terry was helpless to assist his brother, but rather thought Evan had this coming. When her rage was spent, and Evan was sitting in the middle of the road, Judith picked up her valise, took Thomas's hand and began to walk toward Bristol, giving Terry such a menacing stare that he dared not say a word to her.

"Judith, wait, you didn't hear me out," Evan called, hobbling after them. "I was just so afraid it was Father that I wasn't considering your feelings."

"What difference does it make who it was?" she protested, pushing him away. "And I'll thank you to watch what you say."

"All the difference in the world, and do not try to get away from me, for I won't let you. How could you think I would care about such a thing?" Evan asked, glancing at Thomas and finally getting her to stop. "I have not exactly been a saint. Besides, I wager it was not your fault."

"He promised me marriage. He promised to take care of my family. He lied."

"And you left him, not the other way round."

"Your father arranged everything. He went with Helen and me to Harrogate."

"Then what are you worried about, unless you want me to shoot this fellow for you? I will if you insist, but I would just as soon forget him."

"Who are you going to shoot, Evan?" Thomas piped.

"Uh, Thomas, I think Terry needs help driving the team." Evan boosted the boy into the curricle, to stand between Terry's knees, and Terry patiently put his hands on the reins behind his own.

"Don't you see?" Judith whispered. "He lives in Bath. What if I should run into him?"

"I wager he will be more embarrassed than you. No man is going to claim a child he would have to support. Ten to one he does not even know about Thomas.... I just thought of something. Helen! That's why she is having another baby. To prove that it is still possible, to convince people Thomas is her own."

"Yes, that is part of it," Judith said, wearily brushing away a tear.

"I knew she was courageous. I knew she would kill—do anything for you, but to put her life on the line in this way is the ultimate sacrifice."

"I know that. Everyone has been so good to me," Judith said, wiping her cheeks with the back of her hand. "And now I have stolen Thomas away, which I never planned to do. I am so confused."

"You must not think much of me, to not confide in me."

"I lied to you."

"You were caught in an impossible tangle, but you must know I would never ask you to choose between Thomas and me. But then, you didn't trust me with the secret of the porcelain, either. That's another thing. If you are going to be my wife you are going to have to put a little more faith in me."

"Am I?"

"Are you what?"

"Don't play games now, Evan. Am I going to be your wife?"

"Undoubtedly," he said, hugging her. "What about Thomas? Do you want him back?"

"Yes," she said with trembling lips.

"It is your choice, though I do not know what it would do to Father. They will have to give him to us."

"Us? But you don't want children. You said so."

"Only when I thought you could not have any. I would have said the sky was green and the grass blue to get you to marry me."

"I know you think me foolish. At best I shall have him only another six or seven years, until he goes off to school, but I do want those years."

"No! He is not to be sent to some damned school, where he'll be cut off from his family. We can teach him all he needs to know."

"Do you mean it?"

"Yes. We had better go home now, especially as you have absconded with Thomas. They will be searching for him."

"It was stupid of me to carry him away. They love him, too, and he knows them as his parents, not me."

"Perhaps he can merely spend a lot of time at the dower house. In a few more years it may take all of us just to keep him out of trouble."

"You won't mind raising another man's child?"

"Not even if it had been Father's."

"You must be insane to have thought such a thing of us."

"Well, I told you I was."

"Yes, I suppose you will need more looking after than Thomas."

Judith hugged him to her, and they stood locked together until Thomas shouted, "Look at me, Evan. I am driving two horses."

Terry had turned the team and followed them, so that in their abstraction they would not get run down. Evan now helped Judith into the curricle, handed her bag up and crawled tiredly up himself. "Thank you, Terry, you are a lifesaver."

"Don't mention it," his brother replied with a weary smile.

They found Helen in the garden with a terrified Miranda. When the nurse spotted Thomas, she gathered him up possessively and took him away, raining kisses on his cheeks.

"She needn't have snatched him away quite so brusquely," Evan muttered.

"She is probably afraid you will ride him on your horse again," Judith said.

"No, that can't be it," Evan said. "If you recall, she appeared after you had got him down. To be sure, she never knew anything about it unless Thomas told on us, and I bet he did not."

"What are you both gabbling about?" Helen asked. "You sound like a couple of children."

"We're getting married," Evan said.

Helen's mouth dropped open as she stared at him and then Judith. Evan began to wish he had not blurted out the news so suddenly.

"I told him, Helen. I told him about Thomas, and he doesn't care."

"Well, I told you it wouldn't matter to him, but you wouldn't listen to me."

"What?" Evan gasped. He dropped down on the bench beside Helen and covered his eyes. "Judith..." he said finally. "I wish you did not have quite so many scruples."

"It was a matter of cowardice, really. I couldn't face telling you."

"Then how did you manage it, dear?" Helen asked.

"By realizing how much more I was hurting him by not telling him."

"What do you think of me that you did not expect me to understand?"

"I had no idea what your expectations were for a wife, but I assumed it would matter if I—"

"My expectations? I expected to die in Spain. I never expected to come home, let alone find someone like you. I can see I should have pressed my suit more urgently instead of respectfully submitting to that Banbury tale about your religious vocation."

"There was something else," Judith said with a frown.

"What?"

"I couldn't stand for you to think me so stupid as to be taken in by such a false promise."

"I believed Banstock, too," Helen said.

"If the greatest mistake you made was in trusting someone, you are doing far better than me. Look at the mess I made with Father, and it was mostly my fault."

Helen looked at him. "I wish you would tell him so. He has spent a deal of time blaming himself."

"I did."

"And Thomas," Helen continued, "is not a mistake!"

"Of course not," Judith said, kneeling by her sister.

"What a game little fellow," Evan agreed. "He is more enterprising at evading his nurse than even I was at escaping my keeper."

"And who was that?" Judith asked.

"An aged tutor I inherited from Gregory—Whitcomb was his name."

"You would wait till he fell asleep and slip out of the schoolroom," Helen said.

"Father told you about that? I didn't think he knew."

"You remember it?" Judith asked.

"More and more is coming back to me. Soon I will no longer be able to fall back on my shocking memory as an excuse for my lapses."

"Well, if my own memory serves me right," Judith said, "I must leave you now, for I have a dress to make. And if Angel has not come to her senses, I may have two to make." She sprinted across the lawn and waved at them before she went into the house.

"So you have been my ally all this time?" Evan asked.

"Not all this time," Helen replied. "You are a hard person to get to know, Evan."

"So are you."

"I didn't do it, you know."

He looked sharply at her. "I know that."

"There was a time I could have killed you."

"No, you're bluffing. You can't kill. You are too caught up in survival. You make a great show of strength, but you are as terrified as I am when the guns start firing."

"You, atremble under fire? I don't credit it."

"Not of the guns, of myself."

"Evan. It wasn't me, but it was someone. Someone in this house hates you enough to do that to you. Who is it?"

"Don't concern yourself. I can manage things," he said evasively, looking away.

"You know and you won't tell me."

"Fair's fair. You would never tell me about Judith."

"It's not . . . not one of us?"

"No," he said, hoping he was lying convincingly. Let her think it was James Farlay. Let her go on thinking it was Farlay at least until her baby was safely delivered. She didn't need to know about Angel. Not ever, if he could help it.

Chapter Fourteen

Evan rose late the next day and stiffly dressed himself. When Joan brought him his shaving water, she informed him that Bose, and indeed all the family except Helen, Thomas and Angel, were already up at the village.

Evan was a little achy from yesterday's exploits, but nothing mattered now that Judith had accepted him. They had told only Lord and Lady Mountjoy of their engagement, although Terry could not help but know about it. It was Terry who had warned them not to say anything to Angel for the time being, since she was spending so much time in Lady Sylvia's company, helping her prepare for the ball.

Evan had agreed, but for a more important reason. If the girl was given to violence when thwarted, there was every possibility that Judith could be in danger now, too. Evan decided he must insist Judith move into the dower house until the wedding. He would sleep on the doorstep if he had to, in order to keep her safe.

He went to inspect the house again. It had been thoroughly scrubbed and had new hangings throughout, though the furniture had merely been cleaned and polished. Evan did not want it changed too much.

He heard voices in the garden and looked out to see Miranda and Thomas gathering bramble berries from the canes that had started up around the edge of the garden.

"And someday," she told him, in the sweet voice she reserved only for Thomas, "you will be a great lord and all the people will look up to you. That is why you must let your mother teach you your numbers and letters."

"But I had rather be playing."

"You're not to go near those nasty dogs and horses again. You stay with me and I will keep you safe."

Evan smiled at them. How lucky Thomas was to have such a loving keeper as Miranda. Even Gram had been rather brusque in her coddling, always warning him that it was the last time she would rescue him if he ran away from old Whitcomb again. How much easier it would have been if he had been coaxed to learn, rather than having to apply himself with his knuckles still smarting from the old tutor's cane.

A flood of memories broke in then, like the opening of a festered wound. He remembered his mother screaming at him. He remembered her ranting at his father. He remembered her being cold and distant. No wonder he hadn't recognized the portrait. He could not for the life of him ever remember her smiling. Then it hit him that Sylvia reminded him of his mother, hence his disgust with her. It wasn't Sylvia herself that put him off, just an unfortunate resemblance.

He went down the stairs and out into the sunlit garden.

"Hello, Evan," Thomas said.

"We didn't know you were here," Miranda said. "Come, Thomas."

"Don't run off, Thomas. I hope you will visit Judith and me rather often when we move in. Otherwise it will be quite dull."

"You . . . and Miss Judith?" the nurse questioned.

"We're getting married, of course."

"I see. Does your father know about this?" she asked, as though it were a reprimand.

"Of course," Evan said with a laugh.

"Come along anyway, Thomas. It's almost time for your lessons." As Miranda towed him away, the boy looked forlornly back and waggled a hand in farewell.

Evan rode out to the village, letting the jogging of Taurus work the stiffness out of his muscles and joints. Judith, Terry and Ralph were engaged in surveying and staking out a rectangle along the downhill side of the porcelain factory, which Evan could only assume would be a dock for the canal. Bose was having the workmen begin their excavations in this area. Evan walked over to Judith. "So you have discovered I am a sham?"

"What do you mean?"

"That there is really nothing to surveying."

"Oh. As to that, I am only following Ralph's directions. He has plans drawn up already for the dock. You will be careful not to hurt his feelings if they are not right?"

"I think we should put Ralph in charge of this part of the project. It is exactly the sort of complex problem his mind will thrive upon."

"For instance, what to do in case the water level varies from season to season."

"An important consideration, Judith. You are always thinking, aren't you?"

"There is so much that could go wrong. Sometimes I can't sleep at night for worrying about it."

"But there are always solutions, a hundred ways to solve any problem. I have been thinking about Ralph. It would be a hardship to me to send him off to school now. Don't mistake me, I want him to go, but in a few years time, when this project is finished. Right now we can't very well spare him."

"It would mean a great deal to him to know that."

"Then I think, if he is of the same mind, that we should speak to Father about it. Where is Father?"

"Inside, going over the plans for refurbishing the factory."

"I am sorry I doubted you even for a moment. Do you forgive me?" he asked, taking her hands.

"Of course. You have forgiven me for something far worse."

"You only say that because you don't know what all I was up to in Spain."

"I shall have to get that out of you before the wedding."

He kissed her lightly and she let him. Ralph stared at them and grinned. Evan motioned for the lad to follow him inside.

"Have you a mind to go back to school right away or would you rather stay and work at this?" Evan asked, as they walked around the kilns that lined the back of the building.

"You know the answer to that, but will Lord Mountjoy let me?"

"We can only ask."

His father looked up in surprise when Evan came into their temporary command post in the porcelain factory. From the window they could see almost to the river.

"You've obviously made a start here," Evan said, walking with Ralph to the table where the plans were laid out.

"Yes," his father said. "There's so much to do."

"When do you need the money?"

"We don't need yours yet, at least not for this. Judith had been trying to sell those jewels your grandmother left her."

"Jewels?"

"Yes, you remember her diamonds, don't you?"

"Not even vaguely, but go on."

"They would not have been worth nearly as much, broken up and sold, but the previous owner of these lands is a widow who lives in Bristol. Judith had the inspiration to appeal to her vanity. Once the woman saw the diamonds, she had to have them."

"Judith has an instinct for business. I think she will do a good job of running this place."

"Aren't you going to take a hand in it?" Lord Mountjoy asked.

"I know nothing about porcelain or farming. I leave that to Judith and Terry, your able generals. What I wanted to talk to you about is the matter of Ralph's schooling—"

"Ralph? School? Oh, no, no, no. It is not even to be thought of at the moment. We need him here. He is very nearly as good as you in a pinch."

"But...I—" Ralph began, but fell silent when Evan laid a restraining hand on his shoulder.

"Sorry, Ralph," Lord Mountjoy said. "We can't afford to send you back for a year or two. Once we are on our feet here, I mean to send you to school. I don't doubt you will get more out of it, having been in the field, so to speak. Don't you agree, Evan?"

"Since you put it that way, I quite see your point," Evan conceded, winking at Ralph.

Ralph was gaping at him and barely smothered a laugh behind a cough.

"I didn't mean to belittle you, Evan. Of course, you will be in charge of things."

"Certainly not. I leave that to you, Father. I shall merely be a retired captain of engineers who rows up and down his canal looking for leaks."

Terry came in. "Unless we get back to work there will be no canal to row in."

"I still don't see how shipping porcelain will make it worth your while building one," Evan said.

"Porcelain?" Lord Mountjoy asked with a smirk. "Whatever gave you that idea?"

"Well, you did. At least you didn't contradict it, and you did leave all those books on porcelain laying about the library."

"That was for Sylvia's benefit," Terry said, chuckling.

"But what are you going to fire then?" Ralph asked.

Lord Mountjoy looked at Evan with a grin, which spurred him to frantic thought. Something heavy that used clay and possibly coal... "Bricks!" he said, his eyes lighting up. "Why didn't I think of it before? You have the clay, the furnaces, the lime and sand, or you could get them here on the canal. And use it to ship the bricks to Exeter and beyond."

"Quite right," Lord Mountjoy said proudly. "It took you long enough to figure it out. Judith is still interested in making porcelain, but only as a side business. Making bricks is much easier, and there is a growing market for them in the cities."

"What about coal?" Ralph asked.

"Down the Exe and up the canal," Lord Mountjoy replied.

"There are even some iron ore deposits here that may prove worth mining once the canal is in operation," Terry interjected.

"You are into everything," Ralph said.

"But the canal is the key," Lord Mountjoy said, pointing to the map. "Nothing is possible without it."

"Speaking of able generals, here comes Judith," Evan noted.

Judith whisked through the door then and looked commandingly from one to the other. "Well, why are you all standing about? Haven't you any work to do?"

"You see what I mean?" Evan asked as they all chuckled.

"As for you, you should still be in your sickbed. We were getting a great deal of work done before you came to interrupt."

"We weren't laughing at you, Judith, just at the fact that you are the hardest working among us," Evan said as he came to take her hand.

"You don't understand. This has been so long in the planning that if I could, I would dig the canal myself to get it done faster."

"Let's hope it won't come to that," he said as he led her to the table.

"Is this what you meant by moving the canal?" His father pointed at the map.

"More or less. Actually, I was thinking of putting a bend in it thus. I know that makes it look like we will be moving more earth, but—"

"Moving it to bypass Sylvia's lands adds... What did you figure, Ralph?" Terry interrupted.

"A fourth, almost."

"In length, but by taking it through the barrens, we avoid all this rocky ground and gain one spring," Evan argued.

"Also, we would not tear up all those good acres of farmland," Terry added.

"You would know about that," Evan answered. "Remember, I am better at destroying things than making them pretty. The key thing is that there are roads running through the farmland that would necessitate bridges over the canal. There are no roads through the barrens. By going that way we save ourselves the building of three bridges."

"Is that significant?" Judith asked.

"It is to me," Evan replied. "I hate bridges. Sooner or later you are compelled to go wading waist deep in icy water."

"Poor baby," she said in that way that made him shiver inside.

"Plus, for every bridge, you have to unhook the tow rope and pole or walk the barge through."

"That's two-thirds of the survey to do over," Ralph concluded. "When shall we start?"

"After Lady Sylvia's party," Lord Mountjoy declared. "We wouldn't want to spoil that triumph for her."

"Who gets to tell her?" Judith asked, smiling wickedly.

"I think Father should have that honor, don't you?" Terry asked.

"Yes, but not at this party," Lord Mountjoy decided.

"Saving it for a quiet moment when you can relish it more?"

"No, you rag-mannered soldier. One does not do that sort of thing when one is a guest in someone else's house."

"My manners never were the best."

"See that you behave yourself at the ball."

Evan saluted and winced.

The Mountjoy carriages were not the first to arrive, nor were they the last. It was not much of a crush by London standards, but for Devonshire it was a respectable gathering of nearly fifty: some few neighboring families, half a dozen officers on leave and a crowd of Sylvia's friends from Bath, who were staying the week.

Evan had the suspicion the country folk were being paraded to be laughed at, but he had nothing to blush for in the Mountjoy ladies, whose gowns were copied from the latest fashion plates. He could have wished Judith had kept a diamond or two to dazzle people with, but the pearls he gave her went charmingly with her cream silk gown. Angel was wearing a rose pink gown and a locket on a ribbon. She was sweet to everyone except him. She looked through him as though he were not there, and it gave him a chill. He claimed the first dance with Judith and the last.

He had left off his sling and merely kept his arm tucked inside his coat when it was not in use. When not partnering someone, he fetched and carried for Judith and Helen. Lord Mountjoy had deserted the main rooms for the small office where a card table had been set up. Angel spent the evening breaking hearts and, to Evan's surprise, looking longingly at Terry.

"Angel hasn't forgiven me yet," Evan said to his brother. "How about you?"

"I have been afraid to try my luck with her. Bad enough she was so angry at all of us at home. I don't want a temper tantrum in public."

"True, but I have missed the little wretch. She kept the evenings lively."

"She has been over here every day, helping with the preparations and flowers."

"Yes, I know," Evan agreed. "It really is important to her that the evening be a smashing success. I think she may be disappointed if you do not let her break your heart again."

"Oh, well. I shall but ask," Terry said, draining his glass of champagne.

"You still love her, don't you?"

"Yes, damn her. And I don't know why."

"I had supposed that when she shot you, seeing her with a smoking gun would have put you off."

"Oh, I did not actually watch her shoot me."

"What did you say?"

"I saw her carrying the gun later, quite inexpertly, in fact. She said she found it. Then when she saw me bleeding, and Judith trying to staunch the wound, she went quite hysterical. The thing that always puzzled me was that she managed to hit me at all."

"But if you didn't see her shoot.... I should hate to have you on a jury trying me. It could have been anyone. It happened before anyone knew I was coming home, right?"

"Yes. Well, Father might have known, but—"

"But at that point you were the heir. Someone had only to put you out of the way, then Father..."

"What are you saying? Ralph?"

"No, not Ralph. He was at school."

"He was in London, or so he says. And he came home the day before someone shot at you in the home wood."

Evan looked across the room at Ralph, who smiled at him. "I can't accept it. I know him."

"What are our alternatives? It's back to Angel again. I could forgive her doing it once to me, seeing as I deserved it, but not to you."

"It can't be, Terry," Evan whispered desperately. "She had no reason, at least not then."

"Who did you see?"

"I never clearly saw anyone. I only thought it was a woman. Now I come to think of it, to wield that saber takes considerable strength."

"Angel could not have done that. Not my Angel!"

Evan glanced around the room, and his eyes lighted on James Farlay. Evan didn't really believe he was a suspect, but would have grasped at any straw to divert suspicion from Angel. "Farlay has been home since March, and he is extremely jealous of Lady Sylvia. I could see why he might want to kill you when he thought you would marry her, and why his anger would now be directed against me."

Terry made as if to go up to him.

"Don't," Evan warned. "We haven't the slightest thread of proof, and we are not likely to get it if you jump him now. Go and dance with Angel. She keeps trying to look at you without acknowledging my existence. If you don't go over to her soon, her eyes will cross."

"Very well, but guard your back, Brother."

To Evan's relief, Angel rose to meet Terry with a brilliant smile. Evan really began to believe she could not have done it. He racked his brains to try to remember if the footsteps leaving his bedroom had gone down the hall or down the stairs. He tried out both scenarios in his mind, and they were equally convincing to his addled memory. Hopelessly, he realized it could have been either way. He would no doubt pretend they had gone down the stairs, and yes, that he had heard the front door slam behind Farlay. Eventually he would even believe it.

Could he let his brother marry such a woman as Angel? She had not committed murder, but she had come close. One look at their faces as they danced gave him the answer. He would tell any lie he had to in order to keep them happy, and damn the future and the truth. The truth was what you believed. If he believed hard enough that Angel hadn't done it, that lie would become the truth and would protect these people he loved.

He realized the champagne was going to his head, and not seeing Judith about anyway, he went outside to the garden for some air. There were one or two couples strolling about as he walked toward the area of their picnic so long ago.

"Evan, thank God you have come."

"Judith? What is it? Have you torn a hem or something?"

"If only it were that. He is here."

"Who is here?"

"This is no time to play games, Evan. The only he that matters is here. I knew this would happen. Why did I let you talk me into this?"

"Come back inside. I will seek him out and have a little talk with him. You're sure you don't want me to kill him?"

"I don't even want you to meet him. I want you to take me home."

"If you run from this now, you will always be running. You are courageous all the time. I'm asking you to trust me on this."

"Very well, I will point him out to you. But if there is a scene, I will tell Lord Mountjoy it was all your fault."

"Fair enough." Evan took her arm, patted her hand and walked back inside with her. "Where is he?"

"There, talking to Lady Sylvia. His name is Banstock."

Evan took in the man's foppish coat, artistically dishevelled hair and smug countenance. "He's a bit of a fribble, Judith, and older than me, I think."

"I was desperate, if you recall. Damn, Evan, he is looking this way."

"And blenching and breaking into a sweat, as you perceive. Go sit with Helen. I'll introduce myself."

"Evan, you were joking about killing him, weren't you?"

"Oh, yes. There are worse things than killing a man."

Judith watched Evan in fascination as he walked toward her persecutor. It was odd, but she was no longer afraid of the man. She was not even blushing. She smiled and went to sit with Helen, who had now recognized Banstock.

"Oh, Evan," said Sylvia. "There's someone here I want you to meet. I believe Mr. Banstock knows our Judith."

"Do you now? You must have met when they lived in Bristol."

"Yes, we scarcely knew each other, of course. She probably would not even remember me."

Lady Sylvia slid away from them to chat with someone else.

"Oh, you are wrong there. She remembers you very well. I asked her if she wanted me to kill you, but she can't quite make up her mind about that yet."

"Now see here—"

"Oh, don't worry. I wouldn't murder you in your bed. It would be a fair fight."

"You have no right—"

"I have every right. I am going to marry Judith, and you hurt her. She's mine now, her future and her past. All her past hurts are mine, as well. What you did was unforgivable. How many people have you told?"

"No one, I swear, no one!"

"Ah, now that is something I had not counted on. You haven't told anyone?"

Banstock shook his head vigorously.

"Perhaps your case is not so serious then. I have no particular hatred for you. I feel no more animosity toward you than I did toward all those French, poor fellows...."

Banstock gaped at him.

"Of course, they were soldiers. But then, so were you." Evan eyed the scar on his cheek. "Do you know what they do in Spain to a man who brutalizes a lady in such a fashion?"

"No!"

"Let me tell you." Evan placed his arm around Banstock's shoulder and turned him slightly away from the crowd. When he whispered the punishment, Banstock gagged and almost wretched, pulling out his handkerchief and holding it to his mouth. Evan remembered his own reaction to his first battle and waited without sympathy for the man to recover.

"Of course, if you haven't told anyone, I see no reason why you could not simply leave."

"May I? For I had no idea what Lady Sylvia wanted. I didn't even know why she invited me. Will you let me go?"

"Yes," Evan said, the scar below his lip crinkling wickedly. "Just remember to stay out of our path and keep this in confidence."

"I will. I will."

"Have I sickened you? I am sorry. That was very bad of me. You must understand, though. I am still fresh from all those atrocities in Spain. I could do as I promised without blinking an eye. Do we understand each other?" Evan asked quite close to Banstock's ear.

"Yes. May I go now?"

"Yes, of course. Don't let me keep you if you are not feeling well."

It seemed to Evan that Banstock evaporated before his eyes. Then Evan walked toward Judith with a wicked smile.

"What did you say to him? We demand to know."

"Yes, Evan," Helen agreed. "He looked like he was about to be sick."

"He nearly was. I should really be careful where I tell my war stories. I suspected they would not do for polite company and I was right."

"You're not going to tell us, are you?" Judith surmised.

"Suffice it to say he will never bother us again. He may even emigrate."

Helen raised an eyebrow at him but said no more.

"It's Evan, isn't it? Evan Mountjoy?" An elderly gentleman with a cane came up to them.

"Yes, it is, sir. Do I know you?"

"Ethan Pike at your service. I know your father."

Evan introduced Helen and Judith.

"We did meet once under unfortunate circumstances," the old man continued. "When your brother died. It was my carriage he ran into."

Evan reeled a little. "I'm sorry if you were injured."

"No, I was perfectly all right. Too bad about your brother, though. That is what happens from young men showing off."

"He was teaching me to drive. He should never have let me handle such a team."

"But he was driving. I saw it as plain as day. He was talking to you and took the turn out of the drive much too fast. Even if I had not been coming along he would likely have upset your rig."

"*He* was driving?"

"Yes, and he paid the price. So glad to see you took no permanent harm. I always wondered, you know. That's why I was so relieved when your father said you were doing well. Nice to meet you, ladies. Must be off, pay my respects to everybody. We don't do enough of this in the country, you know."

"No, we don't," Evan said numbly.

"Evan, what does it mean?" Judith asked.

"It means I didn't kill Gregory."

"But we never thought of it that way," Helen said.

"I wonder why I did? Excuse me. I have a bone to pick with Father."

"Evan, lad, have you tired of dancing?" his father asked jovially. "Take my place at the table. I shall be in hot water if I don't stand in the room with Helen for at least part of the evening."

"I just ran into an old friend of yours."

"Really? Who?"

"Ethan Pike."

"Talkative old man," Lord Mountjoy complained, as he rose from the table and came out into the hall. "I suppose he told you."

"Yes. What I want to know is why you didn't tell me I wasn't driving?"

"I didn't think it mattered anymore."

"What? Thinking I had killed my own brother, a brother I admired, worshipped?"

"You did nothing of the sort. You never liked each other, and now you don't even remember him."

"Perhaps I don't. It's just that I have always held it to be an unforgivable sin to have killed him, and now I find out I didn't."

"But that's the point, isn't it? The wreck was an accident. It was not something that should have required forgiveness even if you had been driving."

"Hence your neglect to speak of it. I see. How long have you known?"

"A few years. Why is that important?"

"Before Badajoz then?"

"What happened at Badajoz?"

"I threw myself away. I thought it was what you wanted. What you expected of me. I thought that's why you sent me."

"My God, you were trying to...?"

"Not very successful at it, was I? Like most things."

Evan turned to find his father visibly shaken. He had never seen him like that before and did not like it. It made Lord Mountjoy look old.

"I should never have told you that. I am still a clumsy oaf. Why didn't you tell me?" Evan asked more softly.

"If you stayed, I did not want that to be the reason."

Evan nodded and threw his good arm about his father's shoulder. "Come, you had better dance with Helen at least once."

"Do you think we should? The baby, you know."

"I don't see why not. Everyone else has danced with her, including me."

"Evan, I must speak to you," Sylvia declared as they passed her. "Come outside."

Evan resented the command, would have resented it even if Sylvia had not tried to do such a vile thing to Judith. "What is it?"

"Did he tell you?"

"Who?" Evan asked obtusely.

"Banstock, of course. Don't be so dense."

"Did he tell me what?"

"About Judith."

"What about Judith?" he asked, making her say it.

"That they were lovers."

"Is that what you think? You must make allowance for the way some men boast of their exploits."

"Evan, I know he had her in his house for two days. Why would he lie to me?"

"Why would he tell you the truth? Men think they are much more fascinating to women if they have a bit of gossip to spread, something to make you gasp in horror."

"I believe him. Are you going to ask her about it?"

"There is no need. She told me all about Banstock."

"How do you know she told you the truth?"

"I know Judith. Why did you invite Banstock? I mean, how did you even know about him?"

"I wanted you to see what kind of family you had. When I asked Angel why she, instead of Judith, was to marry you, she told me Judith was recovering from a disappointment in love."

"After much prying, no doubt. Really, Sylvia, to be preying on that child is not well-done of you. That is the only reason you asked her over here, to worm out of her any little scrap of information about my family you might be able to use against them."

"I was doing it for you, Evan. We are in this together. Don't you see? You have only forty shares. I need a lever, something that will make Lord Mountjoy trade me shares for my land."

"And Judith is to be that lever?"

"Why not? The scandal is ready to hand. We have only to threaten to spread it about and he will capitulate."

"He would be a fool to do so. You could set the tale about anytime after Father had given you what you wanted."

"He would have to trust me."

"He would not. I know my father."

"We'll see."

"A word of advice, Sylvia. See to it that the tale never gets about."

"You sound upset."

"Upset? I am downright angry. You weren't just flaunting Banstock to worry my father. You deliberately invited him here, hoping to disgrace Judith publicly. That's fighting dirty in anybody's book."

"That's not true. I only wanted you to know what she is really like."

"Why? Why would you care what I think of Judith?"

"Later on Angel said—she said you preferred Judith to her, and she would have to face up to that."

"When did Angel say that?"

"I don't remember."

"You must!" Evan moved closer and grasped her wrists so hard she cringed.

"Evan, you're hurting me. I did it for us, for our future."

"I don't give a damn about the future. If one word of this leaks out, I shall know where it came from, and I will do something about it. No one is going to destroy the reputation of an innocent woman and get away with it."

"What would you do? Beat me?" Sylvia taunted.

"Reputations are destroyed all the time by people as heartless as you. You would have given yourself to me that day I was here, with James waiting outside the house."

"Never!"

"I think you would have, but it doesn't matter. I have only to say you did. You see how easy it would be."

"James would kill you."

"He might try. He has not had much luck so far," Evan added. Her eyes widened at this, but her expression told him nothing.

"Or was it you who wielded the saber?" he pressed. "I was thinking it would have been beyond you, but you are capable of so much more than I ever thought." He let go of her hands and backed away, almost as though he expected another attack from her.

"You are mad to accuse me of that when everything I have done has been for you. I will get what I want, Evan. You'll see."

"Yes, we'll see," he said, going back inside. He found Judith in time for their dance and concluded that the Wells girls had been a hit. There should be no reason why they could not throw such a party at Meremont if it would cheer Angel up. No doubt other families would invite them to any little gatherings they might plan during the summer months.

At the midnight supper Lady Sylvia and her cousin talked intently. Evan decided that if James became privy to the story about Banstock, he might have to have a little talk with him. The opportunity was provided by James himself. While the ladies were sorting out their wraps, the captain pulled Evan into the office and demanded, "How dare you treat Sylvia so? You have bruised her wrists."

"She knows how clumsy I am. She should not have provoked me."

James swung at him and connected, to Evan's surprise. The blow no more than grazed his jaw, and he even caught the vase tottering on the bookcase he had fallen against. When he glanced at James, the man was grasping his shoulder, his arm hanging at his side.

"I assume you will choose pistols," James said coldly as soon as he could talk.

"You have pulled your wound, and you assume a great deal too much. Do you have any idea what would happen to you if I reported this to your commanding officer?"

"You wouldn't dare!"

"Your career could be at an end."

"At least I shall have the satisfaction of putting a bullet through you."

"Not damned likely, unless you mean to shoot me in the back."

"You—you won't meet me?"

"Certainly not."

"What about your honor?"

"What do I care about honor? I have finally won a woman who loves me for my dishonorable self with all my flaws."

"Sylvia?"

"No, you dunce, I mean Judith. I never cared about Sylvia."

"Then why lead her on...?" James's puzzled frown turned to a gape of surprise. "You were using her!" he declared.

"As she tried to use me. The most disturbing thought is that I was better at it than she was."

James stared in disbelief as Evan calmly adjusted his neckcloth, made sure his mouth was not bleeding and let himself out of the room.

Chapter Fifteen

"Lady Sylvia looked fagged to death by the end of the evening," Helen said over breakfast. The ladies, including Judith, had talked of nothing else through the whole meal, but had not yet tired of the topic.

"A party like that is a lot of work," said Angel. "I hope I don't have to help with another one soon. Did you see Mr. Banstock, Judith? I don't know why Lady Sylvia invited him. I told her we were not on good terms with him."

"Did you?" Helen asked, clearing her throat and looking toward Judith.

"Did you say Banstock?" Lord Mountjoy asked. "Was he there?"

"Yes, he was, but I didn't get to talk with him," Judith said coolly, as though he were the merest acquaintance.

"I did," said Evan. "What an odd little man. I think he drank too much champagne. He got ill and left early."

Lord Mountjoy looked from one to the other of them, and finally shrugged.

"I'm so glad you didn't marry him, Judith," Angel said musically. "Then you would not be able to marry Evan."

"Who told you we were getting married?" Evan asked in some concern.

"I did," Terry said, "when I asked Angel to marry me."

"I'm glad to see you young people are getting your affairs in order," Lord Mountjoy said. "We shall expect a lot less confusion around here."

"It will be a race to see who can post the banns first," said Terry.

"We could have a double wedding," Angel said. "I could plan it."

"I thought you said you were tired of such things," Ralph gibed.

"Well, a wedding would be different."

"Judith and I shall definitely elope," Evan stated.

"That takes all the fun out of it," Angel complained.

"I am not going to have Judith sitting up on the eve of her wedding, sewing lace onto her own gown, let alone yours. Her sewing days are over. She has more important work now."

"Oh, yes, the porcelain factory," Angel mused. "That will be fun. Lady Sylvia is very interested in porcelain. She doesn't look down on us for going into trade. 'We must change with the times,' she says."

"You told her about that?" Terry asked, watching in fascination as Angel popped strawberries into her pretty red mouth one after another. She had that odd talent of being able to talk with her mouth full and still be ladylike.

"Oh, wasn't I supposed to? I didn't tell her about the canal. At least I don't think I mentioned it, but it is so hard to remember."

"It doesn't matter," said Lord Mountjoy.

Angel breathed a sigh of relief. "I was thinking perhaps I could help design patterns for you or something, Judith. You know I have a turn for watercolor."

"I think that is an excellent idea, Angel."

"We could design our own porcelain, and our family would have the only set like it in the world. Then we could design unique patterns for other families."

"Actually, that's not a bad suggestion," mused Judith. "I almost wish I could go up to the site today."

"Give it a rest, Judith," Evan complained. "It's Sunday."

"We all deserve a rest," declared Lord Mountjoy.

Lady Sylvia and James called just after breakfast. Evan and his father were together in the library, and they received them there. It was evident she and her cousin had been disagreeing.

"I wish to talk to Lord Mountjoy alone, James," Sylvia declared.

"I'm staying," James insisted.

"And anything you have to say to me can be said to my son," Lord Mountjoy assured her.

"So they have pulled you into their schemes, Evan? Well, it will all come to naught unless you meet my terms."

"Which are?" Lord Mountjoy demanded, as he sat in the great chair behind the desk.

Sylvia laid a document on the desk and seated herself primly on the edge of a chair. "I think you might offer me a cup of tea or something," she remarked to Evan.

Evan tugged the bellpull and waited by the door as his father read over the papers. Lord Mountjoy had nearly finished by the time Joan ran up from the kitchens.

"Sorry, Joan, but we need some tea, and some cakes, I suppose, if you can manage it."

"Surely you don't expect us to agree to this," Lord Mountjoy said as Evan poured wine for James, who lounged belligerently on the window seat, and for his father.

"Those are my terms."

"What are they, Father?"

"Controlling interest in the canal and, to put it briefly, everything else by way of marriage to you."

"What?" James demanded, splashing wine on his sleeve.

"You put a mighty high price tag on yourself, ma'am," Evan said.

"On my land."

"Let's make no bones about it," Evan retorted, "you are selling yourself, not for money so much, I think, as for the power it will buy."

"What if I am? You were willing to sell yourself."

"Was I? Do you know me so well—better than my family, better than Judith, whom I am going to marry?"

"You can't marry her. She's a—"

"Don't say it!" Evan threatened, leaning toward her and resting his hands on the arms of her chair. "Remember, James is here."

"That reminds me, Lady Sylvia, what did you hope to accomplish by inviting Banstock last night?" Lord Mountjoy demanded. "We knew all about him. What sick mind would conceive of such a plot to destroy a woman like Judith?"

"Now see here!" James began.

"I don't have to listen to this," Sylvia complained.

"You will, and a good deal more, my dear," Lord Mountjoy said, handing her back the document. "We don't need your land. We have moved the canal!"

Joan brought the tea tray in, interrupting the meeting and leaving Sylvia fuming impotently. James started chuckling.

"But that's insane!" Sylvia said. "It will cost twice as much to build."

"And will be cheap at the price, considering your own offer."

"Your tea, Lady Sylvia," Evan said, as he poured a cup and handed it to her. He poured one for himself and sat back to watch his father in action.

"You will reconsider," she warned. "You will be sorry for insulting me."

Evan took one sip and gagged. "Don't drink that!" he said, dashing the cup from her hands. "It's been poisoned."

"Have you gone mad? It's tea."

"No, it's so laced with laudanum you would never wake up. I wonder who has been at it."

"Surely no one hates Sylvia enough to—" James began.

"In this case she is an innocent bystander—at least, I think so," Evan interrupted. "The intended victims were Father and me."

"But who did this?" Lord Mountjoy asked. "Surely not Joan?"

"Whoever it was will come to check on the results and perhaps finish us off. We have only to wait. Whoever comes through that door is the one."

"I don't have to wait," Sylvia said. "You are frightening me."

"Yes, you do. Sit down," Evan commanded. "You might contrive to look as though you had fainted or died."

"Stop talking like that," Sylvia demanded. "I'm not used to houses where people are poisoned. Who would want to do that to me?"

"Obviously someone who thought you were of no consequence. But that could be anyone," Evan said, taking a seat.

"Now see here," James said.

"Sit down!" Lord Mountjoy ordered, and James obeyed him.

"I heard someone was trying to kill you," the cavalryman whispered, "but this seems a bit extreme."

"So happy to know it isn't you, James," Evan said. "I rather like you, in spite of you being in the cavalry."

"I suppose I deserve that for threatening you, but you said you would do far worse to me." He drained his glass, then looked dubiously at it. "Rather exciting, better even than waiting for the French." James's eyes were sparkling as he stared at the door.

Evan closed his and listened.

"Evan, lad, you drank some of that. Are you ill?"

"Only a bit groggy. I was just praying. You see, Father, there are so many people I don't want it to be."

Cautious footsteps approached. Evan concentrated, trying to remember if they were the same ones he had heard in his room, but could not tell. The door opened a crack and they sat motionless. Sylvia swallowed, her eyes wide with fear.

"Miranda!" Evan shouted, and leapt across the room. He flung open the door and pursued her down the hall and out the back door. She ran toward Judith and Helen, who had been playing with Thomas on the lawn. Picking up Thomas under one arm, she ran toward the stable. A moment later, Evan pulled up short in the doorway, for she was holding Thomas in front of her with a knife to his throat.

"I want the fastest horses. Harness them now."

"Give them to her," Lord Mountjoy said over Evan's shoulder as the older man gasped for air.

"Don't come any closer," the nurse snarled as Evan edged a step nearer. "You especially have ruined my poor Thomas's chances," she said, pointing at the boy with the kitchen knife.

"Then hurt me, not Thomas. He is the one you have been trying to protect."

"He would be better off dead than in this household, ignored. What is to happen to him? To me? I am the only one who really cares."

Lord Mountjoy laid a restraining hand on Evan's shoulder.

"What if she means to take Thomas with her?" Evan whispered.

"Don't take any chances with his life."

"I won't."

Slipping away, Evan worked his way around to the back of the stable. Not soon enough to jump Miranda, though. After she drove out of the stable, with Thomas crammed into a corner of the curricle, Evan saddled his horse. "Which way is she turning, Father?" he demanded as he tightened Taurus's cinch.

"To the left. What are you going to do?"

"I don't know. At least I shall be there if an opportunity arises."

As Evan took shortcuts across fields and over fences to keep the curricle in sight, the rest of them, including James and Judith, rode out of the stable. Miranda was taking the southern road, so a shortcut over the barrens, even though he would be climbing part of the time, would bring Evan out on the road ahead of her. He calculated all this in his mind without consciously thinking about it and certainly without knowing what advantage this would gain him. Were he to pop up in front of her, would she slay Thomas and herself or try to keep control of the horses? Evan did not know her well enough to predict what she would do. What was he thinking? The woman was insane. Even Miranda did not know what she was going to do.

He was well ahead of her when he came out on the road and saw a hay wagon. "Stop! Stop your load across the road. There's a runaway team coming. They may pull up if they see your rig."

"Here now, what about my wagon?"

"I'll pay for it."

Not liking the fact that Evan hid his horse and himself behind the wagon, the farmer finally got down and did likewise.

Watching under the vehicle, Evan could see the approaching team check in confusion. But at Miranda's urging the horses left the road and came around the front of the hay wagon. He was poised to grab Thomas, but had to change his plan at the last second. Thomas was on the other side, clinging for dear life to the sideboard of the curricle. Instead, Evan launched himself at Miranda, landing in the boot, with his left hand grasping the wrist with the knife in it. He remembered very well how strong she was as she made numerous attempts to stab him. All the thrashing of reins excited the horses so much they again broke into a gallop.

Evan grabbed for the reins, but he could not fend off Miranda and get hold of more than one of them. Thomas could see what he was trying to do and, leaving the safety of his corner, he grasped the rein he could reach and tugged with his small might, shouting, "Whoa!" repeatedly as loudly as he could. To Evan's surprise, the horses seemed to be heeding the boy. At least they slowed to a ragged trot.

There were other hoofbeats now, and a second later James was at the nigh horse's head, pulling it up, and Terry had the other. The team reared unexpectedly at this interference, lifting Terry clean off his horse and nearly oversetting James as well. Evan caught an upside-down glimpse of Judith, her tawny hair whipping about her face as she rode gamely up to the curricle in her muslin dress.

"Thomas!" she shouted. "Get ready to jump."

She had meant for him to leap to her, but remembering his training, he dived off the curricle out of danger of the wheels into a perfect somersault and series of rolls. Judith dismounted to see to him.

Miranda had taken to kicking Evan in the ribs in hopes of loosening his hold on her wrist. Her last blow sent him rolling off the curricle. The nigh horse had wrenched himself free of James, who then made a grab for the reins. Miranda plunged the knife into his arm for his pains. She whipped up the reins then and the team bolted. James dismounted—rather calmly, Evan thought, for a man with an eight-inch kitchen knife sticking out of his arm.

The team ran partway up a bank, taking the right wheel over a rock, which flipped the curricle, pinning Miranda underneath. This freed the harness from the hitch pin, and the horses took off in earnest.

Everyone stared at the crumpled form under the curricle, not knowing what to do. Then Evan, who had never commanded more than a work party, said, "Father, take Thomas back to Helen as fast as ever you can so she does not worry. We shall need blankets and a wagon. Ralph and Terry, follow those horses and see if you can come up with them before they kill someone else. Judith, help me with James."

James had extracted the knife and was futilely trying to tie up his furiously bleeding arm. Evan and Judith added their handkerchiefs to the padding.

They cleared off the road as best they could, since there was a carriage approaching. It was Lady Sylvia. "James! James, what has happened?"

"What a chase! You missed the whole thing." The captain's eyes were dancing with laughter. Evan recognized the light of battle. He relieved Sylvia of her shawl and bound it around James's arm, as well.

"James, you are as mad as the rest of them to be standing here bleeding. Why did you even get mixed up in this?"

"What a piece of action. It was very nearly as good as the war."

"You're delirious," Sylvia said, as Evan helped him to the carriage and deposited him inside. Evan detained her for a moment before helping her in.

"That is no scratch. If you don't get him to a doctor within the hour he may lose the use of that arm, or the arm itself. You understand me?"

"Driver!" Sylvia commanded. "Take us to Tiverton—Dr. Thornton's house."

"Do you want me to ride with you?" Judith asked. "Hysterics will not do James any good."

"Certainly not!" said Sylvia, who jumped into the carriage with no help and rapped for the driver to move on.

"I'll tend to Miranda," Evan said. "Judith, you walk the horses."

Evan picked up the lifeless form and moved it to the side of the road. He took off his coat and dropped it over her head. Oddly, he noticed that it was the coat Judith had mended for him, the one with the saber cut.

Miranda's neck was broken, he realized, and was surprised to find that this did not conjure up any memories for him. Perhaps the death of his brother had indeed been wiped from his mind by the concussion he had suffered in the accident. As for feeling sorry for Miranda, he could not.

He had seen dead women before, and they always looked grotesque. One expected to see dead men. He could only think of little Thomas, keeping his terrible secrets, and marvel that the child seemed so normal for being in the continuous charge of a lunatic.

Finally Evan looked toward Judith, to discover that she was walking not only Molly and Taurus, but Bart as well, the mount James had been riding. Evan went to help her.

"How are your ribs?" she asked.

"She got me in the same old place, so they don't feel any worse than I am used to. I am feeling a bit dozy, though. I took quite a gulp of that drugged tea."

"What?"

"Miranda dumped laudanum in the tea. If that hadn't put us to sleep forever, I suppose she meant to finish us off with that knife she was carrying. What a chance to take! But then, when else could she get at some food that Thomas or the rest of you might not eat?"

Judith was beginning to shiver a bit, so he hugged her. "It's reaction. It will pass in a minute," he said reassuringly.

"I'm thinking of Thomas. She could have killed him at any moment."

"It's over. Don't think about it."

"I thought I was doing right by him, and I have given him a horrible childhood."

"Children have survived worse than that."

"What could be worse?"

"Being hated by your own mother could be worse. At least Miranda loved Thomas . . . after her own fashion."

"Your mother hated you?"

"She hated me so much I turned into a solitary little brute."

"That's why you blotted her out."

"It let me live with myself. I did for a time believe that I wanted Gregory to die."

"But it wasn't true?"

"No. I remember being in awe of him, grateful for any little attention he paid me, much as Thomas is when I spend some time with him."

"You think Thomas will get over it?"

"Thomas has a loving family. I shouldn't think it will bother him at all now that he has been cleared of killing his puppy."

When they returned to the house, Thomas was sitting between Lord and Lady Mountjoy and was being fed sweetmeats by Angel. Ralph and Terry had returned after successfully capturing the team.

"That was an excellent fall you took, Thomas," Evan said.

"Who taught him that?" asked Lord Mountjoy.

"Evan did," Judith said proudly.

"You have done well, boys. I had not thought it could end so luckily. Sorry you had to be worried, Helen dear."

"I wasn't worried, Hiram. I knew the boys could handle it."

"They are a useful lot, all things considered."

"Did I do well, too?" Thomas asked hopefully.

"You did very well," Lord Mountjoy said.

"Well enough to have another puppy? For it must have been Nurse who killed my other one, then blamed it on Evan."

"Yes, you can have your puppy."

"He's not as hard to please as you said, Evan," Thomas confided.

"No, all you have to do is get yourself nearly killed."

"You should know," said Helen dryly. "You have had plenty of experience at that."

"Judith," Thomas called, "Miranda said that you are my secret mother, my real mother."

"Do you understand what that means, Thomas?" Judith asked, holding back her tears.

"That I have two mothers?"

"Yes," Helen agreed.

"And two fathers as well?" Thomas peeked at Evan.

"Most definitely," Evan answered.

"Does this mean I may have two ponies?"

"The boy knows his numbers," Lord Mountjoy said.

Evan laughed. "It also means you have to grow fast so there is enough of you to go around."

"Evan," Helen said, "now that I know who was trying to kill you, I feel mightily offended that you suspected me."

"I am sorry."

"Evan thought you were trying to kill him?" Angel gasped.

"I owe you an apology, too," Evan confessed.

"Me? What have you done to me lately?"

"When I concluded Helen would not have had the strength to attack me with that saber, I actually suspected you."

"Me?" Angel gaped at him, then chuckled, then fell into such fits of laughter that Terry had to support her with an arm around her waist.

"I knew you were gullible, but really, Evan."

"Well, it was down to you or James," Evan said.

"You must have a deal of respect for me to think I would be as capable as James Farlay."

"Oh, more so, for I never know what you are thinking, and James is sadly predictable."

"I will forgive you if you promise never to laugh at me again."

"I promise. I take it that doesn't cut both ways."

"No, oh no," Angel gasped, going off into another peal of laughter.

"I just had a thought," Judith said. "Miranda must have been the one who shot Terry."

"Yes," Terry said, staring meaningfully at Judith and Evan. "That mystery is finally solved."

"Just the other day she was telling Thomas he would be a great lord, and it still never occurred to me to suspect her," Evan said.

Thomas was already tugging Lord Mountjoy toward the stable and the promised livestock. Judith took Helen to her room, to make her lie down for a rest. Evan wandered out of the house, feeling rather well in spite of his smarting ribs. Must be the laudanum, he thought. He went to the dower-house garden as though he were reporting in to Gram.

"It's over and everything is going to be fine," he said, then realized he had been quoting her. Someone had cleared away the weeds, and some roses and perennials were making a gallant effort to look like a garden. He staggered toward a tree and sat down on the grass.

"I knew I would find you here," Judith said, kneeling beside him.

"Judith, let's get married tomorrow."

"We can't. Not till after the funeral."

"Damn that Miranda, a troublemaker to the end."

"Then I suppose we should observe a period of mourning...."

"You can't be serious!"

"What would people say?"

"I don't care what these unnamed people of yours say of us anymore. A family that has been as rocked by scandal as ours can't help but cause talk. With people thinking we are all mad, one insane servant more or less will not raise an eyebrow. Do you really mean to put it off?"

"No, just teasing."

"Angel warned me about your reprehensible sense of humor." Evan found her hands and kissed the ink stains.

She was in his arms, and only after her kisses aroused him almost to the point of no return did he groan at the stabbing in his ribs and the renewed pain in his knee.

"You are very nearly as beaten up as when you first came. Worse, in fact."

"I don't care, so long as you don't cuff me anymore."

"It's my natural reaction. Did you see that scar on Banstock's cheek?"

"Yes."

"I gave him that."

"Good girl. Just remember to pull your punches with me." He sighed and tugged her over to lay on his chest as he leaned against the tree.

"Evan? Evan? Asleep?" She snuggled against him, content to hear his breathing and feel the warmth of him.

Epilogue

"It's not muddy anymore like it was when we first dug it," Judith observed from her position by the rudder. She looked up and down the length of the canal. There was a barge loaded with bricks bearing down on them from the east, but she knew there was plenty of leeway for them to pass at the widening in the middle.

"No, there's a good bit of current from the streams. I shouldn't wonder if we can't fish in here in a year or two," Evan answered.

Thomas was riding the ambling pony that was towing their bark up the canal. A white setter trotted along the tow path ahead of him. Judith steered, and Evan was relaxing in the stern, ostensibly looking for leaks, but almost asleep in the drowsy summer heat. He laid his head softly on Judith's stomach.

"You won't be able to feel him kick yet," she said with a laugh.

"Him? I assure you Father is hoping for a girl. He is fed up with raising sons."

"He has his own daughter to raise now. I'm sure we may have a boy if we want."

"Bridge!" Thomas shouted, and halted the pony.

Evan cast loose the tow rope, pulled the bark hand over hand along the chain that lined the wall of the canal under the bridge and caught the rope that Thomas had coiled up and flung at him.

"There is only one bridge," Thomas shouted with a grin. "I should think you could be watching for it."

"Mind your job, tow boy," Evan called back with a laugh.

Thomas laughed in turn and nudged his pony onward.

"I read in the paper where James Farlay and Lady Sylvia are to be married."

"I know. He wrote me to thank me."

"You?"

"Not only did I make him jealous enough to realize how much he loved Sylvia, I caused the injury that made her realize she loved him. I've half a mind to give them some shares in the canal for a wedding present, just to see what comes of it."

"Don't you dare. Your father would never forgive you."

"But I haven't irritated him in such a long time I am getting out of practice."

"Angel and I are going to design a set of porcelain for them. That will be from all of us."

"What will be your theme, maidens rampant on a field of—"

"A floral pattern. Forget-me-nots and rosemary, I think."

"Must you work on it today?"

"At least I can still get to the factory without having to ride on our bumpy roads."

"Next year for the roads. Do you really want to go to the factory today?"

"What else would I be doing, since you have forbidden me to sew?"

"I have one or two ideas that involve a sunny bank and a willow tree."

"Evan, what are you doing?" Judith demanded as he loosened the tow rope and dropped it into the water. "Where will we end up?"

"Wherever the current takes us." He lowered himself over her to kiss her into submission.

Thomas looked back, realized he was free of his cumbersome burden and kicked his pony into a canter.

* * * * *

Harlequin® Historical

presents
award-winning author

DALLAS SCHULZE

with her new Western

SHORT STRAW BRIDE

A heartwarming tale
you won't want to miss!

Coming this November

HARLEQUIN®

Scandals

A passionate story of romance, where bold, daring characters
set out to defy their world of propriety and strict social codes.

"Scandals—a story that will make your heart race and your
pulse pound. Spectacular!"
—Suzanne Forster

"Devon is daring, dangerous and altogether delicious."
—Amanda Quick

Don't miss this wonderful full-length novel from Regency
favorite Georgina Devon.

Available in December, wherever Harlequin books are sold.

1997
Reader's Engagement Book
A calendar of important dates
and anniversaries for readers to use!

Informative and entertaining—with notable
dates and trivia highlighted throughout the year.

Handy, convenient, pocketbook size to help you
keep track of your own personal important dates.

Added bonus—contains $5.00 worth of coupons
for upcoming Harlequin and Silhouette books.
This calendar more than pays for itself!

Available beginning in November at
your favorite retail outlet.

Merry Christmas, Baby!

A romantic collection filled with the magic
of Christmas and the joy of children.

SUSAN WIGGS, Karen Young and
Bobby Hutchinson bring you Christmas wishes,
weddings and romance, in a charming
trio of stories that will warm up your
holiday season.

MERRY CHRISTMAS, BABY! also contains
Harlequin's special gift to you—a set of
FREE GIFT TAGS included in every book.

Brighten up your holiday season with
MERRY CHRISTMAS, BABY!

Available in November at
your favorite retail store.

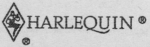

HARLEQUIN ®

Look us up on-line at: http://www.romance.net

MCB

REBECCA

43 LIGHT STREET

YORK

FACE TO FACE

Bestselling author Rebecca York returns to "43 Light Street" for an original story of past secrets, deadly deceptions—and the most intimate betrayal.

She woke in a hospital—with amnesia…and with child. According to her rescuer, whose striking face is the last image she remembers, she's Justine Hollingsworth. But nothing about her life seems to fit, except for the baby inside her and Mike Lancer's arms around her. Consumed by forbidden passion and racked by nameless fear, she must discover if she is Justine…or the victim of some mind game. Her life—and her unborn child's—depends on it….

Don't miss *Face To Face*—Available in October, wherever Harlequin books are sold.

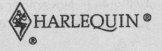

HARLEQUIN ®

43FTF

You are cordially invited to a

HOMETOWN REUNION

September 1996—August 1997

Bad boys, cowboys, babies. Feuding families,
arson, mistaken identity, a mom on the run...
Where can you find romance and adventure?
Tyler, Wisconsin, that's where!

So join us in this not-so-sleepy little town and
experience the love, the laughter and the
tears of those who call it home.

WELCOME TO A
HOMETOWN REUNION

The Murphys and the Stirlings have been
feuding for fifty years—ever since Magdalena
left Clarence at the altar, or vice versa.
Two generations later, Sandy Murphy and
Drew Stirling are unwilling partners in an
advertising campaign, and sparks fly. Everyone
in Tyler is wondering if history will repeat itself.

***Love and War* by Peg Sutherland,**
Available in November 1996
at your favorite retail store.

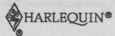

Look us up on-line at: http://www.romance.net   HTR3

Harlequin® Historical

If you're a serious fan of historical romance,
then you're in luck!

Harlequin Historicals brings you
stories by bestselling authors, rising new stars
and talented first-timers.

Ruth Langan & Theresa Michaels
Mary McBride & Cheryl St. John
Margaret Moore & Merline Lovelace
Julie Tetel & Nina Beaumont
Susan Amarillas & Ana Seymour
Deborah Simmons & Linda Castle
Cassandra Austin & Emily French
Miranda Jarrett & Suzanne Barclay
DeLoras Scott & Laurie Grant…

You'll never run out of favorites.

Harlequin Historicals…they're too good to miss!

HH-GEN